ERASED

....

EARLY PRAISE FOR *ERASED*

"Joan Burbick's *Erased* is a novel that revolves around intuition, research and love in a story that wants to know why the past matters. It is a compelling narrative, about an American woman who obsessively researches her Chinese-American husband's past to unravel the truth of his background, one that appears to be a construct of family secrets and lies. She endeavors to write a 'memoir' about his mother's life and death, set against the history of the relationship between China and America from World War Two to the present. The novel includes real photographs and documents and questions what is real and what is fiction and why truth matters. An engaging novel that speaks to our times. Recommend it."

—XU XI 許素細, www.xuxiwriter.com, novelist,
That Man in Our Lives, Habit of a Foreign Sky

"Joan Burbick's travels in Asia have led to her remarkable novel, *Erased*. A Polish-American woman is troubled by her Chinese-American husband's lack of knowledge about his mother. Her desire to find out about his mother leads her back in time, beginning in the 1940s, a period China saw cataclysmic changes during the Japanese invasion and its Civil War. In the end, the wife feels she is living a double life as she tries to live in the present with her husband. *Erased* is a compelling novel about identity."

—JOHN KEEBLE, novelist, *Yellowfish, The Appointment*

REDBAT BOOKS
PACIFIC NORTHWEST
WRITERS SERIES

ERASED

A NOVEL

JOAN BURBICK

REDBAT BOOKS | LA GRANDE, OREGON | 2024

Printed in the United States of America

First Edition: November 2024

Trade Paperback ISBN 978-1-946970-21-3
Hardcover with Dust Jacket ISBN 978-1-946970-22-0
        Library of Congress Control Number: 2024947117

Published by
redbat books
La Grande, OR 97850
www.redbatbooks.com

Text set in Minion Pro and New Spirit

Cover painting:
"Madame Lin" (1938)
Esther Lovett
oil on canvas
16" x 20"

Book design by
Kristin Summers, redbat design | www.redbatdesign.com

....

For Yali

....

"Those to come, who will they be?
Will they grieve someone's
long-ago gone life?"

—Wang Wei,
"Elder-Cliff Cove," 740-761 CE

Table of Contents

....

NOTES ABOUT THE TEXT

To simplify Chinese geography, the author has used
contemporary spellings of all place names.

All letters, photographs, and unpublished manuscripts
are from the private collection of the author.

Prologue

My wife, the writer of this memoir, has tried hard not to alter the truth. Her search to uncover the details of my mother's life, a young woman who died during the war waged decades ago in China when I was a mere child, has been quite overwhelming for both of us. Once forgotten or ignored by all but me, her only child, my mother's life and death had existed in a world apart, a parallel world running next to mine. Because of a series of what seemed to be random events, my wife took up the challenge to right what she perceived as a terrible wrong and, perhaps, bring solace to my broken memories of childhood. What follows is that story of how hard it was for her to find the truth about my mother and her persistence in probing the chaos of those years.

As you read her account, I want to offer a simple suggestion. It may seem an odd one, coming from the person who was left motherless at an unbearably early age. Remember as you read this memoir that I have always felt loved. A mystery, yes, but true. Even I cannot at times believe it.

After the war ended and my shattered family had escaped to Hong Kong, I often took solitary trips by ferry to islands in the South China Sea. Standing beneath a waterfall on Lantau Island as a young boy, I would watch the mist capture colors and know that in beauty my mother continued to live. The nights away were times spent close to her. No other people. No lies.

No heavy footsteps trampling fragile vegetation, only the mist from the falls, holding moisture for the thirsty plants clinging to rock faces and the engulfing sounds of water, sustaining the pure pleasure of rare orchids. Intoxicated, I knew that life was more than war, more than death, more than deception.

It was my private world, rich and abundant.

In those years, if I discovered enough orchids, I would sometimes select a single plant to bring back. I might press it on blotting paper, held tight between bamboo frames and straps, for my collection or, instead, bring my find to the Hong Kong University Herbarium. Sometimes, I would carefully nurture the orchid, finding the exact right pot and placing it on shelves I built on the verandah of our apartment. Once, I photographed one wild orchid, barely ½-inch tall, nicknamed (by me) the candle orchid. This black and white image I have kept with me for over seventy years. I have never lost it during my travels in the United States and China. It hangs on my study wall today.

I know I can't remember the worst moments of my life. The first eight years during World War II and its aftermath are mainly gone, a movie playing a white blank screen with no sound. I know I have lived my life sealed off from childhood scenes of panic, despair over food, and the feeling of parasites swelling in my belly. I live knowing I do not remember. But I also know how on Lantau Island I was freed from the stifling atmosphere of fear and abandonment. My remaining family members offered me no love or solace. But still I felt loved. That they could not destroy.

In 1957, when I was sixteen, I took a Japanese Maru freighter from Hong Kong harbor that traveled through the Panama Canal and arrived in Brooklyn where I disembarked to meet my American guardians and finish my education. Even though I was born in Boston, I did not know this new country. I had left when I was 9 months old to return to a China occupied and under attack by the Japanese. As an adult, my life has continued to zigzag across the Pacific as if I am always in transit. Neither home nor not home.

But always I remember the brilliant star river at night on Lantau, the companionship of a fire, the sardine pancakes I made, and a small blue tarp over my head. I can feel the pulse of the night and hear the insects swirling on the beach above sand and seaweed. I know the world has betrayed me. I have few false hopes. Yet, I can always find my way back to the memory of Lantau, or its later iterations in the stark red cliffs of the Colorado Rockies, the moist forests of the northern Cascades, or the sinuous meadows of the St. Joe River. And I will end my life on an island in the Salish Sea off the coast of Washington state where I can look out and imagine another chain of islands, clinging to China's coast. I have tried to follow a path of beauty and still believe that the world at its core is suffused with wonder.

My mother disappeared from my life when I was a child, but she has always been with me. It is love that abides.

—*Andrew Guo, Guemes Island, 2019*

1

Missing Person

My obsession started as a child when I couldn't stop the feeling that someone was walking beside me, a presence hanging out, nagging. You see, the dead don't stay dead. If you are lucky, they become companions, looking out for you, carrying messages to warn about dangers or false promises, dispelling your nightmares, or sheltering you from harm. Unlucky, there is no limit to the mischief they can inflict. Fury's creatures without mercy.

Almost forty years ago, I fell in love with Andrew, a poet whose past I overlooked; his previous marriages, his strained relationship with his Hong Kong Chinese family, and his reluctance to talk about his childhood or the details of his earlier life before our love. And love, whenever it finds you, seems to exist outside time. That is until, sooner or later, it doesn't and those unexpected walkers who shadow every life reappear in pictures, belongings, and memories, not letting go, never letting go.

One morning at breakfast many years ago, the spring sun flooding a bank of windows on the east wall of our brightly-painted yellow kitchen, I asked my husband about his childhood.

"Cargo planes," he responded, a look of youthful delight on his face. He remembered planes piled high with luggage, crates, and weapons with a few passengers strapped along the interior sides. "C-46s, I think," he said. "Real workhorses."

Trying to imagine the scene, I asked if he was with his parents. I knew that his mother had died in China somewhere during the Second World War. But I knew nothing about her.

He hesitated and stared at me, his warm brown eyes searching my face, as if he wanted to say something, then he simply shrugged. When I rattled off more questions, he tilted his head as if he were listening to someone he could barely hear. Someone standing far away. Perhaps on the other side of a lake. When I repeated my questions, he turned away, his silence filling the kitchen.

Not one to give up, I asked him what he was thinking about. Was it his mother? My directness only made things worse. Once he realized that I wasn't going to stop, he tried to make me stop by saying that he didn't remember his mother. Tapping his fork on the table, he said he was a child when she died. How could he remember? End of conversation.

Exasperated, I insisted that he must have heard stories about her. A remark from his father, or an anecdote from a family friend. Pushing his plate away, he replied, in a voice that made me both angry and sad, "I can't eat any more. I think I'll try and get more work done in the garden."

Why, after seven years of married life, I needed to cross-examine him was beyond me, a mystery between husband and wife that I still don't understand. Once disturbed from its predictable course, however, our marriage entered a hazard zone. That morning, his past became more like an impenetrable barrier than an inviting portal. It was a place I couldn't enter and didn't belong. Sitting across from him, I had become a stranger.

I suddenly felt very bad about what I was doing. What right did I have to badger him about his mother? My American childhood didn't know bombs and invading armies. I believed that family members could not die without leaving a trace. I couldn't accept the fact that his mother was unknown. I felt that someone must have known her. His father must have known her; he died later in Hong Kong when Andrew was teaching poetry at a university in the Midwest. Why was his father reluctant to talk about Andrew's mother. Was it grief?

After I apologized, he waved his hands around the kitchen and told me not to worry. His childhood was "difficult;" that's why he never wanted to talk about it. Instead of memories or stories, he did have a single document. He knew that his mother's name was Katherine Lin, a name written on an American birth certificate that his father had given him on the way to the American Consulate in Hong Kong when he was sixteen and needed a passport to travel to Windsor, Connecticut, for prep school.

Later that day, he handed me his birth certificate as if to prove he was a real person with real parents. I stared at it for the longest time, horrified that Andrew was identified as "Yellow" in the space for race. In 1939 a child was born to Katherine Lin and Zi Ming Guo. That was it. A document with names and no stories. No addendum about how Katherine and Zi Ming fell in love, how they felt during the three years they were in the United States, why they went back to China with a baby during the war, nor how Katherine had died. Somehow she had simply disappeared from his family.

When Andrew left China in 1947 during its civil war and fled to Hong Kong, a British crown colony, he had a new stepmother, Julia, and an infant half-brother, Peter, from his father's new marriage. A refugee in a sea of escaping Chinese, Andrew had never been to school, barely knew English, but could speak three dialects of Chinese.

I was married to someone whose entire life was shaped by the cataclysms in Asia. How could I possibly understand his childhood?

A few days after mulling over what Andrew had said to me about his mother, I couldn't shake the feeling that there must be information about Katherine Lin. I had to find a way. I wasn't sure why I felt so strongly other than my strange, persisting belief that the dead are companions, much closer to us than we care to imagine. And I convinced myself that Andrew would want to know about her. Would need to know.

Breakfast was again the scene of my renewed questions about Katherine.

"No," he insisted, "not a word. Nothing." Whenever he had asked about his mother when he was growing up in Hong Kong, there was a polite, but firm, even threatening silence. He learned to keep quiet.

"Why do you want me to go back to those years?" Andrew asked. I fumbled in my response, spouting some truisms about motherly love and the need to connect with the past. Stone still, Andrew's warm smile contracted into a rigid line.

Accusations followed. Was I trying to affix some label to our relationship, an orphaned child with abandonment issues, a lonely man unable to maintain long-term relationships, a confused soul searching for truth and using poetry as a substitute? "Isn't our relationship enough as it is?" he asked, his eyes searching my face.

I insisted he was wrong. It wasn't like that. I wasn't trying to spin some silly story that would explain him. It was about his childhood and his mother. I felt simply terrible that he knew nothing about her. He had a right to know.

He laughed at that. "Don't you know that life can take everything? Rights? People disappear. It happens every day, everywhere. There is no 'right to know.'"

He insisted that he only had a few memories from when he was living in the French Concession section of Shanghai before they left China, but basically his childhood was a blank. It was as if his life had begun in Hong Kong when he was eight.

Of course, I thought that was impossible. The discord between us widened.

Without consulting my husband, I decided to try and solve the mystery of his mother, or what I perceived as a mystery, and like a police detective set about the straightforward task of uncovering evidence. Who was she? What happened to her? Where and when did it happen? And why? I wanted answers. Answers for my husband. I wanted to fill in the story that he was denied. I felt it was necessary. Crucial. He must know about Katherine Lin. Looking back, I am struck by my naivete. I was convinced of my powers and my right to gather facts and solve her mystery as if I were some television detective.

At first, I tried to think through what I already knew. There must be a reason why his family never talked about his mother. Granted, his father had remarried, but Andrew's mother was dead before he remarried, not a rival. In Hong Kong, his father, Zi Ming, a distinguished though mainly retired psychologist and his stepmother, Julia, a physician and hospital administrator, led quiet, almost sequestered lives.

There were two servants in the home, little if no conversation at the dinner table, and hardly any interest in what the two boys, Andrew and Peter were doing. They were sent to separate private grade schools and high schools.

These facts still didn't explain his father and stepmother's permanent unwillingness to talk about Andrew's dead mother. Might it simply be the result of the bloody, horrific wars in China that lasted for over twelve years? Even with this possibility, I still refused to accept the complete erasure of a human being. When you know someone lived, but every attempt to know anything about that person leads to a dead end, don't you still have the right to find out what happened? Or at least figure out if the silence is intentional, and why?

In 1989, when I first decided to investigate who his mother was, Andrew's father had been dead 19 years and his stepmother, Julia, had already left Hong Kong and settled in California. I was going to have to scramble to get my information and hope that his stepmother was more receptive to my questions.

Andrew periodically received long letters from her, Confucian lectures really, on how he should live his life. She was a ferocious anti-communist and had left Hong Kong well before the Chinese Communist Party (CCP) was going to retake control. By that point, Ida, his older half-sister from Zi Ming's first and arranged marriage was also living in California. This first marriage of Zi Ming before he married Andrew's mother, Katherine Lin, was never hidden. Born into wealth, Zi Ming had a typical arranged marriage suitable for his social class. All I knew was that this first marriage ended in divorce, a new reality in China rocked by the overthrow of the Qing Dynasty and the establishment of a republic. Ida, a daughter of this marriage, escaped out of China sometime in the 1950s after the communists defeated the republic and had won the civil war. She finished her education in the United States and lived in California.

Zi Ming, Andrew's father, had had three marriages: An arranged, traditional Chinese marriage that resulted in a daughter, Ida; A second marriage with Katherine Lin that resulted in a son, Andrew, who was born in the United States while his parents were on a research trip; A third marriage with Julia Shen after Katherine died which resulted in a son, Peter, who was born in China before the family fled to Hong Kong.

Andrew had never talked about Ida's family, who her mother was, or how she got to the United States. He seemed not to know anything. She was simply his older half-sister. Enough said. And I had simply accepted his lack of details. The war seemed to have caused so much upheaval that gaps in the narrative were natural.

Over the years, I came to know both Julia and Ida more since they had come to our informal wedding reception in Seattle and made occasional visits back and forth between San Francisco and Seattle. Both women—Ida, a geneticist with an independent laboratory, and Julia, a retired physician—were no-nonsense professionals. Once they found out I had a PhD in American literature, they seemed willing to accept me as a relative, my whiteness beside the point.

I turned to them for my first forays into reconstructing Katherine's life. After a few weeks of phone calls to Andrew's stepmother and half-sister, however, my nascent sleuthing crashed against their wall of silence. It was tangible. I had the distinct feeling that I was jeopardizing my relationship with them by even asking questions.

I couldn't bring myself to tell Andrew. I felt foolish. Why hadn't I listened to him? But I still couldn't stop. I continued to keep my investigation a secret.

But how could I find out anything, living in the United States, without even a cursory knowledge of the Chinese language or any leads about his mother's family? What had happened to them. Were they all dead? My initial enthusiasm dampened, I was depressed, knowing that my husband might continue to live without memories or knowledge of his mother. Such inexplicable sorrow. His mother would remain a missing person, one of millions, who died during World War II. Cause unknown.

At that point Andrew and I had been together for seven years. For some quirky reason it seemed to work. We backpacked together, played music together—his piano playing ten times better than my cello—and voraciously read literature and history. We both taught at a nearby university and led writer's lives, his creating poems, mine researching poems by the Amherst recluse, Emily Dickinson. Our home on an island north of Seattle was packed with books and art by friends we had met in our travels. It was a charmed life. One you want to go on forever. But, of course, that didn't happen.

One day, our little circle abruptly lost its fairytale charm. My husband received an unexpected invitation to teach American literature at a university in Beijing.

After hurried conversations, we made the decision that he would go alone for the six-month contract, and I would try to visit him if possible. He was surprisingly excited about the journey. He never thought he would return to British Hong Kong, let alone mainland China. For his entire adult life in America, he had never intended to go back. He was fifty years old, set in his ways, and about to return to a life he assumed was gone.

"It's so odd, friends of friends," he said, shaking his head, taken by the coincidence of going to Beijing in the middle of the student unrest in Tiananmen Square.

Ignoring the State Department warnings, he raced around the house for the next few weeks gathering the documents he needed to apply for his visa. He started referring to the trip as his "adventure."

At least to him it was. I had grudgingly agreed to the trip but, really, I hadn't. Why was he leaving in such an impulsive way, as if he had never thought of returning to China until the first chance to return came along, and he grabbed it, despite the dangerous political turmoil? We had watched CNN together, the smoke-choked streets, students running, rifle shots hitting bodies and buildings surrounding Tiananmen Square, the shutting down of foreign media offices, and the government expelling journalists. Political panic. My husband had left Shanghai in a similar moment of chaos after the Japanese surrender but during the civil war that the communists would win, and his return would plunge him back to a political cataclysm of communist struggle as if time was only waiting for him to resume his former place.

I was horrified. He didn't seem to sense any danger. Something was wrong. I tried to push the thought away, but I was becoming convinced that he was returning to find his mother, or, at least, to find out what had happened to her. Her presence was still haunting him as it was me.

I still don't understand why I didn't try to stop him. The political chaos in Beijing frightened me. I was frozen or, more accurately, I felt irrelevant. He had childhood ties to China while I was a stranger to his past, a mere onlooker, agreeing to a series of decisions I couldn't have stopped if I had tried. He was going, that was that, and during the six months away, he promised to write faithfully. Grim consolation.

Before he left for Beijing, it became clear he had never given up on trying to know what had happened to his mother. He phoned his stepmother urging her to recall anything she could about his mother.

Julia simply replied, "I don't want to remember." Defensive, she grilled him on why he was going to Beijing. Didn't he remember how evil the communists were? She was shocked a Chinese person with his background would ever return.

Upset, he wrote her a long letter asking for information. He was returning no matter what. And he wanted her help.

Her return letter was more conciliatory. I read it several times. Short and to the point, it read like a report. Andrew had asked for his mother's name in Chinese. The spelling of Lin in English could mean a bevy of things in Chinese. Julia wrote his mother's possible last name and said it might mean "tree." She drew the character, 林, in the tiniest script; you could hardly read it. "Too long ago to be certain," she added. I counted how many times she wrote, "I don't know." Seven. But she did include some crucial information. Julia finally revealed to Andrew that his mother was in and out of the hospital when they were living in Chongqing, called Chungking at the time, and she had died there after a long illness. The date was fuzzy, probably 1943 or 44. She emphasized that she was under intense strain in Chongqing since each day the Japanese were still shelling and bombing the interior capital in western China. She was sick, unhappy and mentally exhausted. That's all she could tell him.

Why she waited so long to give him this information made no sense.

After reading the letter, Andrew was more determined than ever to go to Beijing. The morning before he left on the shuttle to take him to SeaTac airport and a sixteen-hour United Airlines flight to Beijing via Narita Airport in Japan, we had a jittery breakfast, his packed bags sitting next to the front door. I think he wanted to tell me something, and I think I was waiting for some confession or declaration like I never loved you or I'm never coming back.

Thirty years ago.

I can't remember what happened yesterday or last week or on my birthday, but I remember that morning in technicolor, the wide-open door to the back porch lined with pots of lavender, hyssop, and tarragon, the rows of rose-pink hydrangeas along the fence, the air sweet with the scent of jasmine, the world ablaze, eager to live, tempting us to sink into the moment and never let go.

After all these years, I still wonder what would have happened if he had decided not to go, and we had made love instead, defying our pasts, finding a way to laugh at the ghosts that linger.

What he did do is leave without saying anything he wanted to say and instead gave me a tender kiss good-bye.

2

The Dress

Perhaps the Chinese Taoists are right: past, present, and future evade humans. We misperceive our lives until we die.

With my husband gone, I had fitful nights worrying if I would ever see him again. I dreamt of people running away from explosions, chased by soldiers and armored vehicles. I couldn't see past the evening news. Finally, Beijing quieted down, its bloody suppression of students and workers over, but I lingered in a worst-case scenario. Once, I even had a dream about Andrew's mother, or who I thought was his mother. An elegant, young woman sat amid a pile of rubble counting stones. I never saw her face. The dream fragments were like fractured glass reflecting more fragments, vertigo glimpses, defying reason. I woke up terrified. Why, I have no idea.

Andrew did eventually return, but not six months later. He renewed his contract and stayed for a full year. I have kept the box of letters he wrote, and once in a while go back and read them again as if looking for clues. He would send the letters from three different post offices in case of confiscation by the government, detailing daily life and his students with such intensity I could feel his life changing in each sentence. The letters always said the same thing without words: He had gone home.

After 1989, our married life would never be the same. For the next thirty years, we became him, me, and China.

One letter I reread the most. He had met a young Chinese woman, a waitress at a Hot Pot restaurant near Peking University, who needed his help. There was something about her that reminded him of his mother. It was crazy ,of course, but he couldn't shake the feeling. The restaurant had a fairly decent piano, and the owner agreed to let him use it if he would play for the customers on Saturday night; light tunes, popular American songs like "Moon River," the sweeter the better. It was fun, a lark. He didn't write much about her after that letter, only small references to how desperate she was, how she needed money, how she wanted to live in the United States. I thought it would dissipate, and it did.

Tucked in the letters were poems, beautiful, funny, startling poems about Beijing with flashes of images from the end of World War II, beggars hawking chocolate for food, soldiers marching down dusty roads, and massive entry doors slamming in his confused child's face. Finally, memories. I was ecstatic, copying each poem for a separate file, the first step, I hoped, for his new book.

This doesn't make much sense, but I wanted to experience each of his recovered memories as if they were mine. The memories belonged to my husband, of course, if you can say memories belong somewhere like 'that belongs on the kitchen shelf' or 'that belongs in a book marked with a post-it', or even 'that belongs inside your heart and sustains its beating.' They did not belong to me. And yet somehow they did. Didn't I choose to find out more about his mother? Didn't I make probing phone calls to his stepmother and half-sister?

When he returned from Beijing, we made crazy love like teenagers, often not in our bed, preferring the living room carpet, or the car, or a grassy slope off a hiking trail, and once a large flat boulder in the middle of a mountain stream. Afterwards he seemed even edgier and more restless. He wrote for days at a time, breaking only for love and food.

These intense moments never went on for long. That's the value of looking back from old age. They were breathless interludes, sucked dry. I knew my husband was only on loan. He would never be satisfied living a settled life in America. Within weeks of coming home, he was trying to find a way to return to China.

Three years later, in the winter of 1992, he received another invitation to teach, this time at a university in a northern city, Changchun in Jilin province. This time, I planned to visit twice, and we even set dates and itineraries to guarantee I would join him.

The few weeks before he left, my husband withdrew into his study and worked on his cryptic poem that rivaled *Leaves of Grass* in length, then after this long absence from our daily life, he emerged one morning, poured two glasses of *Black Label*, one for each of us, and asked me to follow him into our daylight porch, its long windows covered in ice crystals, the room warmed by a small electric heater. We drank, laughed, and made love.

Then he told me a story.

When he was about four or five years old and living in China, he was allowed to stand at the threshold to a large bedroom where he saw his mother propped up in bed. He was confused about why *they* stopped him from entering the room. He could still feel their strong hands on his shoulders holding him back. He struggled to run to her. But he was a child. They won. After a few minutes, he was taken away. He never saw his mother again. He wasn't even certain where this happened, other than it was in China, probably in Chongqing, he thought, the wartime capital during the Japanese invasion.

That was the memory he hadn't told anyone since he was a child, and he had decided after much thought to tell me.

"I had to understand something," he said as he held my hand tightly. He needed to guard this memory of the last time he saw his mother's face. All his life he was convinced that if he described this moment to anyone, he might alter what had happened. "We lie when we describe our past." The temptation to embellish our memories is too great. We want an audience. The imagination was a relentless tinkerer, coloring and puffing for effect, leaving nothing as is. Andrew couldn't take the chance. He might even begin to doubt that the memory happened.

Since there were no photographs of his mother, he had to remain vigilant. He was a guard standing in front of her memory shrine. If it wasn't for him, she would vanish into nothingness.

Growing up he had always felt alone, outside the family. He felt it was impolite or even wrong to try and find out more about his mother as if he was expected to play the role of a boy without memories. As if his childhood had never happened. As if Katherine had never happened.

That wintry evening, he betrayed that secret pact he had made with himself to protect his mother's image. Listening to him, I tried to imagine the bedroom in the spacious Chinese villa with nameless adults preventing him from entering the room yet forcing him to stay still in the doorway. I tried to imagine his mother's face, but his description was vague, more a feeling than a photograph. It was difficult to see what he saw, his cherished memory from childhood retained for decades before a moment of intimacy gave him a chance to describe what he had seen.

That night, in bed, I cried silent tears for his cruel childhood.

After he left for his teaching job in Changchun, I tried sketching his mother's face. It was a ridiculous attempt to make her real. With pencil in hand, I drew a generic young Chinese woman, a collage of parts from Chinese movies and novels I had read. In my final drawings, my imagination morphed her into Ruan Lingyu, the Chinese "Greta Garbo," the 1930s star of Shanghai films. Like Andrew's mother, Ruan died young, but there the comparison ends. Ruan's life is the stuff of legend, her suicide, her lovers, and her career still captivate world audiences through biographies, documentaries, and movies. The opposite of Andrew's mother, the tiniest detail of Ruan's life was picked over for public consumption. Maybe that's what lead me to the movie star's face. I wanted to make Andrew's mother totally visible.

Before I left for my six-week visit to my husband in Changchun, my sister-in-law, Ida, called. She was interested in how I would like China and was curious about why Andrew had returned there. I really couldn't give her a straightforward answer. I tried asking her once more about his mother, but as usual she put me off. But then she told me that she was sending me a package. Not to Andrew, but me. She was phoning to warn me and to tell me she thought I would be pleased to have something that belonged to my deceased mother-in-law. At first, I thought it was a joke. She refused to talk about Andrew's mother, but she was sending me something that belonged to Katherine? Where had this *something* been all this time? And why had it suddenly appeared before my first trip to China?

Looking back, I'm not sure I was more excited or alarmed. Ida had sounded genuinely happy to send me this gift, yet she refused to answer any questions about the package.

She simply said, "You'll see."

In a few days, it arrived. I remember placing the box on the kitchen table and staring. I tried to imagine what was inside. An embroidered purse, a sandalwood fan, a string of pearls? Probably something durable, quickly snatched in a move from one place to another. A wartime keepsake.

The box looked poorly wrapped, and I was careful taking the brown tape and paper off. Inside the used cardboard box labeled glass pipettes (my sister-in-law was a geneticist, after all) and folded into a square was an elegant black silk dress that at first looked like a shroud, a fragile relic that might dissolve in sunlight. My first reaction was to wonder, "could Katherine have died in this?"

I fingered the material, my mind throbbing with questions. How did Ida come to have my mother-in-law's dress? And why keep it for so many years and then decide to send this dress to me now? Why not destroy the dress or give it away long ago?

Holding it against my body, I was surprised to see how the length was perfect. Clearly, Ida was too short to wear it since the dress was made to fit a tall, willowy woman. Andrew was slim and tall. It made sense his mother would be also.

But why save it? Ida must have known someone who could have worn it over the intervening years. Or was there something about this dress that made her keep it? I hadn't a clue why my sister-in-law would send me this dress, probably forgotten in a closet and hastily mailed before my journey.

After the dress arrived, I phoned Ida to thank her. She still refused to talk about the dress and why she sent it, or how she had ended up with it, or to offer any information about my husband's mother. I had the dress. That was that. She had warned me about its arrival. "Wasn't that enough?" she insisted.

Enough for what?

I placed the dress in a clothing bag and hung it in my closet, but not before examining it carefully. After a sleepless night, I took it out of its vinyl bag, lightly touched the fabric and held it up to the light before returning it to its protective covering. I don't remember what made me call Ida back again, but I did. I believed that I had tangible proof at last that Katherine Lin was known to my husband's family. She was not a phantom. You simply don't save the clothes of a relative you know nothing about. Had Ida slipped up? I tried writing down my questions before the call; the reasons behind the dress existing and the reasons for sending it to me. Each question generated several more until I felt dizzy.

On the phone, Ida outwitted me. She wouldn't answer my questions and instead began a long droning monologue about her laboratory and patents, the treachery of fellow scientists and investors, the perpetual lack of funds, claims that her daughter later insisted were based on lies. The slightest inquiry about war torn China and where she had lived in the French Concession in Shanghai during the Second World War was meet with silence. There would be no story or anecdote connected to the dress, no history or allusions, no thread of information.

It was as if she had sent the dress on an impulse.

For the rest of her life, Ida never referred to the dress again. She steadfastly refused to talk about it. The dress was like Andrew's mother. It existed, but it didn't. It was an enigma.

Years later at Ida's memorial service, her daughter told me that her mother left behind chests of beautiful clothes and a staggering pile of debts. As if to confirm this fact, besides her plain funeral urn rested a photograph of Ida when she was a young woman in her 20s looking back over her left shoulder at the photographer, a look of contented pleasure on her face. Wrapped in a lynx fur coat, she leaned over a stone wall, not caring to look at the Shanghai garden that everyone else was staring at, her eyes oblivious to everything but the photographer, perhaps the secret lover that her daughter had whispered about when she detailed the lawsuits, scandals, and deceptions her mother had perpetrated.

I was dumbfounded at Andrew's family. Who were they?

Before I left to join Andrew in Changchun, I decided to study Katherine's dress meticulously. It was my first piece of real evidence. If Ida would not talk, maybe the dress would reveal its secrets. I just had to investigate. You might think this odd, but it felt natural to me after years of interpreting Emily Dickinson's poems. Weren't they like puzzles or murder scenes? You had to be a Sherlock Holmes to figure them out. Why not a dress? Katherine's dress was simply a more elaborate piece of evidence that could be a source of crucial information.

I stubbornly believe that there must exist clues that can act as portals to what came before. Why else do we obsessively record our meals, our first dates, our laughter, if not to remind ourselves we have lived and how we lived? Even though the images might make us depressed or anxious, we still are reassured no matter what we feel. We have proof. Time is not merely a gradual eating away of our lives, dumping each consecutive moment into a vast bin of oblivion. The past accumulates instead of disappearing. The visual records are evidence, even if we never look at them again. They persist in digital clouds, on a DVD, or in a file tucked away.

The dress was my portal.

Would my mother-in-law have chosen the fabric because of its fashionable leaf pattern? Did the specific leaf have a meaning in China where everything refers to something else? Words are objects that carry allusions going back thousands of years. My Chinese name was fussed-over by Andrew's colleagues because one character sounded like the surname of an ancient treacherous general. The Chinese language is a minefield where homophones create infinite puns and troubling connections. Everyone at the university had to have a business card in English and Chinese. Since I was slated to lecture while I stayed in Changchun, the task had to be accomplished before I arrived. After many futile attempts, my surname, itself a variation of a Polish family name rendered easier to pronounce for American English speakers, was finally translated into Chinese.

You see what I was up against. The business of interpretation was thrilling but fraught with unstable words, indirect references, and stubborn paradoxes.

The foliate pattern of the dress suggested elongated leaves that swayed, barely touching each other in a complex dance of negative space that descended in long, slim contours. Maybe it was after all a pattern that only suited the fancy of the fabric designer. That can't be, I kept thinking. Botanical books were consulted. Was it a phlox or a coltsfoot leaf? Does that imply fertility or healing? An image of the fabric was emailed to a friend, a plant physiologist.

He passed the image around the lab with the result: No one could identify the leaf. Was it a designer's invention, my friend asked gently, clearly sensing my disappointment?

But my insistent questioning would not accept simple explanations. There must be a reason the dress survived, and why it was sent to me. If the clues were not in the fabric, then what I wanted to know was elsewhere. Underneath the act of folding the dress, placing it in a box, and sending it to me must lie a deeper meaning or at least a motive. Human acts are not random. They express at least a thoughtless impulse or an unconscious intent. The dress must have meant something to Ida even though she always refused to talk or even hint about why she sent it. It was almost as if the dress made a secret visible, like a friend who told you they knew something, but then smiled and kept silent. From that point forward, this secret defines your relationship, their smile taunts you to guess what it was even though they never offer any clues.

One morning on a rare phone call to my husband in China, I confessed how troubling it was that Ida refused to talk with me about the dress. To try and calm my nerves, he wondered if the dress even belonged to his mother. He urged me not to take anything too seriously. His family had never been reliable or truthful. Maybe I should forget about the dress.

I pretended to listen but ignored his advice. A sister, even a half-sister, could not be so cruel as to send a stranger's dress. What could he be thinking? I simply doubled my efforts to find out about the dress. I clearly had not asked the right questions. Did his mother buy it on a whim or a dare? Was it a present from her husband? I turned the dress inside out, looking for a label or a signature of its maker. Something I could trace.

With a trip to the local fabric store, I discovered that the dress was made from velvet cut away from its backing, a process the French called *devoré*, to devour by a chemical bath, leaving behind a firm, sheer background for an opaque, layered silk, a play with one color in light and dark through a sculptured effect or relief where a raised surface created an illusory sense of depth. Cut velvet repeated a single motif in baroque variations, reversing, inverting, and embellishing a pattern of leaves, bells, rose petals, floating clouds, mosaic windows, sand pebbles, or bursts of light in a single luscious, monochromatic tone, shimmering magenta, coppery bronze, deep red, or the inky depths of black on black.

After a few days of research, I found out that velvet rendered in silk was an expensive process, the height of luxury for the modern woman, especially in cosmopolitan 1930s Shanghai. This costly fabric was cut and sewn in the *qipao* style, a break from the traditional clothes for women under the Manchu dynasty. Clingy, with short sleeves and side slits, these new dresses for Chinese women dared to make visible the wearer's shape, no longer covering the female body with long skirts, full tops, and long sleeves. To traditional Chinese men, they were repulsive.

I read everything I could find on 1930s Shanghai fashion, old magazines published before the war, silent movies and talkies, and novels like Mao Dun's classic *Midnight*; heavy social realism, more like sociology than fiction, describing the contemporary manners of the wealthy Chinese. My copy even had illustrations. I read and reread the section when Old Mr. Wu, the patriarch of the main Chinese family, meets his daughter-in-law's sister. He had been living at his country estate and was sickened by the clothing of the so-called new women when he comes back to Shanghai. He described his abhorrent relative as "sheathed in close-fitting light-blue chiffon, her full, firm breasts jutting out prominently, her snowy forearms bare." Disgusted, he turns away from her and looks out the window of his coach at "a woman sitting up in a rickshaw, fashionably dressed in a transparent, sleeveless voile blouse, displaying her bare legs and thighs." Horrified, yet aroused, he imagined for a moment that she "has nothing on."

My dress, or I should say my mother-in-law's dress, marked this radical shift away from traditional clothing for women. A thin black silk cord ran along the narrow Mandarin collar then edged the right opening of braided fasteners, slide down the breast, and ended at the hip, a slip of a dress conforming to a young woman's tall, slender body with side slits up to her knees, leaving her arms completely exposed.

From a distance, the sleeveless dress looked monotone, simply black. From close up, its shallow relief cast reflections, etched magic. The elaborate devices of the velvety pattern created intricate, almost arabesque, patterns that moved over her body, a dress alive to the rhythms of the wearer dressed in black, the color that absorbed light completely or denied it, a color of dark intrigue and paradox with associations at once elegant and deadly, the runway and the funeral parlor, the yin and yang, the Heavenly Emperor and the void. The cut-away technique was elusive since with the absence of contrasting colors, say black on white or green on yellow, the slight modulation of a single color invited closer examination, even a desire to stare at the silk piled in careful layers, an expensive process fit for the nobility and the rich. True velvet enticed the fingers to caress the fabric as if stroking a cat, purring.

When she was young, my mother-in-law wore this dress and left traces behind, a slight shine on a velvet leaf at the left knee, a pulled seam close to the hemline, a wrinkled underarm, the presence of her body in the dress, sweating, pressing, pulling as she sat at the dining room table in the formal living room of her family home, clear signs of a high-born, educated woman, embracing the role of the modern woman in the new Republic, the pre-World War II, pre-communist government of Chiang Kai-shek.

Over twenty-seven years of traveling to China, I have collected several dresses that I rarely wear. They hang in my closet in their sealed bags next to my mother-in-law's dress. A deep-red embroidered traditional Chinese pleated long skirt and jacket, a gift from my husband. A Mongolian dress, hitting mid-calf, in bright blues and sea greens, made to wear with embroidered boots, also a gift from my husband. A contemporary chocolate brown silk Mandarin jacket with a short skirt made for parties in Hong Kong, another gift, this one impulsive as we walked down Nathan Road in 1997, the year of the hand-over of the British colony back to China. Dresses that mark love's endearments even though I don't wear them in the damp and chilly Pacific Northwest, more comfortable in fleece sweats and long sweaters. Nonetheless they are unforgettable clothes. A couple times a year I take them out, put them on, remember what spurred their purchase, marvel at the workmanship, and wish I had somewhere to wear them. They are too large for our niece. What will she do with them when I pass away? I couldn't bear to give them away to a stranger. Maybe they will continue to be handed down accumulating stories with each generation, adding more fanciful events to the life of a distant ancestor.

Dresses are tangible proof that someone lived. Like the stored wedding dress of a long-deceased grandmother that is unfolded from its crispy lining and held up to the light, you can feel the person's presence in the tucked sleeves and shimmery satin. The dead seem to come alive. This is what she wore when she danced and loved. No longer a mere name, her life becomes real. You can touch it. Such beauty. Such mystery.

Before I left for the airport and my long trip to Changchun, I went back to our bedroom, took out the clothing bag, and suspended the black silk dress from a hook on the closet door. At first, it looked rigid, compressed, and dead. I decided on a whim to see if it would fit.

Sliding it over my head, the dress seemed too narrow, its shape a shaft for someone with more delicate bones; then twisting it slightly, it slipped over my hips and came to rest on my shoulders. My clumsy fingers slowly closed the tiny snaps and frog fasteners running from the collar down the side of the dress. My body trembled as I let my hands run down the black silk. It was as if the dress had been made for me.

3

A Portrait Returns

I don't know how to act abroad as a tourist or teacher, never have. Awkward and shy, I can't figure out what is expected. White Americans are generally friendly, all smiles. I find it difficult to smile. I have been returning to China for 27 years, almost every year, and I can say with conviction that I know nothing about China. I have learned how to go through the motions when friends ask me how my latest trip was. The ideas I had about China have largely proven false. Yet nothing replaced those ideas even after teaching Chinese students, taking part in hundreds of dinners and conversations with Chinese colleagues and friends, and reading Chinese history and literature. There is not a single statement about China that rings true for any length of time. When I read American newspaper columns on China, I don't believe them. No one seems to know what they are writing about, but they continue to write as if they do.

During my first trip to Changchun in northeastern China with two short stays in Beijing, a word that literally means north city, I would jot down brief images and impressions: the peach-colored tablecloth in the restaurant at the Summer Palace in Beijing, the infinite grayness of Changchun, a name meaning *forever spring*, located north of north Korea in the region once known as Manchuria, or as the Japanese renamed it Manchukuo after they invaded in 1931; the rank smell of aging pork hung on hooks in the depressed open markets of Changchun, and the rows of grim cement apartment buildings along the immense length of Stalin Boulevard. I collected descriptions of people: the swaggering walk of a Russian with his Chinese thug, both posing as communists, living in a villa built by the Japanese during the Second World War; Wanda, a Chinese professor, bringing oranges as a gift when I first arrived in Changchun and scoffing at the improper *feng shui* of the foreign compound where my husband lived, also built by the Japanese; elderly Chinese men and women dancing in bright orange and red folk costumes in People's Square at 6 am before they changed into their rough gray Mao clothes at 7 am, and my host's refusal to allow me to tour the Chrysler automotive plant even though Lee Iacocca, its president, had just visited. State secrets must be guarded.

In my journal I had an elaborate discussion of a university event. I was asked to lecture on the American women's movement by a group of faculty women. Men were not invited to join, even though they tried and were repelled by several women who used the occasion to discuss the barriers to divorce with the attending People Liberation Army women officers, business leaders, and administrators. The group reverted to Chinese after politely listening to my short presentation in English. I learned afterwards that several voices called for a new revolution. Afterwards, I was reprimanded by a male university administrator that such a meeting could never happen again.

Most evenings, my husband and I huddled together in his sparse apartment, combing our hair coated with coal fumes from the industrial boilers and heating units in stacked apartments throughout the city, screaming at earth worms falling from the bath tub faucet where we washed our clothes, watching television shows about flying Kung Fu warriors and long white-bearded sages guarding mythical, medieval forests, laughing as I struggled to learn Chinese, and listening as my husband read his poetry. Frequently we visited his colleague, Liu, her Korean Chinese husband, and their son, and sat together on their *kang*, a heated platform bed that doubled as a living room couch and kitchen table, Liu's arm hooked in mine, wanting to talk about Toni Morrison, my husband's face, ashen and thin, yet animated with stories about his treks, his colleagues, his closeness to his students.

Does that add up to a definitive portrait of China?

Before we left to go home from the Beijing airport, we ate at the Hot Pot restaurant where I met the waitress who reminded my husband of his mother. In her 20s, tall and striking, she took me by the hand, wanting to know about my life in America. Framed by thick jet-black hair, her gentle eyes and kind smile put me at ease. Only when she talked about her job did her round face age, her softness harden, her eyes recede, growing cold. She had no dreams, she said. They were gone. She wanted dreams.

My husband looked at her tenderly like a father who knows the random obstacles she would encounter in her future, the disappointments, the rejections, the betrayals. I felt the cruel harshness of her having no dreams since I had many and acted on many, born into a white middle-class family in America.

We never meet with her again. My husband never mentioned her again. Perhaps we are always searching for something we have lost, yet pretending we are looking for something else, postponing the inevitable disappointment. Retrieval of the past impossible. Our destiny to live without certain loss.

After we returned from China, my husband received a telephone call at his office from an elderly man who told him that an oil portrait of his mother would arrive in the mail. He had tracked Andrew down through an old acquaintance who knew his mother and father when they were visiting in the United States in the 1930s. The man's nephew was helping him move out of his home into a small, assisted living apartment and felt the portrait should be given to a living relative if one could be found. He had meant to return the portrait years ago but found it difficult to let it go. He had inherited it from his deceased older sister. It was her prized possession.

"What a stroke of luck to find you," he told Andrew on the phone. Andrew immediately asked him about his mother. The man apologized that he hadn't gone to Yale, where the portrait was painted, and was the odd man out in his family, having graduated from Princeton. "Yale?" Andrew asked. "Oh yes, New Haven, you know." The conversation was brief, disjointed, and confusing. The man hung up without mentioning his name or where he lived. When Andrew tried to call him back, there was no answer.

His mother had vanished into a black hole without a single reaction by those she knew, and then two unanticipated surprises appeared, both without warning and without stories, not even an anecdote. The only connecting link between these two packages was Andrew's return to China. I doubt we would have received either if my husband hadn't crossed the Pacific. But how was Andrew found? We were simply amazed that two things connected to his mother had survived after sixty-odd years. It seemed impossible.

It was as if we were living in the Museum of Unconditional Surrender and the docent was the Croatian writer Dubravka Ugrešić, who believed that things extended the lives of their deceased owners. An old coat or a photo album retained the spirit of a deceased human being. Objects were a force field of being. A dress and an oil portrait were loaded with residue of a lived life. For Ugrešić: "That is how souls migrate."

Andrew and I didn't talk much about the portrait coming besides our fear that it would not be his mother. Maybe it was someone else who no one could identify and mistakenly believed was Katherine Lin. If it was her, it would at least be proof that she lived, not only in Boston but New Haven, Connecticut. For how long was not clear since details of her life were nonexistent. The only thing Andrew believed was the image of his mother that he kept in his mind.

Nothing else had value. He even disputed what his stepmother had told him about Katherine's death.

"Why would she lie about Katherine's long illness in Chongqing?"

"Because that's what they do. They are experts, whispering behind closed doors."

"They?"

"Yes, they, my damn family."

When he was a teenager in Hong Kong, a friend of his stepmother had expressed her sympathy about his mother dying in childbirth. His stepmother stood there with a smile on her face. She didn't say a thing. He knew they were lying. He had his memory of his mother when he was a child. He felt danger and wasn't going to refute out loud what Julia's friend had said. He didn't trust her. He didn't trust his stepmother. Nothing ever made sense in his home. It was better not to say a thing.

The following week a large package arrived, three nested boxes protecting a flat 20" by 24" painting, wrapped in butcher block paper and tied with twine. My husband carefully lifted the parcel and placed it on the dining room table. Hardly breathing, he slowly undid the twine. He didn't say anything when he looked at the painting as if there was too much of his mother to take in at one glance. He gently put the portrait down and walked outside for a cigarette.

Signed Esther Lovett, 1938, the oil portrait was of a young Chinese woman dressed in an oyster blue *qipao,* her bobbed, black hair stopping above a wide Mandarin collar. She looked directly at the viewer with only her left sleeve in sharp focus as if she were curious about what was happening outside the picture frame, yet careful to keep her distance. Since my husband was born in early 1939, it was very possible that he was looking at his mother when she was pregnant with him, and, sadly, only a few years away from her death.

When he came back inside, he nodded that it was her, but acted as if the portrait had never arrived. It would be months before we talked openly about it. He eventually took the painting to our local art studio, had it framed properly with inland wood, and hung it in the hallway leading to our bedroom. His silence settled into the portrait like an extra layer of varnish. In strange symmetry, mother and son had made a pact to keep quiet.

This silence was only broken when a Chinese friend from Hong Kong, Wang Wie, a history professor studying immigration in the United States, stayed with us for a few days, became intrigued with the portrait, and declared Katherine a *liberated woman*.

She was defiant, he told us, his face so close to the portrait I thought he was kissing her. Scrutinizing the date, signature and details of the painting, Wei said, "Back then, many Chinese women still twisted their long hair in a bun at the back of their necks. But look, Katherine cut hers."

I had admired her stylish soft waves that she had tucked behind her ears. I was soon to learn it wasn't that simple.

His stubby fingers jabbing at the outlines of her hair, stopping short of poking the picture's surface, Wei gently berated us on not remembering Madame Chiang Kai-shek, the wife of the Nationalist ruler of China and the darling of American newspapers during World War II, who properly dressed her long hair, pulling it back behind her head in a perfect roll. "Long hair in China was a sign of filial respect and traditional values," he explained. Katherine had chosen a liberated haircut as if the old rules didn't apply, even though her world was filled with style police, enforcing length and hairstyle.

Julia, my husband's stepmother, still wore her hair in the traditional style, only letting it loose at night when she sat at her rosewood vanity table covered with French perfumes, grooming her hair with British lavender oil before going to bed. Ida's daughter was enamored with her grandmother, whose shiny black hair she was allowed to brush when she stayed with her grandparents in Hong Kong.

Wei was amazed, "Look at how she's dressed. Those short sleeves!"

I thought she looked prim and proper in her demure blue dress, not like her black silk *qipao* hanging in my closet.

Declaring her "wonderful," he quoted Lu Xun, the revolutionary writer of the 1920s and 30s, and gave us a mini lecture on republican China before World War II. Lu Xun wrote that Chinese men were shocked when they saw women dressed in short sleeves. They imagined "naked bodies, genitals, sexual intercourse, promiscuity and bastards." He hated the priggish values of Chiang Kai-shek, the leader of the Chinese republic, and his harping on neo-Confucian thought through the New Life Movement. Lu Xun wanted social change for his women students, caught between expanding opportunities in education and claustrophobic traditions about marriage and family.

His shoulder length hair flapping about his face, Wei tried to impress on me that everything meant something else in China, and the "something" was not a classroom exercise in metaphor like a fly buzzing meant death. Hair, color, fabric, style, makeup or its lack were status markers, survival tactics, or revolutionary signals for men and women during the overthrow of the Qing dynasty, the Republican era, the Second World War, and the communist civil war. Queues were cut, long hair chopped, dresses burnt, and allegiances forged by what you wore and how your hair was styled.

He added, "You could, of course, deceive by costuming."

That night we drank a ton of red wine, talking about China and, midway through one of Wei's diatribes about Mao Zedong, I realized that I had witnessed a moment of cataclysmic change in Changchun on the day my husband and I went to the opening of a new department store. A massive crowd had surged into its front doors with hundreds of people smashing into each other to purchase new sweaters, pants, and blouses. Crumpled money was thrown back and forth between buyers and cashiers, literal piles of cash changing hands. There was a crush of women at the Revlon cosmetics counter, the first make-up allowed back in the city since the communist mandates. The resulting chaos was so intense that my husband demanded we leave the store quickly. The crowd was turning into a panicky mob.

The style police had written a new set of rules. Lipstick was back. Mao suits were no longer mandatory. The future was fashion.

After Wei left, an uneasy period followed, a false lull. We had decided to hang his mother's portrait in the hallway, a gallery of photographs of family members, alive and dead. Frequently, I would stare at Katherine when I walked past her painting on the way to our bedroom. I had the eerie sensation that her face was fading, her eyes settling into a faint stare. But once, when I stopped and scrutinized her, I had the distinct impression that her slightly parted lips were about to say something that had pre-occupied her for some time. What was it?

I even tried to avoid looking at the painting, and, instead, stay focused on how late I was, or how I had forgotten something, or how quickly I could get to bed. But the more I ignored her face, the more her portrait seemed to be staring back.

Her portrait was across the hall from the picture of my older sister who died right before her 7th birthday when I was a baby. The certainty of her death was absolute, known down to the tiniest detail, woven into the daily life of my large family that talked (probably too much) about the deaths of parents, grand-parents, aunts, uncles, siblings, cousins, nieces and nephews. Poles do not shy away from death. I knew when, where and how my relatives died and who was in the room and held their hand. I have sat at three-day wakes in front of open caskets where the dead are glorified, berated, satirized, and made the brunt of humor. But these experiences only made Katherine's life seem more appalling. There wasn't a death certificate, a date to mourn her passing or for that matter a birth date to commemorate her life. It got to the point where I simply couldn't walk past her painting without trying to comfort her or at least admit how frustrated I was that I knew nothing. There she was, pinned to the wall. A complete stranger.

It might help to know that my grandmother was a supersti-tious woman. She never let her grandchildren open umbrellas inside the house, measure our hands, or wear opals if we were not born in October. Envy was a curse on mankind and humility was its cure. If you boasted and made a friend feel diminished, you were obliged to send yellow roses as an apology. She told fortunes in the old Chicago Polish neighborhood with her bent Tarot deck, the cards stained with tears and a single drop of dried blood visible on the Three of Swords. She was respected for her powers, but nonetheless feared by her daughters (my mother especially) who forced her to put away her cards when too many predictions came true.

Growing up, I remember her stories were frightening: a death foretold through the scent of flowers, cold materializing as a presence that accompanied her neighbor's death, and her dreams warning her family and friends of the grim stalker. Birds, plants, even smells and sounds were linked to the overwhelming power of death. People with the ability to see spirits or foretell death were gifted like our next-door neighbor, the gypsy Elsie, whose basement apartment was crammed with caged birds, trunks of fanciful dresses, and on a wall plaque a beloved, stuffed Chihuahua head.

It's possible that I had simply regressed to my childhood and needed to check myself from projecting onto a painting my un-American experience of death. Had I attended too many funerals when I was a young? Or was I disturbed about Katherine's presence in the house and my inadequacies as a wife? Did my husband need more love and comfort? He seemed to have no problem walking down the hall. And only once did I find him looking at her face when I found myself checking her expression constantly as it shifted from subdued regret to amusement laced with surprise. She seemed to frown on me when I was doggedly running from task to task, and to smile with approval when I spent time trying to discover more about her. Only once did she seem to dissolve, the colors on her face receding into the canvass as if the painting was swallowing her.

That's why it was all the more shocking when sitting at breakfast one morning, my husband confessed that he hated his mother's oil portrait. "It's fake."

"Modigliani or Picasso told me more about a person than Rembrandt or Sargent."

In general, he couldn't stand realistic portraits and despised the founders' paintings displayed on the walls of the New England prep school he had attended.

Looking up from his marmalade toast, he declared the portrait of his mother "a failure." It didn't capture what she was like. He was even disturbed by the redness of her lips.

"She never wore lipstick."

I started to argue but realized how ridiculous I was. It was his mother, not mine. I tried to explain that after four months, I had a special attachment to the portrait, deciding not to add that the color of her lips was perfect for her complexion.

"Attachment to what?" he inquired; his sharp eyes boring into me.

That shut me up.

He also had the distinct feeling that his mother felt uncomfortable sitting for the painter.

"The portrait was full of shit."

His hostility seemed almost directed at me.

From that point on, I knew I couldn't talk with him about Katherine's portrait. I acted as if he was probably right and instead decided to treat the portrait as a tangible lead. If I could work hard enough, I could uncover more about who Katherine was and what happened to her. I started by researching Esther Lovett and New England portrait painting in the 1930s. Discover context. The mantra of a literary critic. Recover the lost world of Katherine. It felt so right.

Esther Parker Lovett was listed in the Yale University online art gallery because of her 1940 painting of Frederick Sheet Jones. The Dean of Yale College between 1909 and 1927, Jones was considered "competent" and "crusty." More interesting was that Esther was the wife of the beloved Yale chaplain, Sidney Lovett, known to decades of Yale students as "Uncle Sid." After he retired, he was closely connected to Yale-in-China and the New Asia College in Hong Kong where he lived for one year in 1958-1959 when my husband's father and stepmother were living there. The college became embroiled in political controversy over its stance toward the People's Republic of China (PRC), the communist state. Co-existence with the communists was an anathema to many people in Hong Kong, escaped refugees from the civil war between the nationalists and the communists, and dear old Uncle Sid seemed inclined to tolerate a more neutral tone. Clearly, he was over his head in Hong Kong, a Chinese city prone to riots between pro-communist factions and pro-a-long-list-of-anything-but-communism groups. The British, of course, were roundly held in contempt by this city's Chinese residents. A cash cow for the flotsam of the United Kingdom, Hong Kong was dotted with British institutions but had very few British living and working in its labyrinth of streets.

Buoyed by these finds, I plunged ahead and dug up my writings from when I was living off Harvard Square in the historic home of Asa Gray, the botanist, a home on whose walls hung portraits by Gardner Cox, a red-faced Dylan Thomas and a pensive Robert Frost.

The painter didn't live in the house, only his neurotic former wife who watched Perry Mason every afternoon and held me in contempt because I was not a graduate student at Harvard, but at a nearby less prestigious university, Brandeis. I once saw the same expression on Katherine's lips when I neglected my research on her portrait, only to receive a reassuring glance, her rich brown eyes radiating warmth when I started again.

A devoted portraitist, Gardner Cox was intent on capturing the mysteries of identity and, what he called, the "fugitive flux of time." In an essay he wrote, *The Artist Explains His Approach*, he even went so far as to state that the "body carries many messages and its shape and bearing identify the person even from the back a block away." The face held secrets, and the painter can "indicate at least two expressions and sometimes even more." The right side of the face was a separate emotional world from the left, and the viewers gaze shifted back and forth unconsciously between contradictory emotions that the portrait painter must record.

With these insights, I plunged back into examining her portrait and found to my amazement that Katherine's left side was in darkness, her right overly bright. The background was of a uniform ochre brown with highlights of umber. No light source. Where was the contrast coming from? Did Esther Lovett sense the impending catastrophe of Katherine's death, or did she see in her a hidden self, best kept away from the light. In fact, if you look closely, a looming dark presence can be seen in the painting from the top of her head, cascading down her neckline over her back and into the shadow on her left arm.

I began to walk more carefully past her portrait, not wanting to disturb her. At first glance, she looked calm, but once you focused on the left side of her face, the illusion vanished. She was suspended in turmoil. Lao She, the Chinese novelist, wrote in 1939, "A calm demeanor is no guarantee of personal safety." Were Katherine's thoughts absorbed with the chaos in China? By 1937, Japan had bombed and terrorized the Chinese population, controlling huge tracts of the country. Was she worrying about her family back home? What did her husband think about the war? Were they glad to be in the United States away from the violence? Did she know she was pregnant with Andrew?

Swamped with questions, I read everything I could about the war in China until I felt like I was living in two time zones. I neglected my teaching and my research on Emily Dickinson. It was necessary to enter Katherine's world. Without Andrew suspecting, I began to live a double life, tethered to a more vivid world of bloodshed and chaos.

Andrew's trips to China had penetrated the barrier to her lost life, but in her portrait, Katherine became a presence in our home. Mailed sixty years after it was painted, Katherine's face seemed to change its expression throughout the day. Alert, withdrawn, amused, disdainful, terrified. Through it, she came to live with us. No matter what Andrew thought, she had returned. She had found her son.

4

Scribbling

For almost a year, Katherine lived with us, a watcher with silent power, who also wanted something. I could sense it. The longer her portrait stayed on the hallway wall, the more her will seeped through the canvas. It was like she was directing me, but I couldn't figure out in what direction to go. I kept researching China until I was exhausted, but it still wasn't enough to discern what she wanted. In my frustration, I thought about taking down her portrait and stashing it in the garage with the other family photographs I had neglected to hang up. How often did I need to be reminded of her haunting demands? What did she want of me?

Irritated with the hours I spent in my study, Andrew tried to interfere. He sensed what I was doing behind closed doors.

"You are chasing a ghost," he would scold, a phrase he repeated frequently, this man who hated repetition. "And you have nothing of substance on my mother. What are you doing?"

Our fights became more frequent, either with Andrew stomping out to walk in the woods, or my yelling with a retreat to the nearby beach to stare into the surf for hours. Our marriage was unraveling; that is, until the unexpected occurred.

Grading student papers at the kitchen table, my husband received a phone call from another stranger, this time an elderly woman who claimed she had known his mother when they both lived in Boston. In her mid 80s, Mrs. Ann Loring had found out from mutual friends that Kitty's son, Andrew, was alive and living in the Northwest. That's what she called Katherine, Kitty.

Andrew listened to her nonstop memories about how she was raised on an estate outside of Boston in Duxbury, a dreamscape of descending ponds with splashes of meadow rue and irises next to a winding trellised path through purple wisteria, a scent unforgettable like a mixture of lilac and bubble gum, and how she spent her youth reading in the grand room with its massive fireplace and deep chocolate wood floor, covered by a dragon-phoenix carpet, a gift from Katherine and Andrew's father, Zi Ming.

In his recounting of the phone conversation, my husband lingered on the grand room in eerie detail as if he had had known it personally. He thought Ann was a wonderful woman, kind and thoughtful, a person with the "warmest heart."

Who cares, I thought, hesitant to show how impatient I was with his account of the conversation. What does the room or her heart matter? What about his mother? Anyway, that kind of room was more familiar to me than him. As a graduate student, I lived in Asa Gray's house in Cambridge above the famous botanist's herbarium. I stayed in two small rooms rent-free and guarded the home at night from would-be ghosts that the owner, Mrs. Cox, felt might at any time appear. Her daughter had committed suicide in her bedroom, and Mrs. Cox could not bear to be alone. Instead, she wandered the house, filled with fifteen-year-old *New Yorkers*, and spent her evenings drinking. It was like peeking into the Anglo-American aristocracy, lives filled with suicide, adultery and ridiculous spiritual beliefs. I was young and scornful of Mrs. Cox. For two years, we treated each other with cold indifference. I couldn't stand her Boston Brahmin arrogance and I wondered if I would also hate Mrs. Loring.

I can still feel my impatience with my husband's recounting of his phone call. Finally, he showed me the notes he had taken.

There was little coherence in what Ann had said, a rambling series of facts about Katherine. She didn't like the food at Milton

Hospital where she gave birth to my husband and had Ann bring her specially cooked chicken to her room. Katherine was beautiful, even stunning. She loved dining at the Ritz in a special room upstairs, rode in vegetable carts at night to avoid the Japanese, changed her name, slept in damp caves, blackened her face, had her family money stolen in Shanghai, and took one and a half years to get to Chongqing where she died from tuberculosis. My husband's rapid notes resembled a scribbled whirlwind with the word 'Japanese' punctuating the chaos. There were no dates, no sequence given, only an outpouring of events Ann Loring was told or perhaps overheard.

If I had done research for twenty years, I could never have come up with a story close to what Mrs. Loring told Andrew on the phone. The Ritz? Hiding in caves? A journey of one-and-a-half years from Shanghai to Chongqing? Stolen in Shanghai? TB? Well, I might have guessed at TB, the death shadow of war, and the diagnosis agreed with Julia's recent admission to Andrew that his mother had died of a lingering illness. That at least made sense. And where was Andrew's father during this harrowing experience of hiding from the Japanese?

It probably wouldn't have mattered what Mrs. Loring had said. Andrew was ecstatic about this phone conversation. I could see his goose bumps. Overjoyed, he told me that Ann had first met him in his mother's hospital room when he was a newborn. "Amazing. A baby. Can you imagine?" His mother had insisted that Ann meet her new baby and didn't care about violating the protocols of the maternity ward. For months, Ann continued to visit his parents' apartment in Boston and watch Andrew crawl around, then stand up, balancing on the edges of chairs, trying to take his first steps. She was an eyewitness to the life he shared with his mother.

Clearly what was most important to Andrew was that he had talked with someone who had known his mother, spent time with her, and could not forget her. At last, his mother was not a private, hidden reality, a *persona incognita*, but a living, breathing human being who didn't like hospital food. The trivial was proof of life.

What I don't understand is why my husband didn't take better notes. For days, he kept repeating that Mrs. Loring was a delightful woman and gushed about how exciting it was to talk with a friend of his mother. He's not a sentimental man, but he was getting sweet.

"A friend of my mother, can you believe it?" he repeated constantly, even when I tried to get him to focus on the details of the phone call.

He was looking forward to more calls from Ann. But there would be no more phone calls. As quickly as she entered our lives, the elderly woman left. We didn't realize at the time that it was an end-of-life call, a chance for Mrs. Loring to reconnect to a precious moment when she and Katherine were young. In that single conversation, Ann told Andrew what it felt like to hold her dear friend's baby in her arms and reminisced about those delightful dinners at her apartment when she showed Ann how to cook Chinese food using a very hot skillet. "Cooked everything in a frying pan very quickly," she said, adding how tragic it was that such a beautiful person died young.

Behind his back, I scrutinized the notes he took about the call. Mrs. Loring's memories were a fireworks display, brilliant sparks quickly fading into a uniform black sky as if life was inherently disconnected, a random series of bright points floating in a three-dimensional array, fascinating to watch, but gone before we knew it. It's up to those left behind to make the connections, put each flash back in some kind of order or time sequence, straighten out events on a horizontal line.

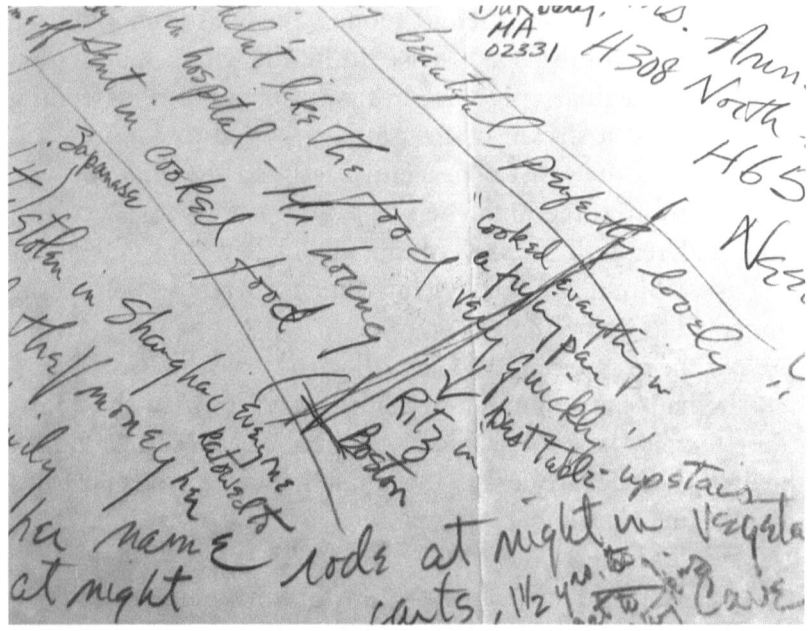

A few days after the call, Mrs. Loring's family lawyer called to say that Ann had died. He was following up to express his thanks that Ann had finally found my husband after many years of looking as if he were the one lost.

Luckily, I was the only one home to answer the phone.

"In my experience, dying people search for someone at the end of their life that they have lost contact with." A probate lawyer, he spoke with authority about the dead.

"But Katherine had died. She was not lost. She was dead."

"True," he responded, irritated at my correcting tone.

"You might want to know that Mrs. Loring talked with your mother-in-law, not really talked of course, but imagined she was with her at the end."

"What exactly are you saying?" I was in no mood for a cryptic conversation. He was a lawyer after all.

"Just that. Mrs. Loring was talking with your husband's mother on her death bed. The poor woman was distressed that she hadn't found your husband sooner. She felt she should have tried harder. It didn't make sense. In her delirium, she pleaded with some imaginary presence in the hospital room, defending herself against a stream of accusations. I tried to comfort her. Everyone did. It wasn't a peaceful death. In the end, she was running from something, her legs propped up in that bed, running. Dreadful. Thank God, she finally died."

I asked him if Ann had left anything for Andrew. Something connected to Katherine.

"No," he responded. "All I can tell you is that Ann was worried that she had said too much to Andrew and terrified she hadn't said enough. The poor woman was caught between loyalties to the living and dead. She was afraid that her call to your husband might get her in trouble."

"Trouble?"

"Yes. Someone she knew but wouldn't name. Someone living who could do her harm. Her speech was very garbled at the end. She was torn between having said too much and not having tried harder to say more. Disturbing. No one could comfort her."

After we hung up, I considered the possibility that the phone call of Mrs. Loring to Andrew was a duty she owed Katherine. Did she have a guilty conscience about having neglected to contact her old friend's son to express her regrets? Weird things can happen at the end of life, strange visitations from past relations and odd hallucinations. My father saw a uniformed Nazi walking around his bed, my grandmother hundreds of balloons. Katherine could have put in a hospital appearance. Emily Dickinson's poems are often riffing on the last words of the dead, those precious syllables that rise above deception as if the dying are the only humans that finally tell the truth.

And what possible trouble could Ann Loring get into by talking with Andrew? That was a stumper. Who was still alive to even care? Could it be Julia or Ida? Or some old American friend from the past who knew Andrew's parents?

With Mrs. Loring's phone call, we were given a few details about Katherine's life and very little to hold them together. Despite that, my husband had made an intense connection with Mrs. Loring. Her voice made Katherine come alive, as if his mother was talking directly to him, the tenderness having never faded. Was that what Katherine wanted, a direct line to her son, refusing to let poor Mrs. Loring die in peace? Was Mrs. Loring an unwitting medium for a mother cut down early in life, perpetually separated from her child? Was Katherine a modern day Ligeia, her willpower lasting beyond death, invading another's life?

When my husband returned home, I told him about the call from the lawyer and Ann Loring's death.

His first instinct was to leave the house and handle his feelings alone, away from people, away from me. The one and only conversation he ever had with someone who knew his mother, and the person immediately died. No follow-up calls. No more stories.

I was used to Andrew's stoicism, admired it in fact, but I needed him to stay. He had gone it alone his entire life. What would happen if this time, he didn't run? It wasn't that he had to open up in some psychobabble way. Share your grief *a la* Hallmark. No. Simply don't run away. Stay.

Tall, athletic, and sinewy, Andrew wasn't someone you could push around. A physically strong man who had worked outdoors fighting fires, smoke-jumping into burning forests, and backpacking alone in the wilderness of Idaho and Montana, he knew how to survive. Sturdy was a good word. Solitude was his friend.

I asked him not to leave or, if he needed some privacy, to understand I would wait for his return. He went outside for a smoke and must have walked around the nearby woods for a few hours. When he came back, it was almost dark.

We sat together on the living room couch and looked out the window in silence. Since it was clear he wasn't going to say a word, I told him what the lawyer had said about Ann Loring's visit from his mother.

"Ridiculous," he responded, jumping up and moving about the living room like a marionette, twisting and turning. Then for no good reason he insisted on running out to the store for pork chops and cooking dinner as if it was the last meal of his life.

Midway through eating the meal in total silence, his face collapsed, his eyes fading into flat brown circles without light. Without a word, he stood up, went over to his favorite recliner, and fell asleep. Where was he? Probably in some hidden place where his secrets were safe. Did his unconscious know what happened to his mother?

No one in his family had said one word about his mother, and in a short span of time her dress and her portrait had arrived along with a burst of details about her life, and, of course, her nickname, Kitty. In one breath, she is dining at the Ritz and the next riding in vegetable carts at night with her son at her side during the Japanese invasion of China that ended with 20 million Chinese dead.

What were his surviving Hong Kong family and friends doing, trying at one point to tell him his mother died in childbirth in China when he knew that couldn't be true? He had successfully guarded his childhood memory of his mother's face, and, besides, he had found out at sixteen when he came from Hong Kong for schooling in the United States what her name was. His father had suddenly located Andrew's birth certificate, needed to procure a passport. Andrew was given a copy of it before he left for the United States along with a brand-new American passport. Like her image, he guarded these documents carefully. He knew her name, Katherine Lin, and he knew she was alive when he was at least four years old. What a ludicrous lie, the childbirth story, contradicted by no one at the time, not even his stepmother. At least Mrs. Loring had provided a cause for Katherine's death—tuberculosis—that agreed with what Julia had written.

Covering him up with a blanket, I left him alone in his chair and slept on the sofa. I was such an idiot to think it was my responsibility to have Katherine materialize. When she did assume tangible shape through the voice of Ann Loring, everything went haywire. Ghosts really should stay on their side of the divide between life and death. Poor Mrs. Loring was hounded by something on her deathbed.

When Andrew woke up, the first thing he did was to call his stepmother and Ida. That surprised me. Their responses seemed programmed as if they had rehearsed their lines together. Both said, "You should have asked your father when he was alive." They could tell him nothing more about his mother. They insisted they knew of no one named Ann Loring.

"It's the art of deflection," he said, his black hair tousled from sleeping in his chair. Question the questioner. Insinuate the person asking was at fault. But above all: answer nothing. Andrew ended up confiding that it had always been this way growing up. The weight of silence. A punishing silence, except for their whispers behind closed doors. When he lived in Hong Kong, his father and Julia often retreated to their bedroom beyond his hearing. He tried to listen, putting the side of his head against the heavy wood doors. Only whispers. He could never decipher their words. "They will never change. They shut me out," he emphasized, his voice growing sullen, burdened by resentment.

His explanation of familial treachery only made me restless, my nerves on edge. I did the dishes like a madwoman, throwing around forks and knives in the sink until the sharp pinging made Andrew come over and put his arms around me. "Glad you are not my enemy," he said, grabbing a dish towel. I continued to fume about the flippant responses from Julia and Ida. I wanted to call his relatives back and tell them off.

Andrew told me not to call. "They refused to help. Let it go. You have to protect yourself from them."

I respected his wishes and asked to look at Andrew's notes. It was dangerous to chase after a ghost, but it was worse to ignore one. I was determined not to give his family the final word on Katherine.

I devised a plan. If I had answered Mrs. Loring's phone call, I would have asked her to slow down and then written everything she said accurately in straight lines. No scribbling in circles. And I would have asked questions, probing questions. I had read about interrogation techniques in the *New Yorker*. Don't lead. Keep listening. Intervene strategically. Look for contradictions. My husband didn't even seem interested in the big question: How did Mrs. Loring know Katherine died of TB? Who told her? Who gave her the information about Katherine's long journey to Chongqing? My husband wasn't thinking. Swept away by his emotions, he didn't have the necessary vigilance to ask strategic questions. And it was too late to call her back. She was dead. The whole thing was absurd. A botched chance at the truth.

Details mattered. Andrew's mother had darkened her face, I assumed, to hide who she was, smearing her pale, upper class skin to appear as if she worked under the sun as a manual street sweeper or farmer. If true, what upheaval had Katherine experienced? Yes, of course, the war. But what does that mean? In 1939, she is upstairs at the Ritz drinking with her Harvard friends and then a few years later she is riding at night on a vegetable cart with her young son, evading the Japanese, a life upended, her protective shell of wealth shattered.

If her journey took one-and-a-half years to travel from coastal Shanghai to interior Chongqing, over 1,000 miles away, she must have faced horrible conditions. China is roughly the size of the United States, and its longest river, the Yangtze, flows from Tibet on its western border to Shanghai on the East China Sea, stopping at Chongqing along the way. The Japanese would have controlled the river up to Wuhan.

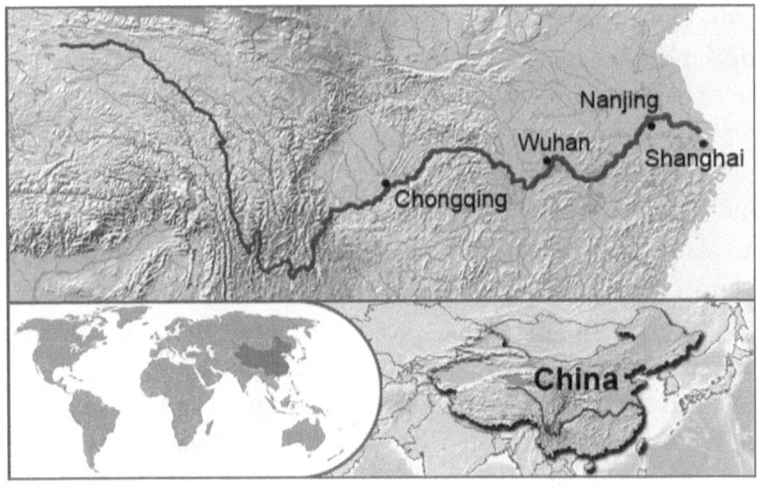

Katherine would have had to avoid it, travelling through arid plains and mountains by indirect routes. Did she contact tuberculosis during that time? Traveling with a young child through a war zone must have required unusual resources. Did she have help? Ann Loring said that she had hidden in caves. That was a clue. On what route were there caves for fleeing Chinese refugees? And what was she doing in Shanghai, on the other side of China? I thought when Andrew's parents left the United States they had returned to Chongqing, beyond Japanese control, on the west side. Mrs. Loring was insistent about Shanghai. At some point, Katherine and Andrew had left Chongqing and relocated to Japanese-occupied Shanghai on the coast of China. And then, they returned to Chongqing. Why, I didn't know.

I purchased a bunch of maps and atlases of China with annotations about World War II. By December 1941, after Pearl Harbor, the United States was at war with Japan. Even though the United States had been providing arms to China to fight the Japanese, it had not entered the war in either Europe or Asia. It was a dangerous game, letting your allies fight your enemies without having to commit your own troops in a ground or air war. Once Pearl Harbor was attacked, the United States quickly declared war against Japan and then Germany.

Let's assume that Mrs. Loring was accurate, and Katherine was living in Japanese-occupied Shanghai with Andrew at some point during the war. As a wealthy Chinese woman, she probably lived in one of its international districts. Since her child was an American citizen, his protection as a citizen from a neutral country was over by 1942. British and Americans who lived in the International District were viciously rounded up by the Japanese and put in camps until the war ended in 1945. Ida had lived in the French Concession in Shanghai during the war, another place that wealthy Chinese lived. Did her life ever overlap with Katherine's? What had made Katherine run from Shanghai and make the dangerous trip back to Chongqing? I knew that Ida had stayed and faced terror and starvation for the war's duration, refusing to talk with anyone, even her daughter, about what she had experienced.

I had scattered facts and no way to string them together.

Ann Sexton and Sylvia Plath, American poets, used to meet at the Ritz and drink martinis, and in my restless mind Katherine had joined them upstairs laughing, sharing gossip, and scoffing at the men that burdened their lives, enjoying life before the horrors of war and her untimely death. She was slipping and sliding through a set of literary anecdotes. Even stranger, I had dined upstairs at the Ritz with a snotty Harvard boy who had granted me the supreme opportunity to see how the better half lives. I didn't slurp on martinis, being a fan of a pink lady, and was instructed in the proper way to prepare a Caesar Salad, at the table with a raw egg and anchovies. But I had been in the exact same room as Katherine once in my life. Astonishing.

Katherine was close.

5

February 18, 1943

I had huddled in the cave with my son for five punishing days and nights. After he fell asleep in my weary arms, I would play a mental game at night, pretending I was a child safe in my Suzhou family home. There was no war. My father was still alive and at work in his study, and my mother was busy in our parlor planning the day's outings. My older sister flitted in and out, my playmate and my friend. The game comforted me. It was necessary. I could feel my body shedding its fears. It was a simple game. I would picture each weathered tree in our garden, the bamboo grove next to the ancient rocks, the waterfall gently filling the narrow stream, the crimson-red flowering plum. Smell the peach scent of Osmanthus trees. I took time to arrange each memory carefully. My sister playing match-my-flower by the white lotus pond underneath the willow trees, a green shelter, next to the Flowering Serenity Pavilion, my father's favorite spot, with bamboo brushes in a red lacquer holder on a square table. In the game, color was important, deep black inksticks, blacker inkstones on a carved white jade stand, and papers, shades of pearl white, oyster white, antique white, glossy green celadon porcelain cups, each detail soothed my mind. Only then could I feel my sleeping child's chest rise and fall against mine, a rhythm in peace.

The game kept the muffled thuds, falling in tight clusters of five or six followed by a single bomb somersaulting from the sky, from destroying my mind. I am mother, I would chant to myself. I must survive. The game was a magic cross I held against the devil Japanese. It restored calm. Only then could my son surrender to a deep sleep that knows no war. But the devil always broke the trance. Like the crescendo of a marching tune, bombs in quick succession would shake the cave's walls and shatter my game.

Under my jacket, my son would gasp for air. There was no escape from the dirty air, laden with kerosene fumes. There was only one truth. My son must have air. He must have air.

When we are dead, pain still sears our soul, warping our sense of time. I remember these events of 1943 until I am exhausted. Yes, I am forced to remember. I cannot forget. Trivial details in the cave loom out of proportion. They are like small whirlpools or rivulets sweeping debris into their shapes and paths. I cannot explain their power.

Nights were long in the deep, limestone cave, the mobbed refugees stuffed inside, pressed against each other, a solid mass stacked on the cold floor, waiting day and night for the bombing to stop. I bought padded jackets from a hunched woman who had bartered them from dying farmers in a village close to Luoyang. Their despair saved us from the damp chill that carried off children from the cave every night. The woman bargained hard, her mouth studded with pointed teeth. She demanded our woolen gloves for the two padded *ushankas* with long earflaps that she had pilfered from the graves of Russian soldiers, stinking of rot. I took the bargain, stuffing them with rags to fit my son's head, wrapping our hands with quilted strips.

In the cave, my husband's private secretary was stretched on the rough floor at my feet, clutching our last blanket to his chest. Beaded with sweat, his flushed face had lost its arrogance. Delirious, he was trying to figure out the distance between stations on the Lunghai railway by counting numbers on his fingers.

For nine months the three of us had bought our way west on the broken train route, riddled with bomb craters, exploded rails, and barricades, until we switched to rail carts, wheelbarrows, and provision trucks. Staying for weeks in churches, we traveled north across Anhui and west over the flat plains of Henan. We walked at night along blackened fields of wheat and millet. Amid the ruins of Kaifeng, we bought space on a stolen truck, filled with Chinese businessmen, disguised as relief workers. A rich farmer let my boy ride his horse for 80 precious kilometers. He offered to buy my son. My son.

My husband's secretary had found me in my family apartment in the French Concession. Insisting that we leave Shanghai quickly, he had received orders from my husband to take me and my son to Chongqing. My mother and sister had already abandoned our family estates in Suzhou for the safety of our apartment in Shanghai only to face fleeing again. They did not want to wait for the Japanese to loot our home. In the French Concession, the Vichy government had collapsed, the last barrier against complete Japanese control. After the soldiers had inventoried every item in our home and affixed red tags, they would throw us out. We would be homeless, living on the street like dogs.

A haughty bureaucrat, the private secretary seemed certain of his power, a master of the events that were swallowing my family. He boasted that he knew the best inland route across enemy lines to Chongqing. Stuffed into his shiny black Western suit and tie, his high white collar tight around his neck, he bragged about the meetings he attended with the inner circle of the Generalissimo. He had written meticulous reports that were essential to the workings of the Chinese Nationalist government. He strutted around the room, speaking nonsense, staring at the silk wallpaper and Soong dynasty paintings, estimating their value. His oily hair pushed back high above his forehead, he tried to sit in our dead father's chair. My mother ushered him to the damask divan. Offended, he sat down and placed his black fedora on the square rosewood table as if everything belonged to him.

My mother had made plans to abandon the apartment and flee to a fishing village on the southern coast, hiding with a relative of our cook. She pleaded with me to come. "You must protect your son. You will never find your husband. You will never survive the journey. You must think about your son."

I was thinking about my son. I did not trust the cook.

My sister insisted on staying in Shanghai to work and live at the medical clinic by the Jardine & Matheson silk factory. She wanted mother to stay and join her. Time was short.

We had to decide. We couldn't decide.

Earlier, an intelligence agent, Mr. Yamaguchi, had visited with questions about our country estate that the Japanese soldiers had seized. Communist guerrillas were threatening to overrun the troops and distribute food and guns to the local peasants. In the countryside and on the streets of Shanghai, grain was gold. Rice was gold.

"Are you communists?" he probed, making my mother stand for hours while he searched through my father's old study and my sister's bedroom.

I remember how the intelligence officer touched the shiny chrysanthemum pin beneath his label, grilling my older sister about her activities at the clinic. Was she working for the communists at the International Relief Committee? Who were the leaders of the guerrillas harassing their troops at the estate? Mr. Yamaguchi would return soon with Japanese soldiers to arrest everyone.

We had to decide.

The silver-tongued secretary kept assuring me. Since my husband had arrived safely in Chongqing after his important work in the United States for Chiang Kai-shek, the president of the Republic of China and the Generalissimo of the National Revolutionary Army, we only had to reach the government's haven nestled among the Huaying Mountains 1,000 miles west of Shanghai.

What husband, I thought? Who was this husband that I had not seen for almost three years? This man who had barely touched me since our child was born. But he was a father, and he would protect his son.

Chiu Chun had pointed at the precious tickets for the Shanghai-Nanjing railway that he placed on the dining room table. He had risked much to obtain the tickets by bribing key Japanese officers. He insisted that they could make our way by rail farther west from Nanjing to Luoyang, then Xi'an, and finally the capital, Chongqing, a city of refugees protected by the Generalissimo's soldiers, anti-aircraft guns and American P-40 Warhawks. They would fly from Xi'an to Chongqing on American cargo planes. He paused and recalculated, counting on his pudgy, bejeweled fingers.

What choice did I have?

I decided. I fled to save my child. We would die in Shanghai. What chance would we have on the streets?

The next morning, we left the apartment, the last place connecting me to my family, the precious souvenirs of childhood, the sounds of those you love. In a few days our home would become an empty shell, a stylish bivouac for Japanese officers.

I knew that the odds of reaching my husband were not good. No one—not a Nationalist sympathizer, a communist guerrilla, a rich landlord from his villa, a poor worker from his shanty, a farmer fleeing his ruined land—was safe on the road west, away from the Japanese. Loyalties changed in seconds, disguises made landlords into peasants, peasants into soldiers, soldiers into bandits, and bandits into communist guerrilla fighters. Death's road.

For the first thirty-one years of my life, I was blessed with good fortune. The proof was the day I held my son in my arms in Milton Hospital, my American friends hovering over the beauty of my child. I was drunk on the sheer abundance of life.

How I fought my husband not to return to China. I was right to fight. I should have fought harder. Four years later I faced terrible choices that no mother should have to make.

Every day bullets riddled the train to Nanjing, their piercing screams shattering the false safety of the passenger car. Every day, guerrillas or bandits fired at the train and vanished into the night, leaving behind smoke-choked cries and pleas to whatever god the travelers hoped would save them. Passengers cowered under their seats and embraced the floor, their suitcases flimsy cardboard shields. My son clung to me, his small body rigid with fear, his delicate face paralyzed. When the battered train arrived in Nanjing, more frantic refugees swarmed the train depot, elderly parents strapped to their backs. They climbed on the roof of the passenger cars and swung from the windows. The train went nowhere. Dazed foreigners stood at the edge of the swirling mob, their luggage tossed at their feet, their servants gone. Two Englishmen rode bicycles along the rail line as if it were a day outing. Japanese planes swooped over the road heading west, targeting refugees. The northern route was too close to the Yellow River where the Imperial Japanese army waited on its northern bank, preparing to cross the river and cut China in two, *Operation Ichigo*.

My sister was right. I had grown up in a school-girl's fog and married a rich, educated Chinese man. I did not know the world as it was. Her work at the clinic held a deeper truth. War was a deeper truth. My journey to Chongqing became my school. My schoolteacher, my death.

In the gray shadows, Chiu Chun's face darkened.

"Damn you and damn your gold." He spewed a delirious litany of complaints about how he could have escaped Shanghai alone. He didn't need my husband's money. He could have traveled the southern route with his military friends whose sideline was smuggling, and joined networks of soldiers and gangsters who plied their trade on the waterways among the Japanese locking down the coastal cities. He could buy rides on military trucks and boats. He could buy medicine, rice, and fish, his lips smacking spittle.

I was silent when his legs started to shake, his feet trembling, making quivering shadows on the cave wall.

To go the underworld route, he would have joined other collaborators, Chinese eager to appease the Japanese in order to run guns and opium or, worse, tin and tungsten to keep the enemy manufacturing more bullets to kill their Chinese countrymen.

Close to death, he lied.

He had to deliver me and my son to Chongqing.

Sickness, like love, always brought impossible dreams. At night he shouted for deliverance until he finally stopped, turned his head to the wall, and in surprise whispered, "Colonel Huang Yishan, you have come to save me."

I waited for his death.

Underneath my frayed sweater, a silken shawl was wrapped around my waist, a gift of my mother's love. How did I face such loss? My mother gone. My father gone. My home gone. My garden, gone, where father retreated before he was killed by treacherous Chinese. In the garden stood a stand of loquat trees, their dark green leaves drooping with clusters of pungent white flowers, long fingers balancing pearls. I had learned to embroider those trees on a silk screen and loved to sit and watch my mother as she separated threads between her thumb and finger and created precise stitches. "To keep you safe," she said quietly, handing me the shawl as if it would protect me on my journey to Chongqing.

Katherine. Kitty. I chanted my English names in silence, names discarded, belonging to a past without war. Better to call me *Nu*, Chinese for woman, one among the millions walking the road west.

The last night in the cave, Chiu Chun's body jumped as if shot with electric current. He twisted and stared with hatred, his only feeling left. I woke my son, urging him to back away from the putrid smell, closer to the piles of straw stacked against the cave wall.

Frightened refugees were still crushing into the stifling cave, new arrivals from the farms near San Hsien, their wheelbarrows and oxcarts stacked at the cave mouth like expectant animals waiting for an evening meal.

A peasant girl, curious about Chiu Chun's ragged breath, came close to examine him as if she was studying a dying frog without fear, but with interest in the end.

Unafraid, the girl had climbed the straw and asked about the dying man.

She was spindly like a twisted wire.

I said nothing. The girl chattered, watching my face for the slightest reaction.

She told me that many from her village were already dead before their wheat crop shriveled. The hail and frost destroyed much of what was left. Their elderly and children died from eating leaves and green slime growing in old buckets and scattered pools. One day Chinese Nationalist soldiers came and took her father and brother. They ignored the rest. Their village became no more. Nothing.

"I saw an English man ripped from his bicycle and beheaded," Li Min said, lifting her right arm in a quick slash downward with a half-smile on her face.

The girl was a chatterbox. She jabbered about missionaries executed, studying my face as if she knew already who and what I was. The girl's chopped hair framed layers of dirt covering her cheekbones and mouth, an odd grin appearing under thick grime. "Husband, dead?"

I shooed her away.

The girl refused to leave. "Li Min," she said, staring at my son, telling him stories about how she had survived. Her grandfather believed life was short and brutal. Survive. On the road, she bartered dried noodles and bean curd for stolen clothes.

She survived by listening to rumors and repeating them: where the Japanese were strafing roads and where the roads were clear for many *li*. Where the railroads were cracked and where they worked, hauling passengers, cargo and oxen over the mountains to Xi'an. Where the robbers were as thick as the fleas on the mattresses stuffed in caves and where the Nationalist soldiers had executed them like summer flies.

The girl would not stop staring. "Son?" she asked, reaching to touch his head. "No talk?"

I yelled at the girl to go away.

Scuffling for space broke out. The smell of urine, excrement and bloody wounds permeated the cave. My son cried when he heard the fighting. I whispered in his ear, "no Shanghainese, no English." No Shanghai words to betray our past. Every English word must slip away. Katherine no more, Kitty no more. The villagers were listening. A foreign tongue or sound conjured demons and evil spirits from the sky. One word would bring bad luck, drawing bombs to the cave and suffocating them beneath mounds of rock.

I distracted him with shadows dancing on the cave wall behind the lamps, but his eyes looked toward the shouting. I picked him up until he could see the cave entrance.

"Air, air," I whispered in his ear as if the words would still his panicked breathing.

Undeterred, the peasants pushed back into the cave where there was no air. Chiu Chun's let out a piercing cry. And his eyes turned into flat, black coins.

As if on cue, Li Min quickly tugged at the blanket Chiu Chun had twisted around his body. A girl of twelve, she was death's familiar, her loved ones obliterated in the ravaging drought, three generations sunk back in the soil.

"Dead," she announced, waiting to see what I would do. She shouted the word back to her villagers, "Dead."

Two men scrambled to strip the secretary's clothes and drag his body out of the cave.

Clutching my son, I ran into the space created by the stench of the secretary's corpse. I had to reach the entrance. I had to find air.

6

Land's End

Our niece, a microbiologist, believed life was random. I didn't really understand what she meant except that events were unpredictable; only probabilities existed. Patterns were guides, not guarantees. The future befuddled us, as did the past, even the near past of yesterday. Such uncertainty rattled me. I would prefer to think of my life as immersed in a stream of time, heading somewhere, not battered by unintended accidents, and definitely not a pachinko ball hurtling in some game whose rules I don't understand yet am forced to play. I enjoyed comfort and I relished stability with a side of mystery. I didn't want a life ruined by chance, upheavals beyond my control, or delusions.

Despite my desire for order, Katherine's ghost had wandered into my life, disrupting plans, dreams, and common sense. She was the random occurrence that pushed me backwards in search of her. Each time Andrew and I returned to China she was a fellow passenger.

In the mid 90s, Andrew received a United Nations grant to conduct background research for his long poem on the Three Gorges Dam in China, our main destinations, Chengdu and Kunming in Sichuan province. My husband wanted to visit Chongqing where his mother died and to travel the Yangtze River, but it was probably not going to happen on this trip. He had fragile images of a villa in the hills where he lived when his mother died. But he thought it would be impossible to find his mother's grave or more details about her death. He knew no one in Chongqing, a city of 6 million, one of the "smokestacks" on the Yangtze River. The closest we came to the city was a quick glimpse out a bus window that showed a dark brown cloud of pollution clinging to a shimmering strip of water.

Besides giving lectures at local universities in Chengdu, we briefly explored the city, our first destination the Wenshu monastery that was in the midst of a Buddhist revival. We had come before the Chinese tourism industry ten years later would transform this working monastery with renovations and regulations, sanitizing it as a center of religious piety. Advertised today as a sanctuary of calm, the monastery in 1995 was flooded with disabled beggars, blind and deformed, crushing to get inside the main gates. Within the walls of the temple, ten-foot-high bonfires raged with believers tossing paper prayers into the inferno. Prayer wheels whirred amid thunderous chants and disorderly crowds surging around statues of demons and bodhisattvas. Feared by the Chinese government, such religious frenzy expressed the anguish of the masses, threatening to overwhelm communist rule and the monks trying to keep visitors from injuring themselves or the temple.

After ten minutes inside, Andrew reexperienced the same terror he felt when he was a young boy among a crowd of people, running in all directions from armed men in pursuit, a war-torn world splitting apart at the seams. Panic was a deep lump inside his chest, a monster ready to spring. He grabbed my hand, and we ran through the narrow back alleys of the temple complex to the back exit. Outside, bent over, he struggled to breathe. Rubbing his back, I realized how trauma has no words: it seizes the body, shaking it, memories kinetic.

He stumbled toward a stone bench by the side of the road and collapsed. I clung to his side, oblivious of the traffic racing past. After dark shadows had lengthened on the apartments across the street, we slowly made our way back to the hotel, stopping by a young woman lying on the sidewalk, her paralyzed legs limp sticks, writing her life story with chalk in beautiful Chinese characters. Passers-by towered above her figure reading her story of poverty, abuse, and neglect. Coins dropped into the small cup by her hip.

Moved by her effort and the elegance of her calligraphy, Andrew whispered, "This is China."

Intense suffering. Intense beauty.

A few days later, we ventured out again to visit a neglected museum, part eighteenth-century scholar's villa, part cottage for the Tang poet, Tu Fu. The renovators had not yet arrived. The ponds were stagnant, filled with weeds, the grounds littered with plastic bags, crushed cans, cigarette butts and paper flyers. No one was there. Depressingly dirty, the home of Tu Fu mirrored his desperate attempt to find a safe haven when he wandered the Yellow River cities and traversed the treacherous Chin Ming Mountains to reach Chengdu in the year 760, never finding any enduring protection for himself, his wife or his children. His life disrupted by war, rebellion, famine, and invasion from northern nomadic tribes and Tibetan armies, Tu Fu wrote poems in whatever stopping place he could find. In his thatched cottage, he spent two peaceful years composing some of his best poetry. "All things caught between shield and sword,/All grief empty, the clear night passes."

The night before we left for Kunming, we read Tu Fu's poems to each other. Like Andrew, the Tang poet was caught between what he sought and what he found. "After ten desperate, headlong years, driven/Perch to perch, I cling to what peace one twig holds." Trauma had shaped Andrew's life, leaving him to fend for himself. Poetry might be the only language to capture its ragged claws. Before we went to sleep Andrew told me about a recurring wish he had. He spoke tenderly in a child's whisper his outrageous request: one chance to speak with his mother, however briefly.

An ethereal world existed parallel to ours. Attached to our lives was another life inexplicable and unavoidable.

In the morning we left for Kunming. We had bought two train tickets for hard seats in its Second-Class compartment. The car was crammed with families traveling with children, their packs overflowing with packages of noodles, dried shrimp, and glass tea containers, their large red and white plastic duffel bags jammed under the seats. We were two feet apart from our Burmese neighbors as we slept on our bunk ledges through the dozens of petrol-fumed tunnels underneath red dirt mountains terraced with rice fields.

Children ran down the narrow aisle screaming while parents shouted, punishing their offspring with blows. While the engine billowed and belched, its whistle screeching, I dreamt of a magical city guarded by a delicate, twelve-year old Chinese girl who encouraged me to follow her through the streets. All I had to do was jump across a three-foot gap separating our worlds.

Once home in the United States, Andrew received a phone call from Mrs. Loring's nephew. The family lawyer had given him the task of cleaning out his aunt's apartment and creating an inventory of her belongings, the expensive furniture, old rugs, piles of books and assorted boxes. He had hauled a stack of her boxes to his study and had finally gotten around to sorting through her bills, tax returns, memorabilia, and letters.

In one of Mrs. Loring's boxes, he found a stash of letters that a Chinese woman named Kitty had written to a relative of Mrs. Loring, a Mrs. Withington from Rochester, New York. Having visited his aunt before she died, he had heard tales about the so-called ghost that came calling and knew about his aunt's contact with Andrew. He didn't know why his aunt hadn't sent Andrew the letters while she was alive, but there they were in a dusty old box. His question was simple: Did we want them?

Stunned, Andrew urged him to mail them as soon as he could. We were going to read Katherine's actual words written by her own hand. What information and secrets would they contain? I could hardly sit still.

Andrew recalled the surname, Withington.

"I met a Virginia Withington at my guardian's house in New Haven. Years ago. She worked for Sikorsky Aircraft and was a whiz at navigation." What she told him when he was sixteen years old, he could never forget it. Once she stood inside the cockpit of a Pan Am Boeing 707 and used her sextant to check whether the pilots were on course. They were off slightly and were embarrassed to admit her antique sextant was better than their instrument panel.

"She took me for a ride in her red Thunderbird convertible."

The time machine was hurling us backwards. We had barely returned to the United States and unpacked our bags when Andrew's mother reclaimed our emotional lives.

I felt like I had hit the motherlode. It's the dream of every researcher to find overlooked or hidden letters that no one else has read. When I was working on Emily Dickinson at the Beinecke Library at Yale, a correspondence between Dickinson's brother and his lover was taken from the library and hoarded, putting it out of reach from anyone else. I was asked by a librarian to request the materials and become a first responder in retrieving them. I declined and the person who kidnapped the letters went on to become a star in the field of Dickinson studies.

Dickinson's letters read like her poems, intimate encounters conveying dark truths, a Victorian Tu Fu. I imagined that Katherine's letters would reveal her inner life as letters to friends often did, especially when long-distance phone calls were uncommon.

Within a week, a small packet arrived in the mail as if it were normal to receive letters written in the 1930s from a woman whose past had been obliterated. My husband read them through and was quickly disappointed. The letters were little more than thank-you notes to an older friend who had taught his mother polite forms of English. "Too bad," he said, dropping them down on my desk as if they should be discarded.

While reading them through, I thought about my own mother. What memories did I have of her? I had never read a single letter she had written. What I did have were weird stories she and my aunt told about their childhood with my superstitious grandmother, my mother's fond memories about her starring role in the high school play her senior year, her repeated laments about the college scholarship in drama she abandoned when her father had a sudden heart attack, forcing her to drop out and help support her mother, her depression, her anger, her incredible love of babies, and her devotion to the Catholic Church. The list was endless, filtered through stories, gossip, and rumors from my aunts, cousins, family friends, and father. Thousands of images, impressions, misunderstandings, arguments, joyful meetings, and conversations with my four siblings after my mother had died. They still go on today when I am seventy-four.

We are born into a web of stories refined, erased, repeated, denied, and embellished.

The phone call with Mrs. Loring had made Andrew's mother come alive. His trips to China gave him echoes and substitutes, images of faces in a crowd, chance encounters at a restaurant, the familiar smells of food, the haunting sounds of an ossified childhood language. Mrs. Loring was a direct line to his mother, a voice on the telephone who had been her friend and was bursting with stories about Katherine.

The first time I was in Warsaw and heard Polish spoken everywhere, I felt undone. I was in an unfamiliar country that I somehow knew. I would smile overhearing women talking on the streetcar, their intimate sounds resonating in some part of me I had forgotten. With my parents and grandparents dead, their voices had vanished; their laughter about Polish relatives and whispers in Polish so the young children would not understand. I had learned to pray in Polish in the old Chicago Polish neighborhood, Polonia, but quickly lost those words when my family moved from Bucktown to Skokie. It was not cool to be Polish. I refashioned myself a true American. English only. But the sounds never disappeared. A known but forgotten language lingered inside me.

Only the sound of Mrs. Loring's voice on the phone, telling him about Katherine, worked any magic for my husband. The packages we had received, the dress and the portrait, were rejected by Andrew as inauthentic. Terrible suspicions shrouded the dress. It could be a family trick, not belonging to his mother at all. The portrait was worse, reflecting the painter's adherence to artistic conventions that imposed a set of rules rather than illuminating who his mother was.

Unfortunately, Andrew did not hear his mother's voice in her letters to Mrs. Withington. The person writing the letters was a stranger. Conventions masked her strained need to be polite in stifling thank-you notes.

I trusted his reaction, but I was searching for his mother in a separate reality. I could never live inside his childhood, his mother's voice and face, locked in his heart. I could only find her somewhere else, through traces of what she left behind. I could only infer, never know. That fact made me determined to uncover what I could. At the very least, I could do that.

I decided to read the letters like I would Emily Dickinson's cryptic messages sent to family and friends. Give a literary critic two lines and they create a tome. Once I started, I wanted to work on the letters for the rest of my life, tracking down every person in her social circle, recovering historical events, creating a timeline, sorting and searching. Where my husband read thank-you notes, I read veiled emotions, hints of sadness, nagging anxiety, and resignation. I don't remember when my task became an obsession, but after only a few months, my notes became copious, sometimes 30 pages to one brief letter, not to mention the long line of books I bought, borrowed, or copied that lined my study wall.

The 31 letters in the packet began on August 10, 1937 and ended on August 18, 1940, with five letters interspersed from her husband, Zi Ming, to Mrs. Withington. Almost immediately I set out to do what any librarian worth her salt would do, place them in archival sleeves, make a numbered inventory, and transcribe each one.

Katherine's handwriting was clear and elegant, not like Dickinson's odd half-print/half-cursive leaning scrawl with idiosyncratic capitals and dashes in every syntactically challenged sentence. I methodically attached my explanatory notes to each transcription, forming its own packet. Emily Dickinson had insisted on telling the truth, but telling it slant. As a critic, I was drilled in how to unpack the coded, tightly knit poems of the Amherst muse. When she wrote an eight-line poem, I wrote an eight-page commentary. It was a matter of expansion. Poetic words went about the business of making the reader stop, backtrack, and struggle. The critic made the poem available to the reader. Dickinson would have hated my breed, probably would have said something like I was trying to lock her up in prose. Critics and authors rarely agree. But my training helped me to read between the lines, paying as much attention to what was left out as what was included.

And I had a firm belief that most words deceived. Poets try to get rid of that nasty habit of language. They work to crack open language and to clear away the ready-made, comfortable phrase. They stood against what most people do: repeat and write clichés like perfect parrots. Ready-made words are less time-consuming and a cover for what one really thinks or hadn't the guts to think or the wherewithal to think, a survival technique to garner acceptance from friends or political lookalikes. Why rock the boat with language that disrupts tried and true beliefs and prejudices? It would require a new vocabulary and syntax.

After many false starts I concluded that, overall, Katherine's letters told a bittersweet tale of momentary happiness disrupted by anxiety and loneliness. Mrs. Withington, or "Aunty," as Katherine called her, a respectful name for an older woman, provided needed support to a struggling young woman. Katherine repeatedly asked her 78-year-old mentor for advice and described the delights and troubles she experienced as she accompanied her husband from coast to coast in the United States.

Their itinerary was straightforward except for the elite status they had while traveling. The couple arrived at the port of San Francisco, settling in Berkeley, California in the spring of 1936. During that time, the Angel Island Immigration Station was still operating to detain and deport Asian immigrants entering the United States, especially Chinese. Traveling with visas granted through the support of American universities, Katherine and Zi Ming were not typical. They had first-class accommodations for their Pacific crossing, probably never coming close to the steerage class where hundreds of Chinese were crammed together. They never had to undergo the grilling of immigration officers.

They stayed in Berkeley for eight or nine months, then traveled in 1937 to Rochester, New York. From there they moved almost yearly. Envelopes were postmarked from Rochester, N.Y.; New Haven, Conn.; Los Angeles, Calif.; and Boston, Mass. One of the last letters was written on stationery from the Empress Hotel Victoria, Canadian Pacific, RMS Empress of Canada, dated Nov. 19, 1939, though I doubt Andrew's parents could have stayed at the hotel since the rabid Chinese Immigration Act was passed in 1923 and not modified until 1947. Instead, "Chinese friends" had "fixed a small but nice apartment" for them while they waited for the RMS Empress to sail. From Victoria, they made their way across the Pacific Ocean to Shanghai, China with a stop in British Hong Kong, finally flying to Chongqing, the interior wartime capital in the province of Sichuan, China.

Andrew was born in Boston on this three-year research trip, then carried to China as a nine-month-old baby when the country was at war with Japan. Reconstructing the time frame of the letters, I realized that even their train ride across Canada to Victoria where they boarded a Canadian ship back to Asia was through a country that had already declared war against Germany. From its first day, the return trip was fraught with danger.

At first, I was troubled when I read through the letters. Why return to China with a baby during war? Even before I had an inkling that the letters existed, I was incredulous. When my husband first told me that he was probably two years old when he returned to China with his parents, I questioned how this was possible. Drag a toddler across Canada, then across the Pacific Ocean to end up in a bombing zone? Shouldn't they have stayed in the United States? The letters confirmed that the risk was even higher. They traveled with a baby. And they knew the dangers that lay ahead.

In October of 1939, the small family left for China despite Katherine's tears and the pleas of Mrs. Withington to Zi Ming. The need to come to China's defense against such violence and destruction was too strong for Zi Ming. Clearly in the few letters he wrote to Mrs. Withington, he was intent on returning to China even before he knew his wife was pregnant. In 1938, he wrote to her, "I fear if I do not go back and join the people in this great struggle, I will do a great deal of damage to my prestige which will handicap my reconstruction plans in the future." He added "I fully realize that if I have to go back it will be very hard for Katherine to bear." This struggle between his life as a public servant for the Republic of China and his concerns for his wife and son was resolved with their decision to leave the United States and return.

Submerging myself in Katherine's letters, I struggled to understand what her polite lines meant. Did she foresee the shattering consequences of her return to China? By going back, she was facing a world of uncertainty and danger, and a few years after her return she had died. Knowing this simple fact colored every word I read. The end point of her life tainted every expression she used. Like the last utterances of the dead, her letters took on a value and power I could not resist.

One evening drinking scotch after a particularly bad day of dead-end research, Andrew asked me how it was going. My study littered with notes, any semblance of order destroyed, I gulped my drink and replied, "Chaos." I was usually so organized, my research generating a solid path forward, but after three months on his mother's letters, I was a spinning top.

"Maybe you should ease up," he smiled, gently moving my disheveled hair off my forehead. "Do the letters deserve such scrutiny?"

"They're primary documents," I retorted as if that justified my growing obsession with his mother's words. I didn't want to admit to my husband that working on the letters kept me close to his mother. I simply had to become more methodical, stay with one issue, follow it, and stop acting like a wimp. I hated self-pitying researchers lost in the abyss of history, looking for facts that dissolved during the dark hours spent in the archive, rummaging in dust.

Andrew was worried about me. I was worried about me. To protect myself I came up with a plan of attack. I had to find a way into Katherine's heart.

After another month of struggle, I discovered a pattern in her correspondence with Mrs. Withington: repeated references to her mentor's summer home, Land's End in Little Compton, Rhode Island. On August 16, 1937 Katherine had returned to Rochester N.Y. after her peaceful stay at Land's End. Before she and Zi Ming left for Yale University where she would be her husband's research assistant in the Osborn Laboratory, she sent a thank-you note for Mrs. Withington's kindness. "Dear Aunty: I always remember those beautiful days in Land's End."

That tranquil summer anchored her when she needed it the most. Away from China for one year, desperate for news of the Japanese invasion of Shanghai, she began a leitmotif of recalling those few precious months alongside her worst fears. Following her thanks, she states her worries about Shanghai: "We are very anxious to get news from China." Land's End, a retreat at the ocean's edge, a small village on the southern shore of Rhode Island, a place of refuge and safety, was juxtaposed with

Shanghai, also on an ocean's edge but ravaged by the invasion of Japanese troops.

On August 14, 1937, two days before Katherine wrote her letter, photographs of bombed Shanghai department stores, banks, and railroad stations were splashed on the front pages of American newspapers. The attacks were billed as an Asian war or the "Yellow War" by naive and racist Americans who did not understand that World War II had begun with the invasion of China by Japan. Shanghai with three million residents was the target of both aerial bombing, naval shelling, and a well-coordinated land attack. Between 200,000 to 300,000 Chinese civilians and soldiers were killed in three months. A harbinger of things to come; in the following eight years, aerial bombings would damage and destroy major cities and their civilian populations, cities like Warsaw, London, Cologne, Dresden, Hamburg, Stalingrad, and Tokyo.

"Those beautiful days" in Land's End, a place apart, remote from an America seemingly at peace and remote from a China about to enter a twelve-year bloodbath.

A small New England village, Little Compton was ruled by the rhythms of planting with fields bounded by wild rose hedges, stone walls, and pastoral meadows for grazing cattle. The village even had its own nineteenth-century poet, Sarah Helen Whitman, who praised "the breath of sweet briar" floating "at night" through her open window. The scent of flowers, not the noxious smells of factories and automobiles, permeated the village, far from collapsing savings banks and bread lines with frantic citizens scurrying to survive panic, and farther from terrorized Chinese running to avoid bombs and artillery shells.

Mrs. Withington gave her one summer of peace.

Katherine's dear "Aunty" was descended from Pilgrim stock, her husband from Puritan, and like many bluebloods in New England overlooked the massacres of indigenous peoples perpetuated to seize the land, preferring to describe how God's Providence assisted their settlement in the wilderness. In an article she wrote for *House Beautiful,* Mrs. Withington defined Little Compton as a paradise for Pilgrims with a town Commons for all. Farmers socialized with laborers and the town's elite. It was a place where the American dream was still possible, where citizens had more in common than not. By the time Katherine met Mrs. Withington, she had established the Village Improvement Society, next to the Commons, to help the town "develop along the lines so carefully drawn by the wise first settlers."

Katherine had drunk the elixir of the American dream. In a later letter, she was thankful that her son was born in Boston and stated her one wish was that he would return for schooling (which he did). His future must be American.

Unfortunately, Land's End was not spared suffering.

In the summer of 1938, Katherine received a beautiful photo of Land's End, but soon after she had troubling news and a new set of photographs. "It is terrible," she wrote. The summer house and garden "where we had a very happy visit" were severely damaged.

The entire beach community at Sakonnet Point was destroyed by a storm surge. Fishermen and fishing vessels were lost. Many summer homes in Little Compton were never rebuilt. The water and sand reshaped the entire coastline. Called "The Great New England Hurricane of 1938" it was the strongest hurricane to hit Rhode Island in 300 years. The storm surge destroyed entire sections of the shore, literally sucking summer cottages out to sea. The hurricane was nicknamed the Long Island Express. It killed almost 700 people, destroyed or damaged 57,000 homes, produced storm surges of over 17 feet, flooded the city of Providence, and obliterated entire forests, toppling 2 billion trees.

Katherine was devastated by the fragility of her American paradise. The summer of 1937 would never be repeated. And 1938 would be a continuing year of crushing losses, drawing her and the world into the cataclysm of war.

On October 21, 1937, writing from her new home in New Haven, Connecticut, Katherine had good news for Mrs. Withington. Letters from her family in Shanghai had taken "five weeks" to arrive, but they had confirmed that her mother and sister and many of her friends were safe.

Sister? Unconsciously, I had thought of Katherine as an only child. She was an individual who had disappeared in war. But Andrew's mother had a sister. That meant my husband had an aunt. And, of course, there must be cousins and more relatives. Not only an individual but an entire family had disappeared from my husband's childhood.

I talked to my husband about this fact, but he seemed less hesitant to celebrate. I thought I had made an important discovery. His reserve reminded me that family was much more than a list of relatives that we might discover doing genealogical research. The names were found, but the souls had departed. The names didn't resonate. They were flat and dead. And worse, if found, the trauma of their life and death could resurface. How had Andrew's aunt died? How had his grandparents died? War gobbled up entire families. Resurrecting past ancestors could create more pain for Andrew.

After his neutral reaction, a survivor's response, I decided to keep my findings about the letters to myself and only when I had gathered my thoughts about his mother's family would I sit down with him and talk.

"My work" is what he began to call the hours I spent hunting down references, a project that started to seem self-indulgent to Andrew. He would chide me about how I was neglecting my teaching and that my graduate students were "in limbo." Truth be told, I was starting to neglect our marriage. Always preoccupied with my research, I couldn't wait to shut my study door and live in Katherine's world. I imagined the steady breaking of the waves on the beach at Land's End soothing her as she sat on Mrs. Withington's front porch, the plaintive calls of seagulls reminding her of home. For one summer, she reveled in the ocean air, the games of anagrams at night, and the quiet conversations with her husband. She would never know such peace again.

One morning walking along Guemes Channel, watching a blue heron fish while above an osprey dove for its meal, Andrew cautioned me that the truth about his family might not be possible. Mrs. Loring's phone call was a godsend. Nothing could change that. His mother's letters were a pale substitute for her voice. He questioned my motives. Maybe I was on a mad hunt to appease something missing in my own past. Or maybe I was trying to help him when he didn't need help. Was I trying to become his substitute mother? Or, was I bored and needed a great mystery to solve?

Irritated, I wanted to disagree. But there was a speck of truth in everything he said. Maybe I was trying to be his mother. How many wives fall into that trap? I felt such loneliness in my husband, a fissure in his heart. Who wouldn't want to help? The problem was that I don't think I could be a good mother. Unlike my siblings, I wasn't a maternal type, didn't even have a dog or cat to cuddle. I loved Andrew because he was so independent. He didn't seem to need anyone. Two loners.

That is, until Katherine arrived. Then I started to live in doubled time. She was more alive than many of my friends, perhaps even more than I was. If anything, that was the mystery: why had she returned?

7

A Primitive Life

On January 6, 1938, Katherine sent the following letter from New Haven to Mrs. Withington:

220 Marvelwood Dr
New Haven, Conn

My Dearest Aunty:

Thank you for your letter and charming gift, I just love it. I keep it on my desk and always look at it when I set down to write

We just settled in our new home, we are living with Li's family their two little children make the house quite noisy but we like it especially in these days of anxiety and worry.

This morning's news makes us

feel very sad. Japanese souldens had looted the whole city of Hangchow and fighting took place on the lake side where our house was located. I think we had lost everything in the house including Zing Gang's big library. Our children are still safe in Shanghai and go to school every day, but they can eat only a little fresh milk, vegetables, eggs and fruits. We do not like to send them some can food because we do not want them to pay the high duties to Japanese. We do not know what we should do now,

With love,

nuary 6th 1938.   K. H.

This letter reveals two facts. First, Katherine had a home with Zi Ming (his professional name was Zing Yang) in Hangzhou, formerly called Hangchow, probably when he was president of Zhejiang University between 1933 and 1936 and right before they had left for the United States. Second, "their children" were "still safe in Shanghai." Since Andrew was their first child, I assumed Katherine was referring to the children of Zi Ming by his first marriage, hence Ida was not the only child of that union. Composing Andrew's family tree was much more complicated than I thought.

Katherine's "sadness" must have been difficult to convey to Mrs. Withington. Would her "Aunty" have known that

Hangzhou and West Lake were places synonymous with the classical traditions of China, where the Temple of the Soul's Retreat, built in 326 CE, was located; where Zhang Dai wrote *West Lake in My Dreams*, where famous hermits retreated from the court politics of the Qing Dynasty, where the President of the Republic of China, Chiang Kai-shek, honeymooned with his wife, Soong Mei-ling, and where Mao Zedong would later reside in his Liu Villa? A place of Emperors, Presidents, hermits, poets, and dreamers; a lake where the writers in the 18th century could nostalgically evoke the vanished pagodas and temples of the Southern Qi dynasty (479-502 CE) that dotted its shores.

Looting the city of Hangzhou was a desecration of China, a destruction of its stunning literary and cultural past. Looting Zi Ming's library was a desecration of modern China in Japan's attempt to stop trained scientists, engineers, economists, and educators in their task of building new institutions. I could only guess at what Katherine had written in her letters to her mother, sister, and friends. They would have known what such destruction meant for Katherine and their country.

In the 1930s, the Japanese Imperial Army was in the process of bombing and looting universities, research institutes and schools in major eastern coastal cities, resulting in the relocation of all major universities 1,000 miles west to the secured interior capital in Chongqing. Reacting to this military campaign, Chih Meng, the director of the China Institute connected to Columbia University, wrote an essay for *Foreign Affairs* stating that by January 1938, "84 percent of the higher educational institutions" in China were unable to function normally.

In this letter, Katherine also mentioned the food shortages that plagued the city of Shanghai under Japanese occupation. Ida's daughter once told me that her mother didn't want to talk about living in Shanghai when she was a child because of hunger. Better to forget. But the reference was to "children," not a child. Who else counted as "our children? Who were these children? I knew Ida was Andrew's older half-sister with his father's early arranged marriage. What I didn't know until this letter was that Ida had siblings, a sister, Ifong, and a brother, William James, named after the famous American psychologist, and known in the family as Bill.

"Left behind," was my husband's simple explanation when I asked him directly. He had seen no reason to go into the details of his Chinese family before. The letter made him rethink that convenient amnesia. When the communists were battling the Nationalists after the end of WWII in a prolonged civil war that lasted until 1949, three of his half-siblings were out of luck with no escape from this fraternal violence. Andrew was uncertain of how old they were, except that Ida was a middle child. After the civil war, Ida was able to reach the United States, fleeing to Taiwan and years later emigrating to the States through the aid of the Nazarene Church. Andrew hadn't realized that his half-siblings were living in Shanghai during the World War II.

My husband had never mentioned Bill or Ifong.

In 1947 after the war when Andrew left China for Hong Kong with his father and stepmother, they must have been at least teenagers. Did they choose to stay, or did they have no choice and have to stay?

Was his silence a refuge since words were inadequate to explain severed siblings? Better to say nothing when no right word can be found. Assured answers and pat explanations were smoke screens covering impossible realities. When I was growing up in Skokie, our Jewish neighbors sold their home quickly and left. The mother in the family had committed suicide by sticking her head inside the kitchen gas oven. I remember feeling so upset that she had survived a Nazi concentration camp only to die in a safe, suburban home in America, but no one in the neighborhood talked about it. A new Jewish family replaced the old and life went forward, the click-click of their mahjong tiles on their screened porch heard through my bedroom window at night.

A Polish friend of my father who survived a camp for Polish Catholic resisters to the Third Reich also killed himself in

America. He had no words for what had happened in the war and spent his years in the States buying expensive clothes and drinking the best liquor, vowing never to touch filth again. This strategy eventually failed him.

I have read that the one way out of trauma was through action, not words. If you are a doctor, save a life. A teacher? Nourish a life. A farmer? Grow food for life. The Holocaust writers Hanna Krall and Eva Hoffman offer hope that trauma does not have to end in suicide. There are ways to live.

Was that what Andrew was doing? Did he become a teacher and poet to live a life that gave rather than taking? Or was his personal biography irrelevant?

How shielded I had been, growing up. My Polish-American family was large and getting larger as siblings married, and more nieces and nephews emerged, marrying in turn. An ordinary family dinner might seat 25 people. To offset our comfortable middle-class life, my father told us terrible stories about his Catholic relatives back in Poland, their violent deaths at the hands of fascists, the incarceration camps for political resisters, and the surveillance state of the communists. He described the genocide that Polish Jews had faced in the concentration camps and left books about the Nazi regime in the living room. Looking at the photographs of emaciated prisoners and crematoria when I was young, my body would freeze. I was a child. There were photographs of children peering out through the barbed wire, their large eyes staring. My father felt it was necessary for his children to know what humans had done to each other.

As horrible as his history lessons were, these events were still distant, removed from the rock and roll of the 1950s, the contagious optimism of my white schoolmates. My husband's childhood was war, his immediate family scattered across two continents. They would never be reunited around the dinner table. They were war's uncounted toll.

Andrew first learned of his siblings' existence when he overheard his father and stepmother talking, whispering really, in their bedroom in Hong Kong. In high school, he met Ifong only once when she visited briefly. He learned years later she had died during China's famine of the 1950s. He also thought he might have another older half-brother besides Bill. There was a person he met as a child in Chongqing that took him for a motorcycle ride. And then there was the time someone knocked furiously on the door of their apartment in Shanghai, and his father grabbed his pistol from the bedroom closet and pulled him inside, covering his mouth with his sweating left hand, in his right the silver gun.

When he finished talking about his scattered family and how he had always been prevented from knowing anything, I was as heavy as lead. I could say nothing. He threw up his hands. "You sense it now, don't you? Can you hear the whispers?"

It was the sound of adults hissing behind closed doors, the shudder of a child anxious, alone, with no one to trust yet filled with suspicions, and the heaving of walls and floors, ready to collapse with no place left to stand. Andrew often had nightmares, terrifying dreams of people chasing him with knives or ghosts searching for him, their deep groans filling the darkness. Home offered no comfort, only uncertainty, a silence laced with secrets.

In her letters, Katherine desired normalcy, a carefree summer, fulfilling work, a graduate education, a home for her family. Nothing unusual. But she didn't know her future. Only the reader of her letters knew that her plans and expectations were doomed, casting over each letter a bitter shadow.

Her New Haven letters were packed with activities. She described the dinners she prepared for her New England friends; her tea party for the Republic of China's national holiday on October 10th (known by Chinese as 10/10); the daily work she did for Zi Ming as his research assistant at the Osborn Laboratory; going there early in the morning, having luncheon club with the other scientists, and working often into the night at her husband's side. In what time she had left, she went to meetings or teas with the Yale Chinese Student Club, the AAUW and the Yale Dames. A packed schedule, she participated fully in the life of Yale with enough scientific training to assist her husband in his research and enough education to join the American Association of University Women (AAUW).

In the 1930s only a small fraction of men graduated from college in China and, of that small number, only 15% were women; even fewer went abroad. How could someone with her education and training simply disappear, with no one alarmed at her demise? Like her husband, she must have come from the Chinese elite. Did the war wipe out her entire family? Was there no one searching for her or her son? No one?

By the summer of 1938, Katherine knew she was pregnant and was clearly experiencing bouts of morning sickness. Instead of staying in New Haven, she moved to Los Angeles, living in a small apartment near the University of Southern California, because Zi Ming had left the United States for the summer to fly to central China where the Nationalist government had retreated from the Japanese army. Katherine's Chinese friends who were working on their PhDs kept her company.

Before Zi Ming left for his summer trip to China, he admitted in a letter he wrote to Mrs. Withington that he was hesitant to return to China permanently because it would be "very hard for Katherine to bear." If not for that, he would have already "been in China for several months." His summer may have changed his mind about returning, at least for a while. In a letter Zi Ming wrote in the fall of 1938 to Mrs. Withington, he hinted at what happened on his trip.

The conditions in China are too horrible to describe. I wish I had not seen them. The distinction of wealth and culture is so complete that it will take at least two generations to recover. The savage behavior of the Japanese soldiers is also very astonishing. I have not heard of any such shameful conduct in a modern army except the Japanese.

By the fall of 1938, the Nationalist army of Chiang Kai-shek had retreated from Nanjing and Hangzhou, no longer protecting their civilian populations. The Japanese army invaded and without mercy killed, tortured, and raped hundreds of thousands of Chinese civilians. The Rape of Nanjing would go down in history as one of the worst massacres of World War II. In six weeks, Japanese soldiers gang-raped thousands of women between the ages of twelve and eighty and then bayoneted their bodies, often burning evidence of their atrocities.

The contrast could not be starker between the summer worlds of Katherine's apartment in LA and Zi Ming's visit to central China. Aware of the accelerating catastrophe for China, she knew she was pregnant and among friends, where food was plentiful and much cheaper than even New Haven. Despite the horrors of the war in China that were reported in the American newspapers, she still held onto her dreams. Even though she could not "study in University this summer," she planned a course of reading and study after she felt better.

I told Andrew about his mother's wish to continue her education, and he decided to check with the registrar at the University of California at Berkeley to see if his mother had ever been enrolled. To his shock, there was a record of a Katherine Lin, born August 18, 1908, in Kiangsu, China, who was admitted into a PhD program in August, 1936, and who had withdrawn a month later. She had attended National Nanjing Central University (one of the top universities in China at the time) from 1930 to 1933 with highest honors, and her home was listed as Hangzhou of West Lake fame as indicated in her 1938 letter.

The registrar was pleased my husband had called before the library placed the 1930s microfilm in special storage. Then, she would have had difficulty accessing his mother's records. Time not only obliterated people: it chewed up every document or trace that they ever existed. Finding a record of his mother's graduate admission imparted substance, clarifying why she could be Zi Ming's research assistant. Clearly, Katherine was an accomplished woman in her own right and was on a trajectory like other Chinese coming to the United States for their graduate education after World War I. As many as 17,000 Chinese students studied in America from 1919 to 1949, a small percentage of whom were women, and Katherine had friends among them at both UC Berkeley and USC.

Why she dropped out of graduate school was uncertain. Perhaps when Zi Ming realized that his appointment at Berkeley was only going to last a semester, they decided to have Katherine assist him in the laboratory instead of pursuing her PhD. We will probably never know, but by January 1937, they were living in Rochester, New York, where Katherine became friends with Mrs. Withington while Zi Ming worked at the University of Rochester.

The Berkeley document provided two essential facts: when Katherine was born—August 18, 1908—and where—Kiangsu (Jiangsu) province on the eastern coast of China. That August we celebrated her birthday, buying her an Inuit stone loon from a gallery on San Juan Island. A simple gesture, the gift was another step in reclaiming her life. Afterwards, I pinned a large map of China to my study wall, marking the places where Katherine was born, where she lived, and where she died. Time and space, the barest skeleton of existence.

Katherine's thank-you notes to Mrs. Withington had helped to flesh out a person with her own dreams, not only those of her husband. Those dreams faltered, however, once she became pregnant. After the summer of 1938, her letters shifted in tone. They described loneliness, even isolation, as she approached giving birth to Andrew.

In the fall of 1938, Zi Ming was given a research position funded by the Carnegie Institution of Washington, then located near Harvard Medical School in Boston. Their cramped apartment in Brighton was a distance from his office where he enjoyed the lively intellectual atmosphere of colleagues. Katherine's absence from his laboratory hurt them both. She spent her days "doing reading, light housework and making preparations for the baby." The spark was missing from her correspondence to Mrs. Withington, except for her wish that her dear "Aunty" could give her parenting advice.

The Lorings made a few appearances with dinners and a Thanksgiving feast but basically, she was unhappy. I had hoped Katherine would write about Ann Loring, but she didn't. Indeed, the letters are painful to read. In one, she wrote that her day was spent "reading and reading". If not for that, she would "feel very lonesome as Zi Ming goes out before eight and comes back after six, whole day I am alone." She commented frequently how happy he was because of his participation in several Harvard Medical School research projects. Her only positive comment was that she was pleased that her baby would be "born in this city;" the rest of her life was tedium. Two months later, the day after Christmas, she wrote that Zi Ming was "home for the whole day. This is the first Sunday he stayed at home. He always works on Sundays and comes back very late in the evenings during weekdays." Since it was Christmas day, I assumed he had no choice but to stay at home. Everything was closed.

Mrs. Lovett, her portrait painter, came to visit briefly in March, bringing the gift of a baby blanket. Katherine's thank-you note was short, adding a sentence at the end of the letter that summed up her new life. "The baby takes most of my time." By April 1939 they were preparing to leave the country and travel to Chongqing, the relocated capital of China. Katherine wrote Mrs. Withington about their problems getting ship passage to cross either the Atlantic or the Pacific. Neither route was safe. And, as it turned out, the Canadian ocean liner, the *RMS Empress* of Canada, that Katherine and Zi Ming took with their baby from Victoria, BC to China was requisitioned a few months later to transport troops for the Australian/New Zealand Army Corps (ANZAC) and was subsequently sunk by torpedoes from the Italian submarine, the *Leonardo Da Vinci*, off the coast of Africa in 1943.

There was a slight hint of optimism in the last letter she wrote Mrs. Withington from her Brighton address. She asked for American books and magazines to be sent to her via the President of Fudan (Fuh Tah) University in Chongqing where she planned to "start a little reading room and let my friends come to get some new information and know what is going on in the world." At least to Mrs. Withington, she put on a brave face. She would create an educational space for her friends. She would not be alone in Chongqing.

Toward the end of their correspondence, Katherine attempted to maintain the persona of a diligent Chinese woman, but she often slipped into describing a woman left alone with a baby, heading to a makeshift interior capital, with a husband who was growing more distant every day.

Their trans-Pacific crossing was uneventful and, on November 19th, 1939, she was able to send a quick note from their short docking at Shanghai. In this letter, I learned that, like Zi Ming, Katherine also had family ties to Shanghai. Her mother had a chance to meet Andrew when they docked there. No details were given about Andrew's grandmother other than she was "very well." When I pointed out to Andrew that the letters had this brief mention of his grandmother, he barely reacted. She was gone to him. Completely.

Once Katherine and Zi Ming reached Hong Kong, she and Andrew stayed for the winter while Zi Ming flew ahead to Chongqing. The winter in Hong Kong was a respite before she flew with her baby to chaotic Chongqing, a city of refugees and bombing raids. By 1940, inflation and shortages were rampant throughout East Asia, but food was still available in the British colony. Not so in Chongqing. Katherine worried about basic necessities and minor luxuries like an alarm clock or a light bulb that she had taken for granted. In Chongqing, "money cannot buy any modern convenience."

Her last letter on April 18, 1940, was crushing. Once again, the problem was loneliness. "After we came two months ago,

I was fixing a home and Zi Ming went out so often." They had relocated 50 miles north of Chongqing, then to an area called Beibei, a haven for transplanted universities where air raids did not reach. But there remained an inescapable danger: continuing inflation. Prices for basic food, manufactured goods, and simple household items were spiraling out of control. "The living expenses are 8-10 times more than the pre-war time."

She did not mince words about her new home. "This is a terrible place, many kinds of diseases around here. We even have to boil our wash water." The only positive change was that Katherine could employ a nurse while she performed charity work.

I am working for the children of wounded soldiers. My work is not interesting. Those children are very stupid and dirty. Many bad habits are not easy to correct, and they have so many different kind of diseases. We have a very little money (most of them came from U. S. A) to opperate the school and give them clothes and food and try to educate them.

We are living on a very primitive life, get up very early and go to bed early too. We could not do anything at night because we have no light, we use the vegetable oil lamp, it is hard to read and write. The water we use is carried from the river by a servant.

Everybody in the war capital thinks the war will last at least for another three years and everybody is ready to face it.

Please write me often.

With love to you and Margaret from both ous.

Kitty

Katherine's world had turned upside down, a modern woman without a modern world, thrust back into primitive living conditions, unable to read or write without difficulty. The American journalist, Theodore H. White, described wartime Chongqing as an old, backwater city filling overnight with sophisticated urban elites. He compared their culture shock to "the most devoted executives of New York, Boston and Washington" arriving in the "hills of Appalachia" to set up their resistance to an invading army.

Katherine's disgust at the "very stupid and dirty" children she was supposed to help showed how ill-prepared she was to understand the daily realities of ordinary Chinese. Aside from the best trained units loyal to Chiang Kai-shek, National Revolutionary Army (NRA) soldiers came from poor villages without schools or medical facilities. Illiterate, they were often forcibly conscripted into the army and mistreated or killed if they did not obey those in command. Their families were collateral damage in a brutal and often corrupt military system.

As in many wars, more soldiers died of diseases than combat wounds. Cholera, influenza, tuberculosis, malaria, typhus, typhoid, bacillary and amoebic dysenteries were rampant in the army camps. Working with these children would have brought Katherine face to face with these dreaded diseases and a China that she had never known firsthand.

When she was an undergraduate at Nanjing Central University, there were massive student protests to chart a new direction for China. Nationalists, reformers, and communists competed for the students' allegiance. Katherine broke barriers for a woman in her social class, but she was distraught when she left her educated world to care for the children of the poor. She had never joined the communist call to liberate the masses, and in her letters was clearly supportive of the Republic of China. And though she and "everybody" else in Chongqing was willing to face another three years of war, by the spring of 1941, a year after she had arrived, she and her husband had left the hardships of Chongqing behind, Zi Ming to the United States and England, and Katherine with her son back to Shanghai and the safety of her family.

Her last letter was hard for me to read. I chafed at her judgmental language. I wanted her to be perfect, a woman who saw beyond her elite status and understood the suffering of most Chinese. Four years after this last letter to Mrs. Withington, Katherine would be dead and, three years after her death, her husband had remarried and moved with his new wife and Andrew to Hong Kong. By 1949, the communist party would have won the civil war against the Republic of China, pushing the remnants of the national government to Taiwan where they still reside. The fate of the "masses," the disenfranchised soldiers, the poverty-stricken farmers, the illiterate laborers rested with Mao Zedong who reorganized higher education, ridding it of American influences. Academic researchers like Zi Ming and Katherine, trained in the United States, would have been purged from their university positions. Katherine would have been denounced as a traitor to the masses.

Caught in the violent events of World War II, Andrew's mother had little power besides retreating to her family in Shanghai once her husband had left for the United States. She and Andrew must have arrived there before Pearl Harbor when there were still pockets of safety throughout this dynamic city, the financial capital of China. Then, for another unknown reason, she had decided to leave Shanghai and travel back to Chongqing with her son. It was there that she died. It was there that Andrew remembered the fragile image of her face, propped up on her deathbed.

Through the letters a picture emerged of a young wife and mother, lonely at being no longer useful to her husband's career and left without his companionship, distraught at the looting of her home by the Japanese, fearful of the conditions in Chongqing, and repulsed by the charity work expected of her social class. She may have reveled in her summer at Land's End, but as this last letter showed, she was brave enough. Conflicted but determined, Katherine was no longer unknown.

8

Stolen in Shanghai

In February 1940, Katherine and Andrew had flown from a warm, subtropical Hong Kong to a cold, muggy Chongqing. The American military had not yet built Peishiyi Airfield so they had to land on a sandy island airfield in the Yangtze River and be carried by sedan chair porters, *ban-ban* men, up 500 perilous steps that clung to the steep cliffs until they reached the interior capital, severely gutted by Japanese bombing raids. Their one-way ticket cost $400, a staggering amount, $7,300 in today's currency. The only other ways to reach the capital were by boats up a maze of rivers and treks overland that took weeks. Bandits, smugglers, disease, and food shortages threatened refugees who risked their lives unless traveling in secure groups.

Bursting with new arrivals, Chongqing staggered under demands for housing. Rickety shacks sprang up overnight, covering neighborhoods charred from incendiary bombs. In a short time, a half-million Chinese had moved to this provincial city of 300,000, stressing every aspect of daily life. Caves were blasted out of the hillside surrounding the city to provide air raid shelters. In one horrific Japanese attack, 3,000 Chinese died.

Graham Peck, an American journalist, more attuned to the daily lives of Chinese than most American writers, called Chongqing in *Two Kinds of Time* a "city of infinite differences. There were people in fur hats, in turbans, in Western-style tweed caps with the visors worn rakishly backwards, people without shoes, with straw sandals, with embroidered silk slippers, with two-color sport shoes from the Bata factory in Shanghai." Rural peasants walked the narrow alleys next to stylish Shanghai arrivals. Resentments were rife. "The Buicks of the officials' wives, in town for shopping and tea, threaded past air-raid caves where the last and most unlucky of the refugee tide lived as crudely as Australian bushmen."

By 1940, when Katherine had arrived, the new capital of the Republic of China was home to essential members of the Chinese population, government staff, university faculty, and factory workers who had transported official documents, office equipment, libraries, research laboratories, machinery, and construction materials to build their interior capital.

Up in the hills, where Chiang Kai-shek presided over the Republic of China, the government was heavily composed of American-educated Chinese like Zi Ming, Andrew's father. Even the Generalissimo's wife, Mei-ling Soong, spent two years at Wesleyan College in Macon, Georgia, then graduated from Wellesley College in Massachusetts, and was a devoted Methodist, as were her parents, who required Chiang Kai-shek to convert to their faith before he was allowed to marry their daughter.

Soon the United States would join with China to fight the Japanese, building its headquarters, airfields, and military bases outside Chongqing. Russian, British, French and American embassies were established in the relocated capital with the international press corps staying in the famous Press Hotel. General Stillwell, or "Vinegar Joe," squabbled with General Chennault about his Flying Tigers, and the two American generals in turn argued with Generalissimo Chiang Kai-shek over strategies for the Burma Road and the Air Force. When Katherine wrote her last letter to Mrs. Withington, she had lived in the Chongqing area for two months, luckily miles from the constant barrage of bombs. In it she expressed her willingness to face the ongoing war, even though she chafed at the reversals in her life. In America, she had been a woman with a professional future until she became pregnant, then she was a woman alone, cut off from the laboratory and further education. In China, she was a woman with a nurse and servants, doing charity work—probably connected to Madame Chiang's assistance projects—that she hated, living in a place that gave her a modicum of safety but had nothing else to offer her, not even adequate housing or affordable food, let alone a scientific occupation or intellectual peers.

After she moved to Shanghai from Chongqing, probably in late 1940, information about her life stopped. We had no more letters. Other than my husband's notes about what Mrs. Loring had said, I really had nothing else to go on for the few years between 1940 and when she died. Extrapolating from Mrs. Loring's information, Katherine would have stayed in Shanghai for all of 1941 and 42, probably living with her family in the French Concession. Sometime in 1943 she left Shanghai for reasons unknown and traveled overland with her son, returning to Chongqing to reunite with her husband. According to Mrs. Loring, Katherine had endured a harrowing journey to reach the interior capitol only to die of tuberculosis.

After his mother died in Chongqing, Andrew, then probably around six years old, would traverse China again, travelling with his father back to Shanghai in 1945 at the war's end. He knew no rest in the first eight years of his life, no stable home, no neighborhood, no family gathering sustained during years of childhood.

In 1947, with a civil war raging between communists and Nationalists after the end of World War II, Andrew, with his father, his new stepmother, and their baby, Peter, resettled in Hong Kong. He was eight, the first year he ever stepped into a schoolroom, and the first time he would have some stability, living in Hong Kong for eight years before re-crossing the Pacific Ocean and the Panama Canal to finally arrive back in the United States where he was born sixteen years before.

His life would come full circle.

Such dislocation was not unusual in wartime. Families moved to wherever it was safe, if they were lucky. Andrew's family had resources few Chinese had access to, and yet their lives were thrown into a perpetual state of flux. Only extremely wealthy Chinese were able to avoid the war entirely, resettling quickly in Hong Kong as early as 1932, and then moving themselves with their money to the United States, staying ahead of the bombs, the invading army, and the economic hardships of most civilians.

The Shanghai that Katherine and her family called home was a dynamic, cosmopolitan city of 3 to 5 million residents, depending on how far you extended its boundaries. In the 1920s and 30s, it produced entrepreneurs, bankers, artists, and hucksters. Called by J. G. Ballard, the novelist of *Empire of the Sun*, "extravagant and cruel," the metropolis contained a sprawling Chinese population of residents and refugees alongside two foreign sectors, the International Settlement (mainly British and American) and the French Concession, worlds unto themselves with their own treaty port governments and municipal police, yet mainly peopled by Chinese, both rich and poor. Foreigners lived in palatial quarters, as Ballard pointed out in his autobiography *Miracles of Life*, the French in Provençal villas, Germans in white Bauhaus boxes, and the English in golf-club elegance while Chinese beggars slept and died on the streets. In Shanghai lived 26,000 Japanese civilians who were amassing fortunes, 35,000 White Russians who had fled the Russian revolution, and 20,000 European Jews who had fled the Nazis, plus pockets of Belgians, Brazilians, Danes, Dutch, Italians, Norwegians, Portuguese, Spanish, Swedes and Swiss with varied treaty rights.

Westerners have long been fascinated by the underbelly of prewar Shanghai. The city's gangsters, brothels, casinos, and clubs appear in novels and movies as clichéd settings with Chinese chorus girls and jazz singers. Its gambling halls entertained both foreigners and Chinese, creating millionaires and paupers overnight. A playground at night, in the daytime Shanghai was mainly a commercial, financial, and manufacturing center for East Asia. It was a landscape of mills: Chang Sing Flour Mill, Zung Yu Oil Mill, Japanese Oil and Leather Mills, Shanghai Silk Spinning Mill and dozens more on both sides of the Whampoa River. British interests were handled by Jardine, Matheson & Co., who managed the Ewo Cotton Mills which employed 300,000 people by 1924. Banks competed for profits and the business of entrepreneurs: Bank of China, Chartered Bank, Bank of Taiwan, H & S Bank, Yokohama Specie Bank, Bank De L'Indo Chine, and the Commercial Bank of China. And Americans represented their energy investments through China General Edison Company and Standard Oil of New York, their kerosene ubiquitous throughout China, supplying both inexpensive lamps and lamp oil.

After the invasion of Shanghai by the Japanese in 1937, both legal and illegal Shanghai businesses were seized. Japanese government agents and businessmen requisitioned banks, factories, and offices, spreading their staff throughout the city. Already a center of opium smuggling, Shanghai housed notorious gangs that aligned with different political interests, helping to bankroll the military campaigns of both Chiang Kai-shek and Chinese warlords. The Japanese wanted these funds for their war effort, an enormous drain on the Japanese economy. Besides drug profits, opium helped the Japanese to maintain control over the local population. They pushed drugs even to the poorest Chinese to deter resistance, lacing cheap cigarettes with opium.

In his 1947 novel, *Fortress Besieged,* the novelist, Qian Zhongshu, described how under the Japanese the extremes of Shanghai worsened: the "struggle for survival was gradually stripped of mask and ornament to reveal a primitive brutality." Some Chinese collaborated with Japanese to run guns, opium, prostitutes, and illegal goods needed for their war effort while "slums gradually spread like ringworm over the face of the city." Terrorists used the city streets as their theater and "men of good will" disappeared underground.

Because the Japanese army had also invaded the countryside, refugees overwhelmed Shanghai, a city that had already experienced prior waves of refugees from flooding, warlord conflicts, and famine. In 1937, after a few days of bombing and artillery fire, a million Chinese became refugees in their own city. Most sought out family members for shelter, others relocated to emergency centers, and thousands were forced to live on the streets. Children represented between a third and a half of these dislocated Chinese families. In addition, the French Concession, where Katherine's family and many wealthy Chinese lived, was flooded with impoverished Chinese seeking shelter.

The number of homeless continued to grow during the war. After the 1941 Japanese attack on Pearl Harbor, "enemy nationals" from the Allied countries were forced from their homes and incarcerated in detention centers. And, of course, there were reverse waves of Chinese that fled Shanghai and headed away from the coastal cities.

China became a refugee country, almost 20 percent of its population of 475 million people fleeing for safety. Rana Mitter, the British historian, concluded that this internal migration destabilized China during the war years and well beyond. Whether to the safety of Chongqing (for the Republic of China) or to the caves of Yan'an in Shaanxi province (for the communists who arrived there after their Long March), the Chinese attempted to stay ahead of the Japanese armies and planes, and at key moments fought each other's troops.

Andrew was only two years old when he left Chongqing with his mother. How they traveled to Shanghai in 1940 is unknown, probably by a combination of boat and plane since, for the right price, it was still possible to travel to Shanghai in relative comfort. In the beginning, the Japanese wanted to keep Shanghai a financial hub open to commerce with the neutral United States. That quickly changed, of course, after Pearl Harbor. Katherine and Andrew survived in Shanghai for probably two or three years until she decided to leave and journey west in search of her husband. Following Mrs. Loring's estimate, Katherine might have left Shanghai in 1943, the year when Vichy France turned over the administration of the French Concession to the Japanese.

Andrew has no memories of being in Shanghai with his mother. His earliest memories happened in Chongqing after he returned in 1944. He had no memories of their perilous journey to reach the city, only the image of his mother's face. After that there were glimpses from his childhood; scenes of people running, a large villa up in the hills, probably in Chongqing, a goose that chased and bit him in the villa courtyard, a family Chow dog left behind that his father told him would be eaten, a capsized boat in a river where people flailed around in the water, their floating possessions picked up by other boatmen leaving the owners to drown, and a servant slamming the main gates as he peeked at soldiers marching past on the road below. He also remembered the motorcycle ride with someone he thought might be an older half-brother, someone older than Bill, his half-brother.

His memories of Shanghai commence after his mother had died and his father had returned with him in 1945. The war was over, and the streets were filling with American soldiers and returning Chinese. Relief packages floated down from the sky. He could see vivid images of the apartment where he lived, where beggars squatted outside its gated entry.

Andrew wove these images into his poems, not expecting them to cohere into a story. Mere childhood impressions, never reaching beyond the moment. He composed them as if polishing a small jewel, brilliant and solitary, cut away from its hard rock home.

I wanted the hard rock. I wanted to know the connections to his mother. Frustrated, I read and reread his poems. At best, she appeared as an ethereal presence, a flicker of a woman. If Katherine was to be given form and shape, I was the one who had to use my research tools as paintbrushes and paint. I felt like I didn't have a choice.

Before giving up on Andrew's ability to recall his early life, I decided to talk with him again about his mother's letters. Since I spent months submerged in Chinese wartime history, I wanted to tell him who I thought his mother could be. And I kept thinking he knew more than he was telling me. I hoped I might jar something loose about Chongqing or Shanghai. But I didn't know how to move forward. I was stuck, uncertain of how to talk with Andrew anymore. I was out of words.

So, having grown up with food as my family's social glue, I did the next best thing: I cooked a feast. Remembering a highlight of my visit to Changchun—a dinner with Liu and her family for which she prepared cold sesame noodles and green beans sauteed with ground pork—I tried to reproduce the textures and flavors, the unforgettable scents (that I failed to duplicate). I gave up on the spun-sugar dessert that Liu's husband had made, an intricate web of foot-high springs and coils that broke off into bite-size ornaments and melted in your mouth like sweet air.

After dinner, my husband and I lounged on the day porch reminiscing about the evening we spent with a woman faculty member at Jilin University who described in detail the warring Red Guard factions that took over the university in the 1960s, one group of engineering students improvising a tank to ram into the other's barricades, shooting at buildings without any plan, losing sight of any goal except anarchy. We talked about Liu, one of the few dedicated socialists we met in China, and how she had to live under a communist government in the Northeast corrupted by the Soviet system into a brutal bureaucracy of con artists.

"Enough chatter," my husband said, never one to linger over memories or the futility of politics. "What's on your mind?" He had seen through my carefully orchestrated evening meal.

"It's your mother," I replied, unsure of how to bring up again what was either a painful reality or maybe, at this point, a colossal irritation.

He waited. I presented my grand narrative of her letters, hesitating midway through since I realized I was telling him that his mother's pregnancy had fucked up her life. My hunting for the bigger narrative had overlooked this basic fact: It would have been better if Andrew had never been born.

"Stop," he interrupted. "I have always thought that the day my mother met my father her life was ruined."

I didn't know what to say after that other than to say how he was alive and how grateful I was and how certain I was that his mother wanted him more than anything else in the world, a mealy-mouthed string of platitudes that only made things worse.

He ignored my blabbering. After a considerable silence, he informed me that he couldn't figure out if I was ignorant or arrogant. My interpretation sounded like bad fiction, spinning bullshit. Then, he went on direct attack.

"You read a bunch of books, and what? You know my mother? I hate it when you call her Katherine."

I tried to defend myself. "Do you want me to stop?" I asked.

"What the fuck? Do what you want," he responded, looking with contempt at the table, strewn with half-eaten dishes.

In the matter of a few seconds, he had gone from criticizing my work, to attacking it, to seething disdain at who I was. The few strings holding our relationship had snapped.

As usual, our fights led to mutual retreat. I, a car ride to an overlook along Guemes Channel. He, to his study and computer.

He was still up when I returned home after midnight. I hadn't accomplished anything while I sat in my car except to ferment my toxic feelings and wonder what to do next.

Andrew wasn't still angry, but he was withdrawn and suspicious. A half-empty bottle of Johnnie Walker *Black Label* was perched on his desk.

"Don't you have any demons?" he asked when I came over to apologize.

I didn't have demons like he did, but I wanted to tell him I was giving up my project while knowing that I never would. I could become a calculated deceiver. It might be possible to appear less eager and fool him into thinking I understood his point of view. Which I didn't. He was becoming an obstacle to finding out about his mother.

"You're not even a good analyst," he said, mockingly. "You misread my scribbling."

"Scribbling?"

"Yes, my notes from Mrs. Loring's call. Not such a great critic, are you?"

After a few more drinks and some signs of truce, he seemed to think my work was amusing, a game with his past that he could observe, evaluate, and ridicule. I went into my study and retrieved my Loring file, reading his original note over again, twisting it upside down and shaking my head.

"What have I missed?" I asked, in an appeasing tone.

"Stolen in Shanghai," he said laughing. I had assumed that Mrs. Loring meant the Japanese found a way to bleed Katherine's family of some of their wealth. From what I had read, when they occupied Shanghai, extortion became a way of life to fund their war. In his autobiography, Ballard wrote that his White Russian nanny traveled with him every time he went in the family car. His parents were convinced their chauffeur would kidnap him for money.

"I was stolen in Shanghai."

"What?"

"Yes, me."

When he was a teenager in Hong Kong, he had heard the story that he had been kidnapped in Shanghai. He couldn't remember who told him, probably a servant, definitely not his father or his stepmother. He never forgot it. How can you forget something like that? Mrs. Loring confirmed it. He had been kidnapped when he was about two years old.

"You know, *roupiao,* or meal ticket; that's what kidnapping was. How else could you make money?"

He didn't appear upset at all. It was simply another piece of information, nothing more nor less. And I had missed it. Ha, ha.

It wasn't exactly vertigo I felt, more like total disbelief. Why hadn't he said anything? I mean it's not a board game question. Have you ever been kidnapped? He acted like it was no big deal. Doesn't everybody have a trauma like that hanging about in their childhood?

He wasn't sure it had actually happened until Mrs. Loring confirmed it on the phone.

"Why not tell me when you were convinced?" I asked.

No answer.

No answer.

"Who knows?" he finally replied, as if that would settle the matter. Belligerent, he smirked at my oversight. He then launched into a pseudo-apology and resumed his attack. He thought I was becoming pathetic. He didn't want to become someone chasing after a ghost, someone like me.

That shut me up. I left the house again and started brooding. I didn't have any handy explanations to help me understand him.

Was my husband so traumatized he didn't even know he was traumatized? Was it possible that a two-year-old can simply bounce back once they're returned to their mother? And what about Katherine? What did she go through? Quicksand, that's what it felt like. Not vertigo but quicksand. Was I inadvertently making my husband reexperience his childhood? What was I doing? My growing up was like a fairy tale compared to his first eight years. Maybe I should stop. I had to remind myself that Mrs. Loring called him; the dress, the oil portrait, the letters were sent to our home after his 1989 trip to China. I was unpacking the trail of parcels.

I returned at 2 am and wanted to wake my husband up. He probably didn't want to talk anymore, but I thought I needed somehow to make him talk.

Walking into our dark bedroom, I faltered once I heard him pulling back the bed covers.

"You might as well tell me the rest," he said, his voice weary and cautious.

He sounded so exhausted. I was immediately worried. "Maybe I am pathetic, but God, a kidnapping? That's horrible."

"Is that all you have to say?" he replied, straightening himself up.

I gathered myself together and admitted that I hadn't uncovered anything to do with why his family never talked about his mother or, to add on to that, why they had never talked about his kidnapping.

I followed him out to the kitchen, and he went right to the liquor cabinet. Pouring himself a drink, he stared at it and then laughed as if the whole world was a colossal joke.

He confessed that he had made another phone call to his stepmother before I had returned home. Julia was upset that he had called so late. The conversation was strained. He didn't tell her about Ann Loring's call or the letters of his mother's that were sent to him, although he suspected she knew already.

What he had done was to ask Julia about his kidnapping.

She confirmed it and said a great amount of family money was spent to get him back. Too much money.

"After all these years, she was still irritated about the money, as if it was her money."

He asked her again about his mother's death. This time she said his mother had disappeared after her long illness. That's what she remembered.

"I asked her if she had signed my mother's death certificate," said Andrew. "'No,' she barked. I think I pissed her off. My mother didn't fucking disappear."

"No," I agreed, "that doesn't make sense."

"Of course it doesn't!" He reminded me that his stepmother was a physician. "She knows what happened to my mother. She won't talk. I can't get her to talk. And she knows that I know she won't talk. What a fucking family."

"Katherine would never just disappear and leave you, especially after having lost you once to a kidnapping and then having traveled for more than a year with you 1,000 miles through a war zone to reach the safety of Chongqing and her husband."

His face seemed stricken by my words. "What I'm saying to you is that we will never know what happened. This is now. I should never have called Julia."

"This is now?"

"Yes, live now."

"You mean forget everything."

"It's not your battle. And it's not mine."

We negotiated the terms of our truce and became neutral partners, spending an hour together on a long beach walk. Back home, the windows wide open, the scent of the salt air drifted in from the hillside below. From the deep blue of the sky, I knew it was around 3 am. The fog having cleared, I wandered onto our back deck and stared at the stars, listening. There were hardly any sounds. Not even an owl or the whistle of a diving bat. It was as if the earth stood still.

"This is now," I whispered to myself, trying to relax. Within a few minutes, I could hear a stronger voice insisting, "Don't abandon me." There was something about the way my husband talked with me that evening that made me think there was an unwritten pact between us that I should go forward despite what he had claimed. The present had folded backwards. We lived in a crumbled time of reckoning.

I had to find more evidence. I had to keep searching. I had to be a sleuth in the Old Norse sense of the word, a tracker. A bloodhound on the scent of a killer or a search for a dead body. Dogged. A shadow away from the sun. A spy, a snoop. I couldn't stop.

9

February 19, 1943

Leaving the cave was foolish, you might think. Deprived of air for five days, perhaps I was not thinking straight. On that wintry night, I chose to flee from the huddled refugees, going against what I had up to that point believed, that I could not survive without Chiu Chun, my husband's private secretary. But he was dead and I was glad. Call it my graduation.

Outside the cave, I had no guideposts; I zigzagged the rocky summit, dragging my son behind me. After a frantic search, I found a steep path down, illuminated by the cold light of the night sky. Stunned by the freezing air, I lifted my son up, his body shaking against my torn jacket. "Breathe," I urged him. "Breathe." With each small gasp, I could feel him relax, his breath warm against my neck.

The black mouth of the cave receded into the darkness as we made our way toward a cluster of dim lights below. Nothing looked as it did when we had climbed days before with the refugees to hide from the bombs. Then we were like sheep running, climbing, and scattering from the deafening noise, our minds screaming "hide, hide." Now the silence of the night wrapped around Andrew and me like a cloak, the sky ablaze with stars, not diving planes, black angels spitting bullets, hunting for their prey.

I remember thinking that starlight from millions of years ago was brightening our path. Freed from the burden of my husband's private secretary, I felt strong for the first time. I believed that I could find us shelter. Ever since we had left Shanghai to find a father who hardly knew his son, a man protected by his American friends and the Generalissimo, I had resigned to my fate, following the commands of Chiu Chun. No longer, I would find a way.

The cold air had become an elixir. How much I wanted to learn to fight like my sister. On that mountainside, I realized that she had seen the future correctly. Being among the first woman scientists from China wasn't enough. We had to stand up and cast off our restraints. But how was I to do that, a woman alone and carrying a child? I knew then there was no easy answer. There never have been any easy answers. I would have to learn how to fight in my own way.

Stuffed in my pockets were old rice cakes and dried plums, a handful of sunflower seeds, and a strip of twisted sausage. Andrew had hoarded some watermelon seeds that he kept tightly clenched in his left hand, salty with sweat. We had food. I would find us shelter.

How brief that moment of clarity was, the total belief in my power to survive. How necessary it was. And yet I know that, like all moments of clarity, it was a passing sensation. Something I tried to cling to, unafraid. Instead, the mountainside became a movie about flight, a playground game of run and chase, a pantomime of what we try to do and yet can never do: get away, find safety.

Hearing footsteps behind me, I remember how my body twisted, a toy top spinning without balance, a mother with a child about to be flung onto the icy snow.

The shape was on us in a second, tattered rags with flaying arms shouting, "Stop, stop!"

"Run!" was my only instinct as I righted myself and Andrew. I fled down the dirt path that snaked between scattered boulders like giant soldiers looming out of the dark. Legs burning, arms on fire, I didn't pause to breathe.

At the bottom, the girl caught my jacket, yanking.

"Take me!" her shrill plea resounding in the night.

My son jerked out of my arms.

Determined, the girl grabbed him, his frail body teetering until he collapsed on the ground.

"I can help! I can help," she shouted, her voice spitting frosty air.

Terrified, my son quivered, taking in air too deeply, drinking the air.

I collapsed beside him, my feet bleeding, the soles of my shoes torn away.

A gush of river wind carried the scent of dead bodies, gun powder, metal shards and tearing smoke up the hill.

The girl pleaded, her thin voice choking. "I can help."

Villagers desperate for food were selling their own children. I knew that the girl might kidnap my son and sell the boy to a rich farmer who needed an heir. Or sell him to a trader heading northwest as a slave. Money meant food. A boy meant food.

My arms flung up as if to ward her off. "Go!" I screamed. I would never let anyone steal my son. Never again. Even the sight of her enraged me. She was like those desperate girls roaming the streets of Shanghai, their eyes vacant, starving, eager to steal anything to trade or sell, scooped up by Japanese soldiers to rape or use as slaves, shadow girls pouncing on what was weaker than they were, hiding in alleys, only to end as frozen corpses tossed on the sidewalks.

The days of waiting for his return, the nightmare thoughts that imagined him stuffed in a closet, no food, no water, the desperate cruelty of exchanging a life for food, drugs, why him, why take him, my lovely boy, betrayed by number 4 amah, let her burn in Yama's hell. My child returned unable to talk, a two-year-old's words gone. The authorities told me he was alive, I should be grateful; "See, nothing to cry about." My son could not even cry, a child with no words, no sounds.

And then my sister, lurking in the apartment, her resentment etched on her face, the family gold spent on my child for the ransom, rather than feeding the thousands dying on the streets, one child from wealth valued above those thousands walking into Shanghai from the countryside, the steady stream of children, lost, orphaned, fleeing the Japanese soldiers. Her silent scorn pushed us apart, two sisters who had once dreamed about our shared future.

The girl stood back, almost sniffing my anger like an animal surprised but unafraid. Her large saucer eyes shone. The ripped sleeves of her padded jacket exposed spindly arms, her feet covered in layers of rags, tied with twine.

"Go!" I screamed again, pointing back up to the cave.

But she did not go. She stepped back and stared until we were almost out of sight and then she followed, always behind us, a shape moving in and out of the shadows.

An hour later, on the path ahead, a light flickered from the open door of a shack, a slanting pile of wooden boards with twig brooms hanging from a collapsed roof. Shelter at last, I thought, the dawn sun exposing our frozen lips, my son's numb face.

From out of nowhere, the peasant girl raced past us and dashed inside, coming out with two jackets and three sets of leather shoes, spreading them on the ground.

"Don't go, death." The girl gave orders, her small hands stuffing the shoes with rags from the hut.

I touched the coins sewn inside my jacket. "I have nothing. Go back," this time pleading. My exhaustion was no match for her determination, hewn for thousands of years in peasant work, the way instinct is not learned but is there in full force, untempered.

My only thoughts were of food. I did not want to buy food for the girl. I kept thinking that she must climb back to the cave, vanish in the blur of refugees, rejoin the scavenger children that had pawed at my son since leaving Shanghai. But she would not. No force of my will could push her away.

The girl grabbed Andrew and ran inside the crumpled hut. This time he did not resist. I yelled at her to stop. "Do not touch my son," my voice fading, three steps behind.

A glowing lantern hung from the rafter inside, a tiny flicker about to die. Slouched bodies rested against a wall, parents and three children. Steam rose from the newly dead, their arms and feet exposed from the girl stealing their jackets and shoes.

I grabbed my son.

The girl laughed, her eyes scanning the hut for more booty.

A red lantern swayed above the dead family, a paper riddle twisting from its frame as if they were trying to guess its meaning in this year of the monkey. The girl tore the strip off, cupping it in her hands. She could not read the riddle scratched on the paper. How could she? Her full name was Wang Li Min, and she could not even read the simple character of her surname, Wang, 王. She handed me the red slip, pointing to the crossing black lines, urging me to tell her what it said, as if the riddle would explain the deaths of the family she had robbed.

Only in death can I see how years of arrogance shaped my response. I had no sympathy. I was not like my sister. I felt nothing but repulsion. I threw the paper on the floor. The riddle's solution came from classical texts, not a guessing game for children. An illiterate, what did Li Min know of the Yuan dynasty or the *I Ching*? She had never read the beloved novel, *The Story of the Stone*, or had a relative pass the imperial examinations. The riddle required knowledge of the Peach Leaf song, a door god, and the legend of love between a famous calligrapher and his favorite concubine. Would the girl know of peach-wood charms?

The girl picked up the riddle and stuck it in her pocket. Maybe the riddle brought back memories of her family gathered to eat sweet bean-paste dumplings at the end of the New Year festival. Before the war, our cook labored to combine glutinous rice flour, rose petals, sesame seeds, bean paste, jujube paste, walnut meat and dried fruit to create exquisite dumplings that my ancestors had eaten once a year for hundreds of years.

The dead family meant nothing to the girl, no more or less than mannequins at the Sincere Department Store. To Li Min, people were either dead or alive, nothing more. It was the riddle she wanted, taking it out again and shoving it into my face.

"Go away." I hated the girl because she would not obey and would never obey.

"No good!" the girl shouted, pointing at the dead man as if he were the enemy, throwing the riddle at his feet. She rifled through the pockets of the children's pants, turning them inside out, even the clothes of the baby were not spared. Stripped of his jacket, the dead father's body was shrouded in a long, deep blue *changshan*.

"Take him outside," the girl ordered, looking at the boy. "I am clever, not like this man."

I wanted to hit the girl, my hatred welling up in me, a thousand fists. My son walked outside as if the girl's voice had replaced mine. "No," I yelled after him, fearful of what the girl would do and fearful of the dark road ahead.

In the fading lantern light, I saw the girl stick the dead man's Mauser inside her pack and collect the few scattered bullets at his feet. He must have killed his family, then turned the gun on himself. He had found an escape that repulsed the girl whose only goal was to live.

"What do you want?" I demanded, knowing the girl would not go away. She would haunt us the entire road to Xi'an, then leave us in the hands of bandits or Japanese smugglers. She might even kill us one night while we slept.

Gathering her treasure up in the dead child's tunic, the girl stood tall like a soldier, her body tempered by suffering.

She came close to me. Chiseled in moonlight, I dared to look at her. Underneath layers of filth, the girl's long oval face conjured not a fiend but a Qing beauty; a small, delicate mouth appeared beneath rows of cracked sores. She looked like Lin Daiyu from *The Story of the Stone*, not a fierce orphan scavenging for shoes.

Unused to scrutiny, the girl glared back.

"I want your golden shawl," she snapped, wiping her face.

10

Proof of Life

My husband grew up without family stories or photographs; no baby pictures, no graduation prints, no vacation shots. In one photograph my father took of me on a trip to Mackinac Island, Michigan, on a ferry ride, I was sticking out my tongue at the camera, a defiant eight-year-old. I can't remember why I was angry. I loved this photo. It reminded me of how unreasonable I could be and how childhood had many torments soon forgotten. I tried to imagine what it would be like to have no family pictures. My mother had a photo album dedicated to each child with studio shots from when we were a baby to adolescence. She gave mine to me when it was clear it was time to distribute these records to her children. I kept it in a box labeled "Memories." Every few years I glanced through the album, random thoughts floating through my mind. I have no idea what will happen to it when I die.

Trying to imagine my husband's childhood made me soften my Cold War mentality of our marriage. After our last fight, I wanted to stay mad at him. Stick out my tongue every chance I could get. Andrew wanted my project on his mother to go away. My corkboard in my study, studded with maps, quotes from Chinese writers, photographs of the French Concession, and internet images of Nanjing Central University were circumstantial evidence of her life. I could fill up the entire study with pictures from China in the 1930s and 40s and still be no closer to her life. She was a still a phantom.

He never came into my study any more, to remind me to take a break or to rub my shoulders. It was enemy territory.

Our relationship shifted into neutral. I could feel the engine idling, impatient to either move into drive or stop. A sort of marriage limbo.

It might have stayed that way for years if Andrew hadn't received an email message from Charles Withington, Mrs. Withington's grandson. He was sending a set of 11 small photographs in a manila envelope. Charles had saved a few boxes of his father's photographs, and on hearing from Mrs. Loring that my husband was still alive, searched through his old albums for some snapshots of Andrew's mother. He was astonished at his luck and stripped the fading photos from their black backing and sent them to my husband. His email emphasized that he didn't know anything about Andrew's parents.

On the back of each photo was a penciled date and place, 1937 Rochester, 1937 New Haven, 1938 Rochester, 1939 Boston. Having created many photo albums throughout his life, especially of his camping trips with friends in the Cascades, my husband put the snapshots in archival sleeves and spent time studying them.

Andrew wanted to talk. He was taken aback at how his mother's life kept resurfacing. "Why now?" he asked. "What do I do?"

At fifty-seven years old, he was suddenly in possession of baby pictures. His mother and father were standing in a backyard smiling. After a complete blackout, they saunter back as if the world was filled with their happiness.

Not studio images or posed pictures, the casual backyard photos seemed more like what a family friend would take without much fussing or arranging. "Here she is," he said, raising an archival sleeve, peering at each photograph.

My husband was a great skeptic about photography, having worked in a darkroom on his own black and white negatives, developing and printing, dodging, and burning, altering the image to create visual impact. He'd studied photography with Minor White while he was working on his MFA, and despite the ways our eyes reduce reality to conventional images, he felt it was still possible to record some glimmer of reality with the camera's lens. A good photographer sensed the second the face dropped its mask, and sometimes the causal photographer accidentally happened upon a moment evoking something beneath the surface.

"That's her," he said, placing the archival sleeve back in its three-ring binder as if the images were personally taken for him to look at years later. There was nothing he wanted to say about the photographs other than he had the good luck to have them. It was simple. There she was. No mystery. No contorted family stories. No shifting account of how she died at childbirth or of tuberculosis, or worse, had not died but disappeared after a long illness.

Taken in 1937, the earliest snapshot was of his parents stopping for a second in a garden flooded with sunlight, their faces relaxed as if a friend had surprised them. The location was Rochester, New York, probably at the Withington's home on North Goodman Street, perhaps before their summer trip to Land's End. Likely, Sidney Withington took the photograph since he loved taking pictures according to his son, and his son had decided to preserve the old family photo albums.

Unearthed sixty years after it was taken, the picture of his parents was what we commonly call a *candid* shot, a shot supposedly without artifice, taken outside the studio, but, of course, that is impossible given how we behave and dress in highly stylized ways.

In his 1924 short story, "A Happy Family," Lu Xun wrote that in China the ideal modern couple married for love, had college degrees, and spent time in the West, preferably the United States. "The master of the house always wears a foreign suit; his collar is always snowy white. His wife's hair is always curled up like a sparrow's nest in front, her pearly white teeth are always peeping out, but she wears Chinese dress." Except for the "swallow's nest," Katherine and Zi Ming fit the bill.

The problem was that Lu Xun's narrator-writer can never figure out where in China the ideal couple lived because these two "exquisite specimens" were nothing but a fantasy of modern marriage. The reality was more treacherous since women were anything but free, and modern men were driven by confused ideas about family stemming from centuries of Confucian morality. As in the popular romance novels of the time, these two butterflies or love birds awaited a "cruel or unkind fate."

But to Andrew, these photographs brought his mother closer. They were not ironic short stories. They documented her presence. They were proof of life. Date, time, location.

How much had to happen for this image to survive? Most material things were washed away, torn up or disposed of from one generation to the next. Often one generation's belongings were the next generation's junk. The memories kept alive through clothing, furniture, letters, books, and even recipes are tossed, recycled, or put in boxes and forgotten. Henry David Thoreau thought this obliteration good. Ideally when someone died, everything they owned should go up in smoke from the flames of a giant bonfire, even though he kept in the family attic his unsold copies of *Walden*. Henry aside, within three generations most family histories are permanently destroyed. It is simply too much to preserve, let alone organize. Is there a designated family historian or keeper of the goods? And what happens when that person dies? By the time grandchildren are grown and decide to ask questions about their ancestors, the dead and everything they possessed has been composted. Americans might be eager genealogists, retrieving names from online searches or the Archives of the Church of Jesus Christ of Latter-day Saints, but they find mainly strings of surnames, family trees. Ancestors remain inert, attached at best to a date and a place. Photographs also give limited information. Antique shops are stacked with tossed photo albums of the unknown dead. Like their recycled clothes, no one knows who wore them. Nothing, not even a name, that persistent remainder etched on burial stones or a mausoleum wall.

Once my husband was "found" by Mrs. Loring, an entire network of her New England relatives who saved letters and old photo albums sprang into action, literally resurrecting a dead Chinese woman whose son was also assumed dead.

Since our cold war was thawing, I wanted to spend some time with the photographs and talk with Andrew about his reactions, but he refused.

"I don't need to look at them again," he said, pushing the binder over to me.

"Never?" I was itching to look at them sequentially. Katherine's letters had created a story of her life in the United States, and I wanted to see if the photos would give me more clues about what happened to her.

"You go ahead," he replied. He didn't want his stepmother or Ida to know about them. And he didn't want any friends or family members to see them. He had placed them in his memory and that's where they belonged, away from the threat of voyeurs or scoffers. Like the childhood memory of his mother sitting up in bed, the last time he saw her, he must protect her image from forces that might want to harm or erase her, those who kept secrets for reasons that were not clear. At best, these voyeurs might be neutral, treating his mother's photograph as an object to pick apart.

"You are the only person other than me who saw these photographs," he emphasized, his hand resting on the album. "Take care."

No posting on a website for the world to see. No hauling out the photos to entertain my sisters about his past that he had up to that point kept hidden. No viewers but him and me. The circle was small and necessary.

"Necessary," he repeated. "Maybe someday, it can change."

I didn't understand Andrew's need to protect his mother's image, even in these found photographs. He refused to let Julia or Ida see them. They must be kept for our eyes. Why? Was the distrust so deep? What had happened to Katherine that would make her son continue to protect her image. What were the threats against her and him?

It took twenty-five years more before the time was right for Andrew to show these photographs to someone beside himself and me. Their public exposure in this narrative happened after decades of detours, dead-ends, side-shows, confessions, deaths, and even neglect until my husband's vigilant need to protect his mother's image could cease. Only after a certain amount of truth was revealed could the story be told, and the images displayed.

I had no expectations that this book would be read by anyone other than family and close friends. If it was, I hoped that these photographs would not be viewed with eyes inundated by the shallow rush of billions of images, photos circulated on the internet via Instagram, Facebook, Twitter, Imgur, Google Photos, Dropbox, Flickr, Smug Mug, or Photobucket. Here today, gone tomorrow. Multiplied disposables. A precious few, maybe, retained for comfort or reminder: These are the people I want and need to remember. The photograph not as nostalgia in the sentimental sense or the desire to imprison the past, but the photograph as *nostalgia* in its Greek sense of a return to home that evokes pain. The haunting melancholia due to prolonged absence from home, life lived with full awareness of loss and separation, an embrace of mortality that deepens the value of living things.

The photograph in its present form as a digital image is a hyper-electronic reproduction, circulated with dizzying speed, too often gutted of its power to evoke presence. A target, easily shamed, reviled, and ridiculed, its context stripped. Or as a focus of jealousy or confusion. If embraced, easily forgotten. Once in the land of multiplicities, it loses what made it precious to someone, anyone, its only value residing in how many times it has been viewed.

Two years later in 1939 on a sunny May afternoon in Boston, the lovely couple were photographed with their five-month-old baby.

By this time, the decision had been made to return to China, and Zi Ming was aware of how the return would affect his wife. As noted earlier, Zi Ming defended his position, insisting that "if I do not go back and join the people in this great struggle, I will do a great deal of damage to my prestige which will handicap my reconstruction plans in the future." Lu Xun's ideal couple predictably moved along a track that split them apart, his path ambitious, hers domestic.

With letters and newspaper reports traveling back and forth across the Pacific, Katherine and Zi Ming knew the dangers ahead. They had changed since the blissful summer at Land's End and the 1937 garden photograph in Rochester. No longer her husband's research assistant, Katherine had one role alone—mother—and her husband seemed most engaged away from home. In a letter a few weeks before this photo was taken, Katherine wrote to Mrs. Withington, expressing her gratitude. "I will never forget what you have done for me." She will also let her son "come back to see your family when he is grown up and will come back to his country to study." She sounded resigned yet confident about the future. The war would end, and her son would know both China and the United States like his parents. There would be continuity even if only through her son, an American born Chinese.

What was harder to understand in the 1939 photograph was Zi Ming's expression. Katherine leaned in, touching her son, smiling at the camera while Zi Ming squatted next to his wife, looking directly at the camera with a look I found hard to decipher. Was it apprehension, indifference, or fatigue? He touched neither his wife nor son. Had he become the man that Katherine lamented in her letters, a man at ease only when he is traveling to meetings and conferences, presenting lectures, and planning his future in a postwar China, a man never at home, restless to leave?

The silence of the photographic image has always invited idle comments and silly noise from the viewer, struggling to provide context and meaning. In this way it is a misleading relic from the past refusing to talk, like the dead. If the image is infused with our memories, we might retrieve them partially or place them in an ever-changing story of the past.

These speculations didn't bother my husband. This photograph proved one thing: he was by his mother's side, a baby alive to the infinite textures of his senses. What difference did it make that he couldn't make a coherent narrative out of this photograph? A single moment was reality: that is what I did that day, that is when my mother soothed me, that is how I had a home. It was more than enough.

11

Observatory Road

Trudging uphill along Observatory Road on a balmy October afternoon, Andrew suddenly stopped. He had caught sight of the two banyan trees that still hovered over the courtyard in front of his childhood apartment building. He thought they would be gone, replaced by urban clutter. Engulfed in their dense green canopy, he used to sit on the lower branches, relieved to be outside his home.

"Still here," he said, touching a massive root sticking out of its trunk as if it were an old friend.

He pointed farther up the road to what used to be called the Royal Observatory of Hong Kong that still signaled storm warnings in a code of color, number and geometric shape, the worst level-ten typhoon by a bold cross in the daytime and a night signal of red-green-red. With the excitement of a twelve-year-old, Andrew told me about watching the signals change as a ferocious typhoon formed over the Pacific and headed toward Hong Kong. A competitive duplicate bridge player, he was fascinated by signals and codes, studying cryptography and bidding conventions as if they could solve the problem of human language, bedeviled by deception and ambiguity. One meant don't worry. Ten meant run and hide.

Andrew had jumped at the chance to return to China in 1989, but Hong Kong held no such allure. Having arrived there in 1947 when he was eight from mainland China, he attended elementary school at the Canadian Catholic Tak Sun, and high school at King George V, which had only recently allowed significant numbers of non-European students to attend. When Andrew attended, he and two others were admitted, two from China, one from India.

Over the years, Andrew had told funny stories about his schooling, especially his truculent Scottish history and literature teachers who scorned English patriotism and the kind Canadian nun who taught him how to slide into second base and how to respect classmates, but he wasn't nostalgic enough to return and find old school friends. The shadows over his homelife on Observatory Road made it a place to avoid.

When the opportunity to live with full support for a year in Hong Kong came, he hesitated at first, then agreed with trepidation. We both had received academic appointments, mine in research, his in teaching and lecturing at local universities with plenty of time to travel to mainland China and Vietnam. It was also 1997, the year when the Crown colony was to be handed over to China, and, unswayed by American news coverage, the Chinese in the city were celebrating.

Everything and nothing had changed on Observatory Road. The apartment building was now a boutique hotel with banyan-themed rooms without the noise of neighbors nor any trace of his father, his stepmother, or their son, Peter. His father had died in 1970, his stepmother had moved to Berkeley, California, in 1988, and Peter was teaching piano in the Chicago area. Even though Andrew had kept in touch with Julia, he had little contact with Peter, a sullen man who seemed permanently angry with him.

Busy Nathan Road, down the hill in the section of the city called Tsim Sha Tsui, across Victoria Harbor from Hong Kong Island, was crowded with shops and shoppers much like it was in the 1950s when Hong Kong was fast turning into a commercial and financial hub, with money flowing through its companies and banks from East and West, a linchpin in the world economy

offering goods and financial services to a vast network of transnational corporations.

"A place to make money," Andrew often repeated every time
we watched the Hong Kong news or read about some charity
event or jewelry extravaganza.

We had been living in Hong Kong for three months when we
took our trek to Observatory Road. The trip was not to recapture
the past but to recognize that the past had occurred. More like
returning to the scene of a crime.

Sweating, we sat outside on red hotel chairs placed under
the branched umbrella of the banyan trees, listening to the street
noises and the squeaking of fruit bats. Lost in silence, Andrew
stared at the second floor where his family had lived.

"Why was it so bad?" he asked, as if coming up for air. "I have
no feelings for anyone. No one. Not even Peter."

He couldn't understand why they never played together or
why they never tried to contact each other after they both had left
Hong Kong. Each had stayed in his own bubble. They had gone
to separate grade schools and high schools, but that didn't explain
the continuing distance. Why had he occasional contact with
Julia and Ida, but not Peter? Andrew had pushed him far back in
his mind, but seeing the apartment building made Peter reappear.

The humid smells of the city—a sickly-sweet mildew—
intensified as the sun went down. The dusk seemed made of
glass splinters.

Something was wrong on Observatory Road. The two boys
were like pieces moved around on Zi Ming and his stepmother's
chess board. Julia once accused Andrew of trying to kill Peter
during an air raid. He couldn't remember where they were living,
either Chongqing or Shanghai. A baby, Peter was screaming in
his crib. Frightened, Andrew had tried to stop his cries. Julia had
walked in when he had his hand on Peter's shoulder. She never
stopped accusing him. "I didn't do it," he protested, as if trying
once again to claim his innocence in a house that wanted him
judged guilty.

Andrew kept talking to the darkening sky. He knew from Julia that his half-brother was living in Maywood, Illinois. Five years after Andrew left Hong Kong, Peter also left to continue his education in the United States. He too never wanted to return to Hong Kong and had permanently settled in the United States, pursuing a career as an artist like Andrew, defying their parents' wishes for them to become scientists or physicians.

None of these facts mattered. They had no connection. Any possibility of ties between them were broken in childhood.

Standing up abruptly, Andrew headed down the hill for drinks, leaving me behind. I raced to catch up. On the harbor's promenade was a quiet bar serving double martinis in tall, iced glasses. We could sit at a small table and drift away to live jazz, gazing at the neon lights of Central's waterfront, the scent of white orchids intoxicating. After a few drinks, Andrew proposed a new rule. No more talk about childhood.

We would never return to Observatory Road.

My office in Hong Kong looked down on the back of China's People's Liberation Army headquarters, its scrubbed, crew-cut soldiers practically invisible on the city streets. If I strained my neck, I could see the angel Moroni atop the recently built Hong Kong China Temple with young Latter-Day Saints in small groups on the sidewalk below. Unlike Andrew, I was mesmerized by Hong Kong, a mixture of Miami Beach and *Blade Runner*, its Star ferries, MTR subway system, and minibuses moving millions of people safely and efficiently. A feast of humanity from the garish rich to the pinched workers, Hong Kong was modernity on steroids, the planet's future and possibly its demise.

Doing online archival research on Dickinson, a recluse poet living in rural Massachusetts, felt ridiculous in Hong Kong. Instead, I opted to walk the city streets, not taking pictures or notes, only walking, smelling, and tasting the richness of city life. I was heady from the sensation of merging into a crowd moving on and off the underground trains, hurrying to work or home for dinner. I became an unhinged tourist, pausing only to listen to a solitary Buddhist monk ringing a single silver bell whose pure tone floated over the sea of commuters on the ramps leading to downtown Central, the heart of Hong Kong Island.

Our offices five blocks apart, Andrew wasn't aware of how many days I would skip work and roam. Wandering, I listened to the sounds of Cantonese, quickly learning street curses and polite phrases. My ears popped. I had awakened from the slow rhythms of the Pacific Northwest and the laziness of the native speaker. My English words paled. One morning I wandered into a small store, a mere closet with stacks of rolled fabric, selling clothing made of mud silk. The friendly woman owner explained how a group of village women in Guangdong province in southern China had not forgotten how to make mud silk, a folk textile. She had opened the shop to support them. No one cared about mud silk anymore.

A glossy black jacket with an interior lining of cinnamon brown caught my eye. Its carefully crafted frog buttons, silk edging, and mandarin collar reminding me of Katherine's dress. How elegantly her black silk was sewn, a fashion statement for the rich. How sturdy this basic mud silk jacket felt, a treasure for the trousseau of peasant women.

Taking the jacket off the rack, the owner asked me to touch the fabric.

"Incredibly strong," she said. "Light as a feather. Like wearing nothing no matter how hot the sun."

The newly rich Cantonese from southern China who had emigrated to Hong Kong as peasants before 1949 had no interest in folk textiles from their peasant background. The glittery high fashion chains in Central or Tsim Sha Tsui caught their fancy. They obeyed the imperative to display wealth in clothes, watches, eyeglass frames, and jewelry. Mud silk belonged to a past they wanted to forget.

A white Western woman, a *gwaipo* or ghost woman, especially a *tai-tai*, or wife, was expected to spend her days in Hong

Kong shopping, collecting Chinese antiques and curiosities like mud silk. Since I was an academic, short on funds, I couldn't fulfill this role, especially the part of three martini lunches with other *tai-tai* at the American Club, yet I reached in my purse and ordered a black jacket and long skirt that I would wear once. I was afraid of posing, having known Europeans and American expats who only dressed in antiquated Chinese clothes, affecting the air of a Chinese scholar in his *changshan,* or a Chinese beauty in her *cheongsam.* I was afraid of looking ridiculous.

That's why Louise Chan was a godsend. A colleague of my husband and a slip of a woman, petite and powerful with a wit like a knife, Louise was a Hong Kong native who taught Shakespeare with a decidedly British accent and quickly noticed how uncomfortable I was with the role of *tai-tai.* Once a week, she would take me on an excursion to visit the Hong Kong she loved; Taoist temples, Tin Hau (goddess of the sea) shrines, oracle bone exhibits, open air markets, subterranean archaeological sites, and skyscraper apartments where the majority of Hong Kong people lived in tiny rooms. Against the rules of her upbringing, we usually ended up at Chongqing Mansions eating Malaysian coconut rice and sambal sauce while global immigrants from throughout Africa and countries in South Asia, like Nepal and Pakistan, crowded the narrow pathways lined with stalls. Off limits to a prim and proper British Literature professor, Chongqing Mansions had a reputation for drug dealing and violence, but to Louise it was an escape from the narrow, commercial world of Chinese Hong Kong. With me along, she had an excuse to experience the Hong Kong her wealthy Cantonese relatives wanted to deny.

After a trip to a massive hillside cemetery, a city of the dead facing the sea, and an historic coffin house, a transit spot where dead Chinese were kept before their final burial in their ancestral homes, I confided in Louise, telling her about Katherine and making her vow never to tell Andrew about our conversation. Her response surprised me. She didn't want me to forget Katherine. It was urgent that I stay committed to knowing the truth about Katherine's life and death.

"It's dangerous work," she cautioned, citing her grandmother's, whom she called her *Popo,* deep fear of dead ancestors. "Dig away but remember the dead can protect or injure. You must appease them."

"You believe that?" I asked. Even though we both had superstitious grandmothers, we were complete skeptics with no religious beliefs, seeing human foibles and absurdities through an ironic lens.

Laughing, Louise spun around and then stood stock still. "*Popo* said that Confucius said, 'Respect ghosts and spirits but keep your distance.'"

I countered, "My grandmother, or *Babusia,* would worry that Katherine was a dead ancestor with a grudge. All those packages in the mail? Creepy. A spirit time traveler. 'She wants something,' I could hear her saying. 'The dead are dangerous.'"

To Louise, Hong Kong Chinese had two faces, one pragmatic and money grubbing, the other, superstitious and terrified. "This place is haunted." Chinese victims of Japanese massacres roamed Stanley Point where sharks still return, hoping to eat more bodies bayoneted by Japanese soldiers and then dumped in Tai Tam Bay. Once I told Louse that Katherine and Andrew had lived in Hong Kong during the winter of 1940, she wanted to figure out where that might be. Her best guess was mid-levels in Central since it was close to the University of Hong Kong and had upscale residences for both white expats and educated Chinese.

We spent an entire day walking up and down the steep stairs of the mid-levels area, peeking down alleyways, dreaming up scenarios for Katherine and Andrew. Wild speculations that went nowhere.

"We could try a fortune teller at a Taoist temple and pay for *fuji* or spirit writing." Louise's *Popo* was clearly a match for my *Babusia.*

We took the covered escalator to Man Mo Temple where the God of Literature and the God of Martial Arts were venerated with other heavenly gods lined up in side-altars and courtyards, the ceilings covered with cone incense, its overwrought gold and red interior, incense-laden air, and ornate god sculptures like a baroque Polish church on steroids. I felt right at home.

We had trouble finding a Taoist priest willing to practice *fuji*. We bought bundles of incense and paid our respects, placing three thin incense wands before Man Tai and Mo Tai, bowing three times, and reciting a prayer. Louise told me that it didn't matter if the prayers were from my Polish Catholic background. They should convey respect and reverence. I recited a Hail Mary in Polish at both stops.

I wasn't ignorant about Taoism, having studied it and Buddhism in graduate school, but that didn't mean much. Reading sutras was not equivalent to believing in what they said. I was more an "all-religions-are-one" type of person who understood these ancient systems as a repository of human wisdom, and enough of an historian to know how oceans of blood were spilled because of these religious beliefs. My God against yours. As one of my theologian friends told me, "If you can get people to believe that God is behind what you are doing, you have real power." Apocalyptic power, I would add.

"You haven't heard the last of her," whispered Louise in front of the small office of a Taoist priest who was open for fortune-telling. We could see him inside with a woman, their heads bowed. Once she left, he waved us inside. Louise explained our request and negotiated a fee. From a side desk he pulled a large sheet of rice paper and a forked red bamboo writing pen. He was concerned that Louise did not know Katherine's Chinese name. He had other questions about her life. Where had she died and when? Did we have anything of hers?

The only help was a small photograph of Katherine and Andrew when he was a baby sitting on her lap that I kept in my wallet.

The priest held it carefully and set it down next to the paper.

After a few minutes of complete stillness, the bamboo pen in the hand of the priest started to quiver and move across the rice paper as if searching for a spot to begin writing.

Starting from the top right and then gliding down, the calligraphy spurted on the paper with clicks and bangs, fluid characters at war with each other. The message was a jigsaw puzzle that Louise spent quite some time discussing with the priest who kept looking away. Maybe, he could sense our disbelief that an immortal had descended into the pen and established a connection with the spirit world.

Handing my photo back, the priest wagged his finger at the door. He wanted us out of his office. There were three other people waiting outside. He looked disgusted with me as I tried to thank him.

Louise wasn't happy when we walked outside the temple.

"He told me to tell you not to try and find Katherine. It would bring bad luck. The only other message he deciphered was that there was already a message from Katherine. He asked what was wrong with my friend's ears?"

"So much for the spirit world," I said, trying to make light of what had happened.

"I'm convinced the spirit message said something else," Louise whispered. "Before he burnt the rice paper, I saw the character for 'rage.'"

A character, Louise added, that is said to contain a warning since it combined the script for slave and heart, and slave contains the character for woman. "Tread carefully," Louise insisted. "Something is wrong."

12

Ku Woman

Six months into our stay in Hong Kong, Roger, a British historian of science, came calling. Arrogant and cagey, his sandy hair swept over his right eye, a boyish look, he was eager to interview Andrew and discuss what it was like to grow up the son of a famous Chinese scientist.

Zi Ming's work was being rediscovered by American, British, and Chinese psychologists who were busy reprinting his research articles and books in English and Chinese and writing biographies of the pioneering scientist who turned the nature versus nurture debate on its head. A radical anti-instinct psychologist, Zi Ming had proved with his studies on chick embryos and the behavior of cats and rats that much of what passed as instinct was merely learned behavior, even behavior learned in the womb.

Eager to make his mark, Roger had made several trips to the United States to interview Andrew's stepmother and visited archives that housed Zi Ming's letters to a string of famous American psychologists. More relevantly, he had traveled to three Chinese universities, interviewing contemporaries of Zi Ming. Zi Ming's Chinese past was under his microscope. The walls that kept China, Hong Kong, and the United States apart since World War II were crumbling. Researchers were free to move across borders, piecing together information long kept behind the bamboo curtain.

I always felt Zi Ming was a threat to my work on Katherine. I had resisted researching him since I felt he had participated in erasing Katherine's existence. He was the man who left her alone for years in the United States and in Chongqing when they returned to China. He caused her loneliness. More information about the great man would only further black out her past. His legend would overshadow her brief life. No one would want to know about her. Only his life would become worth recording.

We ended up spending too many evenings with Roger listening to his discoveries until my husband decided he'd had enough. Early on my husband had warned Roger that he didn't know that much about his father's research. He had typed a manuscript for his father right before he left for the United States, but he hadn't kept in touch with him. It didn't seem to matter to Roger. He was heady with his chance to publish a comprehensive intellectual biography of the great man. He liked visiting with Andrew, as if Andrew brought him closer to Zi Ming.

For a few months we didn't see Roger. Then one of his publications on Zi Ming appeared in the mail. The article barely touched on Zi Ming's personal life, mainly outlining his psychological research and theories. A single footnote listed Zi Ming's children. Before Zi Ming left China for his PhD at Berkeley, he had two sons with his first wife; when he returned, he had three more children, five in total. Andrew had two half-brothers older than Bill. The oldest son had died, the second son, Yaoming, was alive in China. Andrew was then mentioned as the son of the second wife, and then Zi Ming left China with his third wife to live in Hong Kong. There was no mention of Peter.

The day after we received the article, Andrew's stepmother called him long distance in a rage. It was all about the footnote that listed the children of Zi Ming. She called him at his office. "Don't talk to that man!" she screamed into the phone. "Don't listen to what he says." He had tricked her when he visited California. Andrew must not believe rumors or scandal.

We found her anger baffling. What possible difference could it make that this list of children was printed in an academic article on the history of psychology? Who would care?

"She's crazy," was Andrew's reply. "The whole family's crazy."

I think he was amused by the feathers flying over the Pacific. From what I knew, my husband had one half-brother and two half-sisters from his father's first arranged marriage: Bill, Ida and Ifong. Katherine had known about these children and wrote about their well-being in her letters to Mrs. Withington. She was worried about Ifong because she had throat and respiratory problems, and it was difficult to get her the right medical care in Japanese-occupied Shanghai. These children of Zi Ming by his first wife were not hidden from sight. Katherine was open about who they were, including them in several letters when writing to Mrs. Withington about "the children" back in Shanghai.

I also kept notes on how Andrew suspected there might be another older half-brother from his father's first marriage. There was no mention of such a child in Katherine's letters. Was this Yaoming? I put a giant question mark in my husband's family record.

Despite his siblings, Andrew experienced his childhood like an orphan, the son of deceased wife number two with an ice-cold father and a treacherous stepmother. His Chinese family was a loose net of tenuous lines without clan loyalty or filial duty, the opposite of the stereotypical Chinese family built on Confucian principles of filial piety. The war had created fault lines, splitting husbands from wives, brothers from sisters, creating suspicions and anguish, offering no means to put the pieces back together. Andrew's family was a casualty of war.

Then my husband received a long letter from his stepmother. During the war in China, she had been married to Yaoming, the older half-brother, and had a child with him who was given the English name Peter. She described the wartime chaos of Chongqing, how Yaoming had betrayed her by sleeping with a servant, and how he had been banished from the family. Rejected and ill with beriberi, Julia was left alone with her baby, Peter. After Katherine's long illness and death, Zi Ming was also alone with Andrew and severely depressed. Both in distress, they supported each other at the Chongqing villa until the war ended, then left together for Shanghai. Julia insisted there was nothing wrong with her decision to flee Shanghai with Zi Ming. The communists were threatening. What was she to do?

Julia blamed Yaoming for what had happened. What she did was to preserve lives by forming a new family in Hong Kong. It was necessary.

Whatever her reasons and rationale, we now knew that Peter was not Andrew's half-brother, he was his nephew. Also, Julia was his former sister-in-law, and his stepmother. She had been married to Yaoming, Andrew's older half-brother. Further, Zi Ming was Peter's grandfather, but he had protected his third wife by passing as Peter's father. This was Julia's secret, which she had guarded for over fifty years. She insisted on her innocence, the victim of an adulterous Yaoming; her only crime was to want a future for her son.

I felt like a large stone had been dropped on my head. The family's relationships were so dizzying, I had to make a list of this new reality, the familiar public connections, and the secret, but real, bonds.

1. Zi Ming married First Wife. Yaoming is their son.
2. Yaoming marries Julia. Peter is their son.
3. Yaoming banished.
4. Julia joins with Zi Ming, her father-in-law, and escapes to Hong Kong with Peter and Andrew
5. A new family is invented that lasts from 1947 to 1998

Because of one letter, Julia had shape-shifted from stepmother to sister-in-law, and Peter had changed from half-brother to nephew.

My husband had no reaction.

I repeatedly tried to rearrange his family in my mind. It wasn't like learning that you had a new half-brother or sister because your father had an affair or kept a secret wife, or your mother put an unwanted child up for adoption. Andrew's father had married his daughter-in-law and pretended he was the father of his grandson. How Andrew's family managed to keep this secret was baffling. "Kids know," was what my husband said. He had rightfully suspected that something was wrong on Observatory Road. He had grown up in a home where family members were not who they claimed to be.

The footnote revealed a revised list of Andrew's siblings by the first arranged marriage of Zi Ming:

1. Unnamed half-brother, died in China
2. Yaoming, half-brother, living in China
3. Bill, half-brother, living in China
4. Ida, half-sister, living in the United States
5. Ifong, half-sister, died in China

The dreaded name from the past, Yaoming, had reemerged in Roger's biographical research on Zi Ming that he conducted at Chinese universities. Andrew's trips to China and Hong Kong were clearly a danger to Julia. She feared that old friends or enemies would tell him the truth about her. Instead, a biographer dug up the scandal, alluding to it indirectly in a footnote. If truth be told, we barely skimmed Roger's article and only went back to it after Julia mailed her confession. Ironically, she had taken charge and exposed that Peter was her son by Yaoming. Once the name Yaoming was in print, Julia must have felt she had no other choice. Scandal never lost its sting. Better to fess up.

Andrew folded up his stepmother's letter, carefully placed it back in its envelope and tucked it under a stack of files on the living room table. His movements were so deliberate and slow it was as if he was ritually closing her words up and binding her voice.

I didn't intrude on his silence. I knew he would want to talk eventually. It was our pattern. Our life together was punctuated by long silences, interrupted with intimate conversations. It wasn't family news to yak about over breakfast or with friends. Who would understand it? What good would it do?

My family irritated me, stumped me, puzzled me, but with them my life deepened, its details and textures intensified. I had never cut them out. It would feel suicidal. We laughed the same way, told inside jokes around the dinner table, teased each other, and would do anything for each other. I knew I was lucky in spades.

I wanted my husband's life to feel like that, not betrayed, not deceived, not abandoned. I couldn't do anything but wait. And the silence was painful.

Finally, I had enough. After a long dinner in a local dim sum restaurant, crowded with families sitting around large round tables dotted with revolving trays, and waiters running around with carts stacked with dim sum baskets, I said, "The secret's out. That's something."

The din was deafening. Not the best place to have a serious conversation.

Maybe it was the ridiculousness of sitting in a restaurant packed with Chinese families each talking louder than the next that made Andrew laugh.

We finished our meal and walked to a bar in Tsim Sha Tsui, not far from Observatory Road, and proceeded to drink too many vodka martinis.

Perched over his drink, Andrew scanned the night skyline, trying to locate the old Bank of China, dwarfed by a wall of skyscrapers.

"I don't believe her," he said.

"Believe what?"

"The bit about her marriage to Yaoming makes sense. And Peter. The rest is a pack of lies."

The disgust in his voice settled on each word.

He urged me to listen. He didn't want to get dragged back into his family. He was drowning in their lies. Couldn't I see that? It wasn't a game or a hobby or a research project. He didn't want to blame me. I didn't know what it was like in China during the war or afterwards in Hong Kong. He had tried hard to separate himself, create a new life, not get sucked down in their deceptions. He had to warn me. He didn't want to drag me into the same dark place. But I needed to understand. My obsession with his mother had to either stop completely or stop being naive.

Then he told me what was really on his mind.

Since he was a child, he had suspected that his stepmother had killed his mother with white arsenic powder. He didn't know exactly why he felt this was true. But after his stepmother's letter about her marriage to Yaoming, his suspicions turned to belief. She was trying to get into his head and direct him away from what she had done in Chongqing. A terrible thing had happened in his childhood, and it wasn't about Peter. His stepmother knew that he knew something. She counted on him not remembering or at least not being able to put into words what he remembered. His memory needed to stay locked in a subliminal space without language. But she wasn't totally sure. She was on the attack. Julia was trying to fill his head with an alternative story in which she and his father were victims of grief and war.

"She's a *Ku* woman. Her words are poison."

I had never heard this phrase before.

"White arsenic powder, a Chinese family weapon." Andrew explained that *Ku* women killed their rivals in love with poison or sorcery. If they fell in love with a married man, they plotted to murder the wife and harm their children. They usually succeeded, spinning stories to cover their crime. They were smart.

"My stepmother was a physician in Chongqing, not some weepy, bed-ridden woman, betrayed by her adulterous husband, Yaoming. Really? No one gets exiled for sleeping with a servant. She must think I am totally stupid."

I had to admit that her account contradicted everything I knew about wealthy Chinese families. The *Story of the Stone*, the eighteenth-century Chinese novel, was filled with cheating wives, husbands, servants, and practically anyone involved in running a large clan mansion. Masters routinely slept with their servants, especially those assigned as chambermaids. Exile for sleeping with a servant was ludicrous.

To Andrew it wasn't important that his stepmother was really his sister-in-law. She most probably wasn't even his legal stepmother. He didn't believe that she and his father were married, but they did live as husband and wife. They shared a bedroom in every sense of the word. She was his mistress and that meant that Zi Ming had committed incest according to Chinese values. Even without an historic belief in monogamy, traditional China would have condemned them, and modern China would have too.

"They could have been the only ones left," I insisted, attempting to find a reason for her actions. "But a murderer?"

"She had to invent some ridiculous story to cover up what she had done. She wanted my father, and my mother stood in the way. She admits to what she can't cover up and then throws me off the trail. I was a liability and still am. She should have killed me too."

I was shocked and, I must admit, confused. If Andrew was correct that Julia had not only erased the memory of Katherine but killed his mother, she would not stop trying to manipulate Andrew's memories. His return to China and Hong Kong had begun the process of untangling her fabrications about the Hong Kong family on Observatory Road and about what happened to Katherine in China. The dreaded past, long silenced, was heard in the tiny space of a single footnote in an academic journal.

From then on, Andrew and I were very close in Hong Kong. The truth about his family and his worst fears about his mother had launched us into frantic activity. We were never home. We ate at off-beat restaurants and bars in Wan Chai and Da Pai

Dong, hiked dangerous trails on Lion Rock, and visited obscure art galleries. We hung out at the Foreign Correspondence Club listening to aging journalists who had covered the American war in Vietnam and drank heavily with everybody arguing about the future of Hong Kong under China's rule. Our time was heady, even intoxicating. We'd stay out all night, not caring about sleep or work. The city was our drug.

Oddly, we stopped talking about Observatory Road and his mother. Hong Kong obliterated the past. Each new skyscraper amplified the glittery skyline of the city's future. The dusty relics of China's ancient past and suffering during World War II faded away. Buildings were torn down at dizzying speeds, and in their place new luxury goods stores sprang up like weeds. Many nights we drank martinis with Chinese artists and Italian friends who worked for Prada. Sitting amid the opulence of the China Club, we'd listen to tales of how the Chinese from both Hong Kong and the mainland kept the global luxury goods market alive. Wealthy Chinese were the new big spenders, purchasing with cash complete outfits accessorized from shoes to hats and packed in Prada suitcases. Before leaving the store, the Chinese customers bought enormous Prada handbags to carry more luxury goods from their visits to Hermes, Gucci, Dior, Chanel, Bottega Veneta, Ermenegildo Zegna and Missoni. Only the future mattered, the stock market, the currency market, the latest trends in clothes, watches, and cars.

Sitting at our table on the rooftop terrace of the China Club with its giddy view of neon skyscrapers and twenty-story-high advertising images, we would laugh about this new consumer hell. But it had us all in its grip. Our minds were mesmerized, even fixated on its accelerating and unstoppable movement forward. Consumers in hell. Money the ultimate drug.

Only when I sat alone on our small balcony in the humid nights did I think about Katherine. I had stopped going out with Louise. Now that Katherine's death was explained by my husband's unverifiable belief in murder, the truth seemed out of reach. Impossible to find. How can you find evidence, especially for a murder committed fifty years before in a country at war and with a completely different government in control? My husband never wavered in his belief in Julia's guilt, but he also refused to say with absolute certainty that Julia murdered his mother. It rested on an irrepressible childhood feeling. There was no way forward except to live in the present with a lurid embrace of the future.

Lying in bed at night next to Andrew, I wondered if he was an eyewitness to the crime. Could it be that horrible? I tried to think from his perspective. He didn't seem fazed by the knowledge that Julia was his sister-in-law and Peter was his nephew. I was surprised at how neutral he was, as if he had known all along that he lived in a charade. What we were both running away from was Katherine's death. He had his tenacious belief, and I wanted to find a way to leave this sordid event behind. But the uncertainty gnawed at me. There must be some way to uncover the truth.

I decided to keep secret track of everything I knew about Julia. First, a description: a Chinese beauty with a perfect oval face, fair skin, black hair swept back above a high forehead, crescent-shaped eyebrows above luminous eyes, a straight, thin nose, delicate lips but not too thin, graceful, polished, powerful. An accomplished physician and hospital administrator in Hong Kong, she had written my husband many letters lecturing him on his need to obtain a PhD; a mere poet was not good enough. She instructed him on how to find better jobs and how to succeed. She was a moralizing machine.

How could this person be a murderer? Everything she did or said had seemed to have a moral intent. She was didactic, an enforcer. I had grown used to her sharp criticism of my Chinese pronunciation. I would never forget any word she had corrected. I admired her. When she retired in the Bay Area, she was surrounded by old friends from Hong Kong who doted on her. A group of Chinese unwilling to live under Chinese rule after the 1997 handover with a shared hatred of the communist party that had ruined their lives, they were drawn to her magnetism. She was a Chinese woman physician who had been awarded an O.B.E. by Queen Elizabeth II. She was the widow of a famous Chinese scientist. She had survived the Second World War and triumphed.

Next to her accomplishments I listed whatever I could find about *Ku* women. I read oral histories of Chinese women from the eastern province of Sichuan where Chongqing is located. They recorded folk tales of *Ku* women snatching husbands after poisoning their wives. Some told of how they infested with parasites the children of their rival, the swollen bellies of the young proof of *Ku* women's evil practices. I also had learned that when Andrew arrived in Chongqing with his mother after their long trek across China, he was treated for parasites, his belly a balloon. The tales fit Andrew's childhood belief. Had a servant told him these stories after his mother died? If Julia had left Chongqing with Zi Ming, whose wife was dead, her actions would have reproduced the folk tale. Could that explain Andrew's belief?

Still, the shifting explanations about Katherine's death had always raised red flags. Childbirth, tuberculosis, a sudden disappearance? Why were there multiple explanations from Julia? Was the uncertainty deliberate? Something was wrong. If Andrew had heard servants gossiping about Julia, repeating folk stories about *Ku* women using white arsenic powder to kill unwanted wives, that still didn't account for these conflicting reasons for her death.

P. K., a famous Hong Kong poet, had gathered us together at the Drunken Boat, a restaurant on Hennessey Road in Wan Chai to bid Andrew and me good-bye. We were leaving for the United States in a week. Everyone brought spirits to share. The group was seated around a large round table, Andrew's large bottle of *Black Label* dead center. Three Hong Kong Chinese writers, two Hong Kong Chinese translators, two American-born Chinese, a white American expat journalist, and me, a white American woman academic, debating the essence of Hong Kong. What was it? A Chinese city, a British colonial city, a post-colonial city, an empty transit place of global finance? Everyone's pet theory fell apart, a new one taking its place. Only merriment was shared, not certainty.

Louise sat on my right side. She was thinking about leaving Hong Kong, too, and moving to Brisbane, Australia. "Hong Kong is Chinese and not Chinese." Her British-accented English made her jokes funnier as she imitated the last British Governor, Chris Patten, aka Fatty Pang or Fei Peng, and his ridiculous largesse in giving the Chinese people the vote as he exited the political stage. In a single stroke, he had brought democracy at the last minute to the Crown colony that had been denied it for over a century. Abruptly standing at attention, Louise mimicked, with an imaginary scepter, the British Governor as he bestowed political power on his Chinese minions.

Everyone burst out laughing.

A ferocious rehashing of what China had up its sleeve for Hong Kong followed.

I described how I could see the People's Liberation Army Headquarters from my office window. Every morning I watched as the soldiers did calisthenics and then marched in orderly lines back inside.

"Do you ever see them on the street?" I asked.

"So quietly, so quietly they move among us," sang Louise, mocking their movements.

Mei, a Chinese short story writer eyeing New Zealand, shifted gears. "Did you see the fireworks over Central? We are rejoicing. The British are gone."

"Now what?" asked the young woman graduate student from UCLA studying for one year at Chinese University. Her parents had fled to Taiwan in 1949 and after twenty years moved to the United States, her father a noted Buddhist scholar.

"Are Hong Kong people really Chinese?" she asked. Her father didn't understand why real Chinese had consented to live under British rule.

The question was like a red cape taunting a bull; everyone started talking at once. Mainland Chinese thought Hong Kong people were not Chinese, neither-here-nor-there people. They weren't like the Chinese on Taiwan who were Chinese but in that defeated sense of the old China that had lost the civil war and were forever living in the past like Cuban refugees in Florida, dreamers of ridiculous futures unwilling to see reality. In short, fools.

Only P. K. wanted to defend Hong Kong as the future, all cities moving toward a global mishmash, neither-here-nor-there, hybrids of other places, bits and pieces juggling against each other, recombining, reinventing, free to play.

"Free to lie," added Andrew.

Silence, then complete agreement. "Too many secrets," said P. K., the wars in China shaken and dropped in a pile on this tiny island. "Old spies and new secrets."

I kept a diary during my stay in Hong Kong, mainly trivia that happened each day. Lines from P. K.'s poetry punctuated my mundane chores. Underneath a list of what I bought at the grocery store in Sha Tin was a line from his *City at the End of Time*, "on the edge, I'm nowhere in particular, a smoke-signal in a sandstorm, a border legend, a plotless detail in the weeds of history."

To me it seemed that Hong Kong tried to pretend that the past had never happened, that city had no history, but the past felt like it was everywhere, stinking up its narrow streets. Arriving with suitcases, the Chinese keep coming from mainland China, originally as escapees from the civil war, then as opportunists and conquerors, each generation bringing its own inventions and lies about their past.

Katherine was caught in this web of lies.

Tucked in my journal were notes on Julia next to a quote from Lucretius, the Roman poet, "Uncertainty bred secret violence." Living in Hong Kong as a child, Andrew imbibed this "secret violence." Never threatened directly, he was neglected, discounted, a non-person. He underwent an existential gutting. He had to flee.

Zi Ming was dead, but Julia knew what happened to Katherine. She had guarded the truth about her husband, Yaoming, for over fifty years. She still guarded the truth about Andrew's mother, a secret, I was convinced, she would take to her grave.

When we returned to the United States, I would stand in front of Katherine's oil portrait urging her to say something, anything. Give me a sign. I wanted reassurance that Andrew had solved the mystery of her death. Julia had killed her.

Day after day, her face stared back, her mouth mute. Was I beginning to lose my mind? Why was I so anxious, at night waking up my body drenched in sweat, uncertain of where I was or who I was? One morning I found myself interrogating her portrait. Ridiculous. Thank God, Andrew wasn't at home. What was happening? I tried distractions, for days hiking the woods near our house. It did nothing. Unable to unwind, I listened to music, cooked, practiced meditation, and watched a marathon of movies. Nothing helped.

Katherine wouldn't talk but she also wouldn't go away, fade to black and let me go on with my life. Part of me wanted to go back to China, hire a detective, and hunt down her death certificate in Chongqing. I needed a document, not Andrew's childhood feelings. His accusation against Julia could be the truth, but what if it was a symptom of unresolved conflicts with his father and Julia? Andrew could be lashing out and blaming her because she survived and his mother hadn't.

Tense and grumpy, I avoided meals with Andrew, making up excuses about my need to burrow into my research as if I was making breakthroughs on my Dickinson book. What a lie. I created lies that were making me crazy.

I retreated into my study, manically pinning more images to the cork boards over my walls, covered with an array of Chinese maps, photos, and scribbled notes. I rampaged through my research files, devoured more Chinese novels and histories from the 1940s, and watched old Shanghai movies online. A mental plunder of China.

The Taoist priest's warning had gone completely unheeded. Katherine was in our home. Her dress, her letters, her portrait, and her photographs were more real than my life.

One morning I stopped spinning inside my head and settled into the task at hand. If Katherine's ghost was dangerous, so be it. In his spirit writing, the Taoist priest had drawn the Chinese character for "rage." At night, I practiced writing the word, *nù*, on a large sheet of paper.

With each stroke, I felt my calm returning. Something was missing from the explanation for Katherine's death. Rage was missing. What precisely happened when Katherine returned with Andrew to Chongqing? The long journey with her son must have been plagued by predators and taken an immense toil on her and Andrew. Her reunion with Zi Ming had to have been a relief. So what did rage have to do with it?

I had to keep digging.

13

March, 1943

Before she gave me the embroidered shawl, my mother had sewn two gold coins, one on each side, into the collar of my jacket. They were my secret weapon. The girl may have taken the precious shawl, wearing it around her waist like a trophy, but I had still fooled her. I had the coins. She would never find them.

How did my sister do it, working with the poor peasants flooding into the city and the factory workers striking for food? None of them could be trusted. They would turn on you and take everything you had. Hardened and conniving, Li Min was waiting for her chance to take my jacket, my shoes, my gloves, and even my son. She was the truth of China, predators calculating their chances.

My husband used to talk about revolutionary love when we lay in each other's arms. I was his chance to break free of a stifling, arranged marriage. What I had seen on the road was revolutionary hate, not love, a simmering fire ready to burst into flames, the masses hungry for revenge on whoever they felt had caused their recurring nightmares: landlords, generals, tax collectors, and people like me, the rich. For three thousand years, dynasties and governments had inflicted war, conscription, and famine. Their heritage was funeral pyres darkening the sky as ravens came to feast on the battlefields, strewn with their beloved dead. Li Min hated me. Why pretend otherwise?

Only the gold coins sewn in my collar mattered to bring Andrew and me to the safety of Chongqing.

Once on the road west, we met an elderly couple, Reverend and Mrs. Speer, Presbyterian missionaries from Huntingdon, Pennsylvania, which they called "an inspired place of dairy farms and quilted fields," the hum of church hymns resonating beneath their words. They sat on two handcarts stacked with provisions that the reverend protected with his black Colt pistol, a gift from an American archaeologist who had chiseled Bodhisattvas from blackened stone bases in nearby Buddhist caves to ship to American museums before the Japanese arrived to steal or destroy what was left.

They had waited too long to leave. In a war, timing is all.

After a grueling week, Reverend Speer started barking at his servants, "Go faster," his calm vanishing like the morning mist. The next day three servants disappeared and took one of their carts filled with pots, pans, and knives. Tables, chairs, and a rosewood mirror were dumped in a ditch by the road.

Promised extra food, the only servant left struggled to pull the remaining cart, the Speers dangling on top.

I offered to help if my son could ride.

Covered in yellow dust, I took turns with Li Min. At each resting place, we were rewarded with canned ham and chunks of bread.

Ashamed to admit defeat, the failing couple argued. They lost their sense of direction as if the wide plains of northern China were to blame. They believed any villager might kidnap them and give them to the Japanese. They wanted me to chase Li Min away. They adamantly believed that she was a communist spy.

We made our way over deep ruts and past burial mounds scattered in the distance. The missionaries grew listless on the cart as the sky turned a thick white and snow blanketed the road. From remnants of clothes we built a makeshift tent, waiting out the freezing wind.

One morning when we woke up, the last servant was gone and so was the cart, stacks of *cloisonné* bowls, pale green porcelain vases, and carefully wrapped bibles discarded in the snow. Bundled in layers of clothes, my boy would not stop crying. At first, the gray-haired missionary and his thinning wife tried to walk, then they sat down and refused to move.

"Pray," I urged them. It was the only thing I could think of saying. I had given up on words, other than to warn others to stay away. Only threats were left after a life filled with polite expressions.

No matter what I said, the reverend hung his head. He seemed to fade into the road's embankment, his wife hooked onto his arm, the Colt tucked inside his boot.

Their familiar stillness made us leave them with hardly a thought. The next day, Li Min bartered their bowls for noodles and a bucket. The following morning when we woke up, the bucket was gone.

After that, we took turns carrying my son on our backs.

The road turned muddy with receding flood waters, a touch of spring that turned quickly to ice. At night, Li Min told stories about the Yellow River god whose anger ruined crops, drowning entire villages at a whim. Winds menaced our makeshift tent, a constant whirling.

Back on the road, an ashen man with a puffy moon face waved us away as if we were vermin.

Numb, my body no longer belonged to me. I gave it to the cracking cold.

One blissful night we found shelter in a gutted pagoda close to Sanmenxia where a small group of farmers had gathered. At first, their leader, Sunfu, thought we were beggars and chased us away. When he saw the child hiding behind my back, he stopped and let us stay. In his village, 400 people had lived. Adrift from their homes, they were the only ones left, eighteen men, two women, and one child; the rest of the children had died of hunger, every baby born dead. Then communist guerrillas came and recruited seventeen of their young men. They gave the remaining villagers food, enough food to walk west to Xi'an where there was more.

Thick eyebrows arched above Sunfu's parched face. His eyes squinted in pain. "Our people *eat bitterness*."

My high school mathematics teacher would repeat the same phrase, urging his pupils to work harder and endure their difficult lessons. I and Miss Wu, my best friend, thought we *ate bitterness* sitting at our desks, our workbooks sketched with equilateral triangles, rhomboids, and spheres, the first generation of women to attend Suzhou Girls' High School. We were rare flowers, preparing to bloom into the rarest of flowers, women scientists who would advance to study in the United States.

Fractured sunlight cast shadows on the stone floor of the pagoda. My son played with Sunfu's daughter, an eight-year-old who made twig figures dressed in torn parchment. The two children climbed the ruins, laughing as they looked back to see when we would stop them. The pagoda's broken steps became battlements, the rocks became tanks, the toppled stones became enemy soldiers. Andrew climbed back down, his right hand clutching a dead sparrow with no head, a blood circle around its neck. He held it up like a trophy of war then pierced its body with a stick.

I slapped him, red lines streaking his face. Shocked, he squatted in the dirt and cried.

After a few days their food ran low, and Sunfu decided to risk the winds and have his people walk at night. The night protected them from the strafing of Japanese planes. We followed.

We walked past silent villages. Babies with swollen bellies whimpered on the side of the road, their parents lying dead nearby. Old women with no hair moaned on the backs of their sons. Ragged men fought in an empty field. Ghost men whipped dying horses. The dead blurred. Scarecrows. Skeletons.

There was no sleep, no dreams, only the road. Only the taste of bitterness, our tongues coated in soot.

One night the farmers left us behind.

After that, I scavenged everything we could use from the dead and dying. I survived the road, my son at my side. Li Min was teaching me much.

At night in the frosted tent, my husband would return to me like a courting lover. Slowly your warmth would spread over my body, your hands unbuttoning the long row of woven fasteners across my breast. You knew everything about my body, where to touch tenderly and where to seize. You had memorized my skin.

I wanted to tell you again that I was not a revolution. I was simply a woman in love. In the bedroom, lying next to me, you insisted, "We have chosen each other." My love had liberated you from an unbearable duty to a wife you hated, an empty shell of a woman. Not like me. A modern woman, educated, independent, unburdened by the past. A young Chinese woman scientist. A helpmate.

I remembered how our bedroom in the villa would flood with light. The carved jade vase on the rosewood table shimmered on the heavy damask tablecloth. Built on the shore of West Lake, the pale-yellow walls of our home glowed in the moonlight. On clear nights, we went rowing, drifting past blue and saffron sails, butterflies in the sunset.

On the road, I was obsessed with playing back the same scene, stuck in its repetition, going over it until I wanted to scream. I could not solve the riddle of our love.

I pleaded with you not to return to China. Each fight made you hate me more. "Look at our son," I would plead. Listen to Hu Shih, listen to Miss Wu. Why won't you listen? Even Mrs. Withington tried to talk you into staying. We had to stay in the United States. My Chinese friends at Berkeley, USC, UCLA, Rochester, Yale, and Harvard were staying. My mother wrote me, "Don't come back."

Your silence killed me.

On the train ride back across Canada, you left me to socialize with seven Presbyterian women missionaries who boasted they had impeccable taste in tea, preferring Earl Grey, a blend inspired by a legendary Chinese mandarin who revealed its secret on a perfectly fine morning in his garden amidst white Yulan trees. I would sit with them, listening for my baby to cry, while you talked politics with their husbands.

You refused to listen to me.

Boston to Quebec City to Vancouver to Victoria with luggage handled efficiently by the Canadian Pacific service, one month after Canada declared war on Germany and still you would not listen. My only company were these women and their endless chatter about how they would set up housekeeping in Shanghai and how easy it was to locate good help. The love of Christ hummed beneath their words until on the fourth day they inquired about my religious beliefs, ancestor worship and filial piety.

I tried to explain how the names of my ancestors for thirty generations were carved in stone at a family shrine in the small village, Tai Chung.

They asked why I returned with a baby in arms.

I had no answer, no reason to return. I pretended to explain your role in the government, your commitment to the reconstruction of China after the war, the imperatives of your profession as a scientific leader. I was growing to hate you.

Eagerly, Mrs. Peabody explained her wartime mission.

"I mine for souls like gold," she believed, adding the caveat of 300 million pagans waiting for Christian light. She was raised a strict Covenanter, ready to preach under the worst conditions, even to risk the persecution of invading Japanese.

"We read the newspapers and receive letters from our missions at Jiangyin and Shanghai," another woman interjected.

A solemn pause entered the conversation before Mrs. Peabody returned to the absolute need to stand behind the King "in this grave hour, perhaps the most fateful in this history," amazed at how his speech, broadcast on *Movietone News,* awakened their inner resolve.

I did not tell them of my nights of tears and pleas to convince you not to return and to forget your work.

My Shanghai was reduced to ruins by Japanese bombs and artillery fire. God did not protect the city.

Mrs. Peabody's Shanghai was a slice of *Movietone News* before *Snow White and the Seven Dwarfs.*

My Shanghai was gutted buildings in Nanshi, deep trenches dug along Suzhou Creek, shredded people on sidewalks outside the Serene Department Store, headless bodies tethered together in Huangpu River, herded children cowering in front of Union Church, Japanese bluejackets marching toward the North Train Station. The Bund flooded with refugees, fleeing in random patterns, climbing, hiding, racing, and twisting into the International Settlement, beaten by police into splintering lines that broke apart creating panic, while others buy American flags as charms against the ravaging banner of the Imperial Japanese Army, a red sun radiating blood.

Like these Christian women, you ran toward the spreading horror, dragging me and my son behind. They welcomed war as a ritual expected of their faith. You welcomed it as a grand opportunity. China must win, and in its ruins, you would build your future.

I was invisible.

14

Sunflower Fragrant

We checked into the boutique hotel, Twelve at Hengshan, in the former French Concession of Shanghai where life was advertised as "a Collection of Experiences," their corporate logo floating above the motto, "Let Us Be Your Guide." Not a room for the night, our stay was to be an immersion in the exquisite China of bygone days, extracted from its history of wars, famine, and civil unrest. A garden oasis at the center of the hotel anchored the Zen ambience, each room a haven from the frantic work of 24 million modern Shanghainese.

Our bathroom glowed, every light inserted within a marble niche, even in the shower with its cascading waterfall. The embossed bamboo forest etched on the glass partitions created the illusion of a mountainside enveloped in mist. Every faucet, handle and light were motion-sensitive, vulgar touch banished. The toilet flushed through a system of what seemed mental telepathy. The room responded like a loyal servant.

We were expected at an evening banquet at Fudan University in my husband's honor, or more accurately, his father's honor. Andrew called it a political resurrection, rising from the ashes of revolutionary denunciation and public shame. If Zi Ming had stayed in China after World War II ended, Mao would have executed him or at the very least forced him to make a public confession. His activities in the United States from 1918 to 1947 as a student, a researcher, and a reformer would have demanded full disclosure and complete renunciation. He would have faced purges in the 1950s and 60s, as a fascist dog of the Republic of China, a traitor currying favor with enemy number one, America. The furor of Red Guards in the Cultural Revolution would have destroyed what was left of his reduced life. As an intellectual from a privileged background, Zi Ming had a huge black mark over his name and work. His writings burned or banned, his psychological theories submerged beneath Mao's version of Marx, he was one of those who escaped punishment by fleeing the motherland.

That dire judgment was passé by 2007. With Mao long dead, a new line of leaders had transformed China's economic policies and forged significant links with the United States in trade, science, technology, and education. The past must be rewritten, memories adjusted, enemies reclaimed as former allies.

For the last ten years, Andrew and I had been teaching annually for two months in Beijing, graduate courses on American literature, cultural studies, and creative writing. In 2007, we traveled from Beijing to Shanghai for one week. Andrew had no recollection of his toddler years in this booming city with his mother after they had left Chongqing for the security of Katherine's family in the French Concession. His kidnapping was also a blank, though he wondered about the large burn scar on his leg that had been with him his entire life. For some reason he couldn't explain, he felt it was connected to his kidnapping.

Only from the period when he returned with his father to Shanghai in 1945 at the end of World War II and after his mother's death did he remember anything. By then he was six years old and had memories of a tall-windowed apartment with immense rooms inside a walled perimeter with glass shards embedded on the top. The city was crowded with beggars, cars, pedicabs, American soldiers, and black marketeers in packed streets. He couldn't reconstruct precisely where in Shanghai he lived during that post-war period, but he knew it was in the French Concession.

Nothing clicked when we walked around the plane tree-lined streets, stopping in front of each apartment building slated for restoration, creating upscale housing for expats and wealthy Chinese longing for the pre-war elegance of French architecture. After the war, the city changed from an international, cosmopolitan center to a shabby backwater town of refugees and then back again to a pulsing economic boomtown of wealthy Chinese and global corporations. The one difference: the predatory treaty rights of European, American, and Japanese businesses were gone. Instead, transnational corporations competed for China markets as profits skyrocketed in the sprawling port.

Between 1924 and 1925, Zi Ming had been the acting president of Fudan University, an elite university where students, many intoxicated with communism, eventually forced him out, a fact not lost on our university hosts. Before the banquet we were given a tour of the campus with a stop at the Ziban Yuan Building, referred to locally as the *White House*. In need of repair, it was slated to undergo extensive renovation. Before Zi Ming left Fudan University in the 1920s, he had hired a German architect with his uncle's generous donations to design and build the first psychology laboratory in China, a palatial three-story pure white building at the heart of the old campus, an historic treasure surrounded by green promenades and sycamores.

Engrossed in this relic of his father's past, Andrew stood before the White House's front door, peering inside. Empty except for dust and clutter, the building looked like a giant white ghost. Besides the entryway was a contorted stone, painted white, over six feet tall, with an inscription about the 1925 building. From one angle the stone resembled a decaying tree, from another, an entrance to a cave. Pocked with deep cavities, the stone's twisted branches were meant to evoke the erosions of time, a perfect balance between the forces of earth and the forces of water. The opposite of modern China's fetish of the new, the stone was proof of the wearing away and transformation of earth from time immemorial. The effects of the past were made visible.

And we were here for the past.

Our young guide next took us on a tour of the University History Museum, highlighting the institutions' key accomplishments from 1905 to the present. Inside the building was a black-and-white photographic mural of a street scene of young activists. Taken in 1926 when Shanghai was rocked by protests and before the White Terror when Chiang Kai-shek's Nationalist army had thousands of liberals, socialists, union leaders, and communists slaughtered, the reproduction covered an entire wall, the scale so large I felt as if I was walking among the clustered protesters engaged in intense conversations, oblivious to the camera.

One lone figure stared out of the mural with iron resolve. Not angry or accusatory, he expressed utter determination. Dressed in a dark *changshan*, a loose-fitting long gown with a high mandarin collar, the man seemed poised for action, ready to sweep the dying structures of traditional China aside and seize the revolutionary future. He understood what needed to be done. History would absolve him and the young men and women who took to the streets. The future would prove the nervous, the greedy, the weak wrong.

Unnerved by the mural, I stopped listening to the propaganda of the young tour guide who stood before the immense image, narrating the triumph of communist liberation, omitting Lu Xun's belief that revolution is "a bitter thing, mixed with filth and blood." Her scripted story of revolution freed the poor, the illiterate, and the peasant from their dark hovels into the light of modern China. She beamed with pride.

Confident in her beliefs, I wondered what she knew about the bloodbath and carnage China experienced during the war and the subsequent civil war. Betrayals, deceptions, secret agendas, intrigues, and murders had no place in her tale of glory. Young and rosy fresh, she was China's future: clean, pure, and patriotic.

But I was convinced that the man in the mural knew about blood. He knew about the costs of revolution. The youth around him would be swallowed up by history. They would pay the price.

The violence between the communists and nationalists went on for two and a half decades from 1922, until the toppling of the Republic of China in 1949, a government that buckled beneath corruption, unable to align with its citizens. After 9 million combat casualties, the Chinese Communist Party declared victory.

The toll of blood was staggering. Millions killed, starved, and exiled.

Having seen non-violent movements accomplish change in the United States, I was a skeptic about violence as effective, except as a strategy of self-defense. Most often, women and children paid the price globally.

Lost in my thoughts, the tour guide came over to me, wrapped her arm through mine, and ushered me to the section dedicated to my father-in-law. There were letters, testimonials, a photograph taken when he was president at twenty-six years of age, and a bronze plaque engraved with how much Zi Ming's uncle had contributed to the building of the White House. The philanthropist's photograph was mounted next to the plaque.

We stared at his great-uncle, speechless. We had always wondered what had happened to his father's family. Like Katherine's, they were never mentioned when Andrew was growing up, his father's past cut away in the move to Hong Kong. His father must have had siblings, nieces and nephews, aunts and uncles who were living in China when the family fled to Hong Kong. What happened to them?

Unable to digest this long, lost relative, Andrew shrugged. "How many files do you think the CCP has on my family?"

Walking over to the banquet hall, Andrew told me that when he was ten years old, living in Hong Kong, adjacent to communist China, he liked to read comic books about neighbors helping each other defeat mosquitoes breeding in backyards and street puddles. Distributed by communist sympathizers, he brought the books home. They caused quite a stir.

For several evenings, he could hear his father whispering to Julia behind closed doors. The two adults shared secrets in a special language at a specific volume, pitch, and duration that Andrew was forbidden to hear. Intimate, this shared speech was never heard at the dinner table. Only in Zi Ming and Julia's bedroom did their voices come alive, urgently consoling, cautioning, and planning, a whisper world behind a sealed wall.

When he asked about the mosquito brigades, they said nothing. They ignored him.

They never demanded he hand over his comics with pictures of neighbors pitching together to drain pools of water, singing together "The Sky Above the Liberated Zone."

He had no idea what happened to them. One day they simply disappeared.

The banquet room looked out onto the impeccable gardens of Fudan University with their pebble mosaics, fountains, and sycamores. We were seated in a place of honor at a long oval table with thirty guests. The vice-president of the university warmly introduced us to heads of departments, representatives from the main library, and dignitaries from the community. He then acted as the MC for the feast, describing the contribution of Zi Ming to psychology, the renovation plans for the White House, and the world-class status of Fudan University.

A commemorative booklet was presented to Andrew that contained an account of his father's initiatives to introduce the field of psychology to the university through weekly lectures, classes, and the construction of a major building to house the School of Psychology. It would be the first of its kind in the Far East, equivalent to the Soviet Pavlov School of Psychology and the Princeton School of Psychology. The White House included a human subject lab, an animal lab, a biology lab, a library, an auditorium, a games hall, a picture room, and instruction rooms. Under its roof, departments of biology, bacteriology, botany, anthropology, and pathology were also planned.

The vice-president characterized Zi Ming's tenure at Fudan as an exciting moment in the history of the university. Mimicking the phrasings of public relations and marketing, he reminded me of the business thumpers throughout the United States. Andrew Carnegie reincarnated. He was performing for the group more than for us. After his speech, there was a slide show with photographs from the 1920s; Zi Ming with his students, interior scenes of several laboratories, and faculty gathered on the steps of the White House. His past was unfolding before our eyes. Nothing was said about student protests in the rocky, violent years of the 1920s.

As each photograph was shown, I wondered about who preserved these images. Why were they not destroyed? At one point, I wanted to cry, then I was upset. The group of people in the room were acting as if this presentation was normal, a timely recognition of Zi Ming's educational vision. Erasing sixty years of suffering, dislocation and death was normal. What did the word "recognition" mean?

What else did the luncheon hosts know? Andrew's father never talked to him about Fudan University, yet here were dozens of pictures that the banquet attendees were staring at like it was a simply pleasant slide show at an afternoon luncheon.

When I looked over at Andrew, he sat frozen, unblinking.

I wanted to protect him from what I judged an act of violence. Were the children of war expected to shrug their shoulders and accept a sanitized retelling of the past? Was Fudan University preparing some prize if Andrew nodded his head and smiled, appreciative of the recognition his father was, at last, receiving? Was no one responsible? Would no one recognize what happened? Was the erasure of history necessary?

Andrew remained silent. Once the presentation was finished, he didn't glance at anyone, not even me. I thought for a moment he was going to stand and leave the room. He didn't. He remained silent.

Sensing there would be no response from Andrew, the vice-president introduced the head of the library. He asked Andrew if he would be willing to donate his father's manuscripts and correspondence. They would preserve these materials in their archives for any ongoing research on Zi Ming. The history of psychology in China needed detailed knowledge of what Zi Ming had accomplished.

Andrew had stored a few manuscripts of Zi Ming's that he had inherited from Julia when she moved from Hong Kong to California. She didn't want to haul them around anymore. But he didn't mention their existence to the eager librarian. Instead, he was non-committal. He knew Julia would rather die than give anything to Communist China. She would never forgive the CCP or him for handing this material over.

His delayed response caused the banquet to grow silent. He finally said something like he would see what was possible. After that exchange, the atmosphere in the room decidedly cooled. The precise agenda of the meeting seemed to be thrown off course. I sat there contemplating why exactly we were asked to come.

An exquisite Shanghai dinner followed, a polite and formal affair, unlike other raucous banquets I had attended in China. Courses of grilled duck, fresh scallops, sautéed greens, sweet dumplings and fruits followed in precise succession. It felt like something had gone wrong. As the guests were preparing to leave, an older man approached us and said he had something that would interest my husband. Handing Andrew a stiff cardboard sheet with both hands, he announced, "Your mother."

It was her college record from Nanjing Central University.

The man had heard from someone he didn't name that Andrew had once inquired about his mother who had died in China during the war. His ease in handing over the form and his feigned friendliness stopped us cold. Did he have other information? Andrew and I had often asked our Chinese colleagues how to find information about his mother. They tried to help. Part of the problem was her surname, Lin, was so common. And her given names were not known. It would be like looking for information on someone with the last name Smith.

Over the course of ten years, Andrew had had long talks with the Dean of the School of Foreign Languages in Beijing about his mother. A brilliant man, he sympathized with Andrew, but felt constrained because he did not have Katherine's Chinese name. The revolution and its aftershocks had brought terrible suffering to intellectuals and scientists. So many documents had been destroyed. So many lives lost. One evening, we visited with a horticulture professor for hours, listening to him describe the destruction of his laboratory during the civil war and then again during the cultural revolution. Had one of these colleagues found a way to discover information about Katherine's life?

The man at the banquet had simply presented the document and proceeded to point out a few details. Here was Katherine's Chinese name, Lin Qui Fang, her mother's name, Lin Jing Zhen, and her guarantor's Jiang Yun Yi in Chinese characters. "There was no father's name," he remarked. She had graduated from Suzhou Girls' High School. And for an unknown reason was taken off the university records in 1934. He took a blank piece of notepaper from his brief case and wrote out Andrew's mother's name in Chinese characters:

Andrew had been told by Julia that his mother's surname was Lin with a rising tone. In Chinese, she said it probably was the character for forest, a common surname:

Julia was wrong. A more complex and rarer character, Katherine's surname was pronounced Lin or Ling with a rising tone that meant high or aloft tower:

Julia must have known how Katherine's Chinese name was written and that it wasn't "forest." Had she been so clever as to throw Andrew off the track with an incorrect surname?

Katherine's given names were more common. Qui with a rising tone meant plants with big flowers, especially sunflowers, and Fang with a high tone meant sweet smelling or fragrant, a moniker often given girls whose names were often associated with flowers and their fragrance.

Here, at last, was Katherine's Chinese name in characters and roman alphabet transliteration, Lin Qui Fang.

The man at the banquet who presented Andrew with the college transcript simply smiled and then excused himself since he had a meeting across campus. I can't even remember his face, only the gesture of his hands. He presented the cardboard document very gently as if he was handing my husband a flower.

We left the banquet room loaded down with gifts, bound books on the university's history, beautiful folio pictures of his father and the White House, an exquisite woolen scarf for me, and a set of teacups.

In the taxi back to our hotel, I turned to Andrew and asked, "What the hell was that?" It was like his family. What was going on? What were the real motives? I was under the impression that school transcripts before the war had probably gone up in smoke and how did this man know about his mother? I had a list of questions that I fired off.

"This is China. The world's oldest bureaucracy," he replied.

He was treating the entire country like he had his Hong Kong family. The truth was under so many layers of deception and secrets, it would take one hundred lifetimes to make sense of what had happened to his mother.

"We have this," he said, patting his daypack with the college record tucked inside a protective plastic folder. "Sunflower Fragrant. Perfect."

It was a victory. My brain buzzed with confusion while my husband was satisfied that the banquet hadn't been a complete waste of time.

"Who knows what the Vice-President wanted from me," he added. "I'm too old to figure it out. And I don't care."

15

July 8, 1943

When I was a young girl at Suzhou Girls' High School, I learned that explorers to the North Pole hallucinated during the worst hardships of their journey. Maybe that is why you come to me repeatedly like a flickering movie image in the night, Andrew wrapped next to me, cocooned in the shredded blanket we had found on the side of the road outside Suicheng. Expressionless, you stare at me as if I were a laboratory specimen.

How young we were in our crisp white laboratory coats and pigtails.

The two of us, Miss Wu and Miss Lin, together in high school, college and graduate school, Suzhou Girls' High School, Nanjing Central University, and Zhejiang University, before the ultimate prize, a trip to the United States.

In my dormitory room, you once told me that one day you would change "the accepted view of the structure of the universe." Big words for such a tiny woman, much smaller than me, with a grace I admired and imitated.

I see you walking off the SS *President Hoover* at the port of San Francisco, the same year my husband became a visiting professor in the Psychology Department at the University of California. Remember how you smiled the first time I introduced myself as Madame Lin, a distinguished title for a married Chinese woman, no longer single like you.

You spent a week visiting me, your high school and college classmate, before leaving for the University of Michigan to study physics. That is, until learning that women would be second-class students there, and you changed your mind and stayed in Berkeley to study with the nuclear physicist, Ernest Lawrence. And I had changed my mind too, not attending graduate school in zoology at all, plans dropped, not even starting one class as a Berkeley graduate student, my future life determined by the strong force of my *husband's destiny*.

Miss Wu, my dear friend, remember those lovely summer lunches, comparing dreams and goals with hushed conversations about why one woman waited and the other didn't for love and romance.

Little did I know that my life would decay like the atoms you studied. Little did we know that you would only read about the war between Japan and China in American newspapers while I walked through sniper fields with my son, struggling each day, each footstep forward, to survive. My graduate school became a series of epidemics charted in the flow, peaks, and endings of infections, ravaging the lungs, guts, blood, and brains of soldiers and civilians, babies, youth, teen-agers, young women bursting with love, older women looking back perplexed or resigned, men of all ages, shooting, killing, kidnapping, hiding, praying, wondering what has happened and will it ever end or will their lives cease before the projected, statistical time allotted organic carbon forms of such and such an age in such and such a culture with such and such an income, class or other benefit or loss.

Cessation. Obliteration. Oblivion. Forgotten.

How often you urged me when we were still young college friends not to be tempted by love. Our mentor, Hu Shih repeated one constant refrain, "Do Not Be Distracted by Romance," in lecture halls, small group meetings, private tête-à-têtes, and letters, that you chanted late at night in the physics laboratory and in your 100 square foot single room at Nanjing Central Uni-

JOAN BURBICK

versity with your biography of Madame Marie Curie, while I at
the same moment worked in a different laboratory in a nearby
building under the lascivious gaze of my husband-to-be who
tutored his brilliant young charge in the old story, an old gossipy
story, provoking snickers, sideways sneers and green envy, the
distinguished scientist, married with a wife and four children
at home, metamorphosizing into a lover, the dashing professor
finding his ideal mate, the lovely, untouched student devoted to
his experiments, his success, his every word. Is there a formula
with factors and variations for their love?

It is said that the interior of the sun pulsates as rhythmically
as the interior of the human heart. Did I count the beats when
he fastened me to his side in the laboratory and in his bed? I succumbed to the power of his desire, the promises he made while
you, Miss Wu, on a parallel journey in your solitary room at midnight, studying the universe, its atoms, and vectors, and forces
spinning deep into the darkness transposed into equations easy
to remember if loved, embraced an absolute rule to never have
your heart beat with love until the pieces are in place enough
to build upon, instead searching the interior of atoms with expensive machines, exorbitantly expensive machines, reliant on
funds, grants, benefactors, sponsors, institutes, universities, and
friends in high places to assist in the great subatomic journey.
Husbands and children later.

Hu Shih insisted that you not return to China, your beloved homeland, where parents, siblings, cuisine, classical texts,
temples, pagodas, and Song paintings were under constant
threat. Never return during the war with Japan, wait, wait and see
what will happen, and then never return when the communists
won the civil war and came to power, and then only to return
in 1973, thirty-seven years later, after President Richard Nixon
had "changed the world," deciding instead to work on the Man-
hattan Project and the silver-grey mysteries of uranium, and you
waited. You waited and listened. Your mentor and second father,
Hu Shih, lectured, cautioned, and demanded. And you obeyed.

[177]

You never saw your parents or elder brother again, returning home 37 years too late.

Over time you became Madame Wu. I know because hallucinations have their advantages, futures collapse in pasts and presents. You visit me a mature woman, your long hair wrapped neatly in a bun like our mothers. How distinguished, balanced, in control. You live within atoms, your mind preoccupied, or occupied by beta decay, observed, formulated, admired, when a neutron becomes a proton or the reverse but not the same. Your classic experiment of electron emission (β^- decay) measured the decay of cobalt-60 to nickel-60, neutrons decaying into protons, emitting an electron and an electron antineutrino, decaying further, two gamma rays generated, lost or released.

I want to ask you in the night if anything is lost in the swirling world of sub-sub-atomic particles, breaking into electromagnetic processes, a transitory stew of asymmetry, directions probable only? But you only stare.

Within the atoms you love, quarks behaved in ways charted and uncharted, partly registered by particle accelerators to be built beneath a Swiss mountain range that hunt and measure infinitesimally small, near massless quantities, possibly points or vibrations, that still impact the spacetime of atoms that comprise everything, maybe, in the universe, that means you, your dog, your refrigerator, and the evening stars.

Surrounded by machines, black eyes piercing, you won't stop invading my dreams, a robotic woman whose apparition under the inky skies of China besieged by artillery fire, interrupts my sleep with her dutiful belief in the single word, "later."

But what of me? "Later" was a word that I could not speak. My allotted life was quickly slipping away. Three years in the United States wandering with my ambitious husband, then home to China in 1939 to a life of complete uncertainty until in 1944, my life was absorbed into the gravitas of death, the darkness of a black hole capturing every particle no matter how infinitesimal, no escape, I became a mere footnote in history, two sentences in Madame Wu's biography, mentioning our week in Berkeley together, but not recording any conversation, hope, or dream.

But you see how easy it is to get ahead of a permitted timeline. That is the burden of knowing what came next after the necessary ending, a certain number of words running parallel to a time in the future that will also be enfolded in this story. Spacetime bent, bowed, or stretched.

While you studied in Berkeley, I embraced the promise of a Land of Scientific Opportunity at Yale, laboring in my husband's laboratory from early morning until night, even on weekends, with two free afternoons a week for tea with the Yale Dames, sometimes, and an occasional visit to a zoology lecture, a devoted research assistant, convinced of her necessity until pregnancy randomly sparked new life in New Haven and burst forth at the next stop, the Harvard Medical School. Unwilling to decay, the spark grew while loneliness enveloped me in a chilly apartment in Boston. Laboratory work finished. I was left with writing letters to you, and always Mrs. Withington who renamed me Kitty, a name endearing to Americans.

While our trajectories split like random atoms spinning in an accelerator, Hu Shih continued to ponder the riddle of the modern Chinese woman, their future uncertain, stumbling, a worrisome affair, such freedom, such utter oblivion. The Chinese philosopher studied their fate and mused in essays for Shanghai's *New Youth* and *Crescent Moon*, presenting lectures at the Peking University, University of Chicago, and Academia Sinica in Taipei among others. He cultivated academic venues and engaged in intimate conversations about whether bound feet one year would become glass slippers the next.

For when was later, how long and when do you decide, can you decide or predict when later begin or ends? A time deferred until another time. A decision not to decide right now, later, please. A later that propels one life into a half-life and another's life into a life of complete success, a list of prizes and awards, except for the travesty of not receiving the Nobel Prize in physics, when two fellow Chinese scientists in America, came to you for help, and after receiving the key to success, went on to take the glory with your part an aside. Only recently have the sifters examined what women have accomplished in science, as if in America it is shocking news. You shuddered at the way the term "woman scientist" was a phrase raising the specter of gender, where no dangers, worries, or shadows should exist. A country of powerful men defined science as gendered. How ridiculous, Miss Wu, declared. "Science has no gender."

But war did and power did, and politics did, and the university did. Such inner resolve in the face of men as you explained to me, your dear friend, Madame Lin, that romance for you would have to wait. Did I regret my decision despite the shared warnings at Suzhou Girls' High School, at Nanjing Central University and the laboratories at Zhejiang University, cautioning me to wait, wait, wait? Love will come later.

But later was too big a word for me, too frightening a word since later did not exist in my family already sundered by violence, a father, executed by a warlord, who would not live to see if China would become a republic or another failed state of factious fighting. A mother and sister at risk, waiting for my return. No later. No later. Only now or already too late.

In time, I surrendered to decay, a half-life, no equation given except betrayal, absorbing the shock wave of love. A blast. A flash blinding my scorched life left undone.

Decay, a word reserved for death, feared by humans who imagine their bodies intact then dead, not as part of a sequence of change, inevitable, a breaking of one thing into another over time. Immortality renamed mutability. Whole lives transmuted into half-lives, decay into other lives. Spacetime composed of strong and weak forces, holding or releasing the glue that forms this or that, or a that without a reassurance, matter, then energy, then dark matter, then dark energy filling the universe or universes, our verses, out to the edges of what? A flat surface, a topography of curved shapes, a web with indentations caused by planets, stars, constellations, what ancient Chinese call star houses, everything acting upon everything, everything becoming something else.

Miss Wu, my dear friend, you disturb my sleepless nights.

16

Confessions of a Chinese Scientist

Back home on Guemes Island, we had Katherine's college record framed and placed next to her oil portrait in the hallway. It had been eighteen years since her dress had arrived from Ida who still claimed she had no information about Andrew's mother. On a chance, I phoned her to see how she would respond to Julia's confession about her husband, Yaoming, who was Ida's full brother.

She acted as if we should have known already. "Yes," she admitted. Julia was her former sister-in-law, and Yaoming had been disgraced and exiled from the family. Because she was much younger than Yaoming, a good twelve years, she had no details. It happened during the war in another lifetime. The only thing she knew was that Yaoming "had done something very bad." What she meant by that sentence I wouldn't understand until years later. At the time, she didn't sound upset that her father had married his daughter-in-law. But I couldn't really tell from her tone of voice. Her matter-of-fact response threw me off. Confused, I descended into chit-chat about her research, a topic that sent her spinning in another direction.

"She's lying," Andrew responded when I told him about my phone call. "Ida's never been a good liar, not like Julia." He didn't understand why I continued to bother. Once he had revealed his childhood suspicion that Julia murdered his mother, he became detached from his family. He never contacted Julia again, refusing even to go to her funeral.

One night, I had a dream about Mei, a Chinese woman colleague from Beijing. For several years we had been close, as Louise and I were in Hong Kong, fellow adventurers. She had worries about her daughter, and I had worries about my husband. She introduced me to food from Xi'an, where she grew up, and I brought her homemade pierogis, not unlike Chinese dumplings. We exchanged recipes, family stories, and gossip. A few times we took off from work and went to a nearby coffee shop to laugh about Chinese politics and how irrational our husbands were.

In the dream I saw her across a narrow Beijing street, her back turned, but I knew it was her from the way she fixed her upswept hair. I was about to call out to her when her shape shifted. Another Chinese woman had taken her place, and I didn't want her to turn around. I was horrified she was going to turn around. I didn't want to see her face. I woke up in a sweat, disoriented. It was Katherine. I was certain.

After that, it was difficult to walk past Katherine's oil portrait. I averted my eyes as if her face might be gone. Once hurrying past, I thought I heard her moaning.

I didn't tell Andrew about my dream or my phobia about his mother's painting.

It took a few weeks until I could lift my head and let my eyes glance across her portrait, checking to see if her face was still there. It was. It had regained its composure and seemed almost sympathetic to my fears. As if we shared the same nightmare.

Late one evening after a long walk on the beach, Roger, the British historian of science who was writing a biography of Zi Ming, called Andrew from London. His news was straightforward. Did he know that his father had worked for the Central Intelligence Agency? Zi Ming was on the payroll of an organization called The Society for the Investigation of Human Ecology, writing reports on Chinese emigrants crossing the border into Hong Kong from the mainland. Many American and American-educated academics worked for the CIA in the 1950s and 60s, especially psychologists such as Hadley Cantril from Princeton University. Some didn't even know they were working for the CIA since funds were provided for their research under various covers, others knew and were eager to help their government during the Cold War. They considered themselves "patriots."

Roger wanted to know if Andrew had a copy of his and his father's manuscript, *Confessions of a Chinese Scientist*, written in 1953, but more importantly, *The Chinese National Character and the Myth of Communism* written in 1964. Had he read them?

After digging out *Confessions* from an old box in the basement, Andrew found, tucked underneath, the later unpublished manuscript of his father, *Chinese National Character*. He emailed Roger about his finds but refused to send him the original manuscript or a copy. Andrew thought that everyone wanted a piece of his father, and he wasn't going to cooperate with advancing their careers. Anyway, he didn't want to take the time to make a PDF file, especially when the two manuscripts totaled 717 pages.

He compromised and sent the two manuscripts off to the Archives department of his undergraduate college library that already had a collection of his father's papers. Researchers could access the materials and that would end his direct involvement.

Before we packed the manuscripts, Andrew admitted that he had typed an early draft of *Confessions*. He needed to practice his typing and didn't pay any attention to what he was typing. He never discussed the manuscript with his father, who never talked much to him anyway and spent his time pacing in his bedroom or sitting in a permanent funk beneath a Chinese landscape painting in the living room. Andrew never knew what his father did when he was at school.

Flipping through the two manuscripts, I wondered if there was any mention of Katherine. Dead spouses and family ancestors in China were offered food, paper money, and incense at the Qingming Festival in April. Descendants tended their graves and showed their respect. Some families had indoor ancestor shrines to give tribute daily. Ancestors could provide protection, guaranteeing fortune, if they were respected. If ignored, they could be dangerous.

Had my dream conveyed Katherine's torment? Forgotten, was she a restless ghost out to exact revenge? The memories of past wrongs do not simply go away. They fester. If I knew more about Katherine's husband, maybe I could uncover why she became invisible, outside the ancestral circle of remembrance and respect.

I had purposefully pushed Zi Ming away, afraid that he would obscure my research on Katherine. Something had changed. My reluctance had made me blind to Katherine's marriage. Who exactly had she married? Why marry someone who was ten years older, divorced and the father of five children? Wouldn't she be ostracized for such behavior in 1930s China?

My plan was to read through his unpublished manuscripts for any clues to their marriage. Let me call it forensic criticism, digging into minute details, the odd turns of phrase, the contradictions to extract a profile of a marriage. His *Confessions* was supposed to be about his life from childhood to 1953 when he was living in Hong Kong. Be strategic. Be relentless.

Written six years after his arrival in Hong Kong, *Confessions* was a preemptive strike against the Chinese Communist Party. Zi Ming was haunted by the nightmare that mainland communists would soon overrun Hong Kong and force him to make a "public confession," denouncing his American education, his personal ambitions, and his reactionary way of life as a member of the landlord class and as an intellectual. In Hong Kong newspapers, Andrew's father continually read of colleagues, even personal friends, living under the communists who had already publicly confessed and suffered extreme humiliation. Under duress, they promised to "serve the people" and to "think in the light of Marxism, Leninism, Stalinism, and the Great Gospels of Chairman Mao Zedong." Only after their confessions were they released from jail and allowed to return home and resume their jobs, if they were lucky. Many had to scrounge for work and live in hovels.

Dedicated to "Americans who fight to keep the intellectual light burning," his confessions documented his development as a scientist in America and promoted his belief that only America could "save the world from an intellectual blackout." Once written and published, he could never be coerced into a false confession by the communists. No matter what he said under their intimidation, everyone would know he lied. He had already confessed.

His *Confessions* included descriptions of his childhood, outlining the clan structure of the village outside of Shantou where he grew up, his schooling and college years at Fudan, and his graduate training at Berkeley. He went into depth writing about his younger brother and his efforts to help him come to America for graduate education in mathematics, and how his brother was prevented from coming by the 1924 Exclusion Act, barring Chinese immigration. His brother's anger and subsequent decision to train in Japan, where he met other young Chinese involved in the Japanese communist movement, upended his life. When he returned to China, Zi Ming's brother was imprisoned as a communist, eventually released through Zi Ming's efforts, and then participated in the Long March only to be killed by unknown hands in an unknown place.

In a circuitous manner, Zi Ming touched upon his years teaching and researching in China and his work as an administrator at Fudan University in Shanghai and Zhejiang University in Hangzhou, noting how his wealthy relatives in Shanghai helped him along the way, their money coming from their business as merchants of "black gold," i.e., opium. A product of their donations, the White House encapsulated his academic and research future.

What was glaringly absent were details about the three years between 1936 and 1939 when he returned to the United States with Katherine, his new wife, and had research appointments at Berkeley, Rochester, Yale, and the Carnegie Institution of Washington in Boston, Massachusetts. Only one paragraph listed the institutions where he worked during that time. He then described how in 1940 he returned to Chongqing for "sentimental reasons." He never mentioned his wife, Katherine, or nine-month-old son, Andrew. Instead, he stated that in the year 1940, when he was in Chongqing, he had begun the "wasting" of his "prime." His life as a research scientist was finished. He briefly mentioned his trips between 1941 and 1943 back to the United States and Britain working on the post-war reconstruction of China, but still no mention of Katherine who was left behind in Shanghai. There was a complete absence of her life during their marriage years, 1936-1944. Not one mention.

Since Zi Ming had spent much time in his *Confessions* describing his American education, it was a painful absence that his years as a researcher at prestigious American universities was missing. Just as he had erased his wife, he had erased what he was doing, where he was living, and whom he met during key years in America.

By the end of his confessions, Zi Ming had crafted a story of himself as a man-in-the middle, supporting neither the Republic of China (ROC) or the Chinese Communist Party (CCP). More a fall guy of these two political foes, he represented his life as having bravely resisted both groups. "In this little drama I have tried to portray myself as a little hero in the midst of a corrupt, impotent, and incompetent regime." By that he meant the ROC led by Chiang Kai-shek. He had rejected both the ROC and CCP and lived in an in-between world in Hong Kong, a man without a country, neither Chinese, British, or American. He also winked at the reader, adding that "even a real hero is not perfect or free from blunders."

In *Confessions,* he briefly mentioned his first wife and their children and then spent time applauding his third wife, Julia:

"besides my wife, I doubt that there have been more than five persons in China, dead and living, who have really understood me." The only possible reference to Katherine was to an un-named technician in a laboratory who kept his research on embryology progressing when he became president of Zhejiang University in Hangzhou, the place Katherine listed as home on her University of Berkeley application to graduate school in 1936, and the place that she wrote with alarm about to Mrs. Withington. In 1938 what she called "our house" with Zi Ming was looted by the Japanese, destroying his library and their home.

The dedicated research assistant that worked by his side at Rochester and Yale Universities, the wife that his American friends doted over, was erased.

I wondered if traditional Chinese reserve about grief or a strict separation of private and professional life might cause such reticence. I didn't think that a plausible explanation. Elsewhere in the manuscript he recounted the deaths of his brother and father. Further, Zi Ming was free about other biographical details, admitting that the funds for the White House came from the family business of "black gold." Something felt wrong. A lacuna, a deliberate hole in his confessions.

Maybe Andrew was right. Was there a worse secret in the family that Zi Ming needed to protect? Was Julia a killer? Or would she have been jealous if Zi Ming had lingered on wife number two? Did their unresolved tensions require Katherine's erasure? Unsatisfied, I kept trying to figure out his motivation to hide Katherine. Julia would have known that her father-in-law was in the United States with Katherine since she was probably married to Zi Ming's son when he and Katherine returned to Chongqing in 1939. Nothing made sense.

Only one fact was clear. My search for a hint of his second wife's existence failed. There was none in "Confessions," no mention of their marriage, no mention of her death, no mention of the years they spent in the United States together.

Frustrated, I plunged ahead with *Chinese National Character*, written eleven years later in 1964, expecting a similar problem. I was curious about the CIA connection but leery that it would drag me down a rabbit hole if I strayed too far into his covert life in Hong Kong, twenty years after Katherine had died.

One email to Roger, that's it, I told myself. Get a general sense of how a self-exiled Chinese psychologist could assist the CIA.

Roger's first piece of advice: Watch the 1962 movie, *The Manchurian Candidate*, with Frank Sinatra and Laurence Harvey. He told me that the dates of Zi Ming's two manuscripts, 1953 and 1964, were perfect bookends for the CIA project MKULTRA, a mind-control program carried out with the help of American psychologists at major universities throughout the United States.

If I wanted to know what kind of man Zi Ming was, I needed to understand this direction in his research and writing. I sequestered myself in my study and did nothing but read *Chinese National Character* and books on the history of the CIA.

Hong Kong in the 1950s and 60s was considered a Cold War asset with British and American intelligence services cooperating and competing for information about Red China. Agents from Taiwan and China also operated in Hong Kong since both countries had extensive, experienced spy rings. Dai Li's massive spy network for the ROC during World War II made American efforts look amateurish. The CCP also had networks during the war that had penetrated both Japanese and ROC operations. In Hong Kong both the ROC and the CCP engaged in an elaborate media dance of promoting communist or anti-communist newspapers, movies, and books. And there were moments when the Cold War turned hot. Frequent assassinations were carried out on Hong Kong streets by agents still fighting the Chinese civil war. Called the Casablanca of Asia, Hong Kong was the perfect place for Zi Ming, an American-trained academic, to interview Chinese refugees from the mainland for what the CIA called *Humint*, human intelligence.

What was significant in *Chinese National Character* was Zi Ming's contribution to the enormous CIA effort to understand mind control and find ways to practice it. When American POWs who had fought in the Korean War returned to the United States, some seemed sympathetic to their communist captors. Americans wanted to know why and how this happened. The term brainwashing became an explanation for what the Chinese government had done to American soldiers.

A popular topic in Cold War America, brainwashing was center stage in *The Manchurian Candidate*, pumping up fear of Red China and its communist government. In grade school and high school, Red China was a must-debate item. Righteously, children argued every year about whether Red China should be allowed to join the United Nations. Coming from an intensely anti-communist Polish-American community, I believed Red China was a rogue nation hiding behind the bamboo curtain with a diabolical government strangling freedom and justice, brainwashing its citizens. I was passionate about my young denunciation.

The movie dramatically showed American prisoners of war undergoing intense sessions that transformed their personalities through brainwashing techniques that turned a person into a puppet. In the MKULTRA program, the CIA sought to understand how it was possible to repress and extract memories, how to alter behavior through drugs like LSD and sensory techniques, and how to predict behavior by reconditioning through hypnosis or repetitive suggestions. The answers to these questions they thought could be found in the research of psychologists, hence the plethora of grants.

Zi Ming's conclusion that brainwashing as Americans understood it was a failure went against what the CIA wanted to hear. Funded to interview hundreds of Chinese emigrants crossing the border into the Crown colony, Zi Ming's discussion of their reasons to leave their homeland and their perceptions of communist China were lengthy and complex. The apex of enthusiasm for Mao happened early, when landless peasants were given small tracts of land. It was a simple exchange: land for loyalty. Communism gave the peasants what they wanted. That enthusiasm faded when land reform shifted to collectivization and disastrous agricultural policies. The supposed brainwashed "masses" either tried to flee or became resigned to the antics of another "emperor," some telling jokes and singing songs about the cruelty of their fate.

Denigrating dramatic brainwashing techniques like those shown in the movie, Zi Ming thought Americans needed to understand Chinese history and specific factors that influenced Chinese behavior, such as religion, ethical traditions, and what he called "intellectual slavery."

In contrast, what worked in China was carefully executed training for soldiers, for example, through information blackout, constant supervised activities, sustained observation, constant evaluation, and structured indoctrination to Maoist thought. In the People's Liberation Army (PLA), the CCP succeeded in their quest for a loyal collective.

Brainwashing was not a psychedelic drug, narcotic shot, or hypnosis, but a carefully monitored behavioral system within a controlled and, in some ways, closed social setting. These persuasion techniques needed years to implement and required extreme patience. No intense week or weekend session of brainwashing in a setting cut off from the person's daily life would effect significant change. It was essential to reorganize every detail of the subject's life and patiently monitor activities. Prisons, educational institutions, and the military were perfect environments for control of individuals in a group. The state became the head warden, the university president, the four-star general.

Just as important, mindless repetition of phrases or slogans such as those dramatized in *The Manchurian Candidate* often had the opposite effect. People became bored and then indifferent to the message. Techniques such as drugs, sensory deprivation, heightened stimulus, or hypnosis might work for extracting information from prisoners (i.e., torture), but they might as easily elicit false information or feigned confessions. Subjects under the influence of drugs like LSD and mescaline acted unpredictably, making their actions unreliable, the opposite of controlled behavior.

Zi Ming's overall message was that independent thinking was the best antidote to the elaborate systems of social control that communists were building in their army. At the end of the manuscript, he warned that Americans could face their own challenges. He saw in the McCarthyism of the 1950s an attempt to stifle intellectual thought in the United States. Brainwashing trained individuals to be slaves of the state unable to think critically and creatively. It fostered paranoia and purges. It dismissed evidence and fact. It imprisoned the mind.

The greatest threat to America was not the brainwashing gimmicks in *The Manchurian Candidate*, but the tactics used by the CCP and the Soviet Union to ignore, harass and censor their intellectuals. In communist countries, "Everyone writes on the same theme, everyone sings the same songs of praise." The United States needed to fight back with a three-pronged defense. Keep your own intellectual fires burning. Reward independent thought. Support your intellectuals, scientists, artists, engineers, and teachers. Otherwise, America would be "tempted to race with the communist world not only in electronics, atomic weapons, and air power, but also in intellectual annihilation." Blinded by its own McCarthyism, America could destroy its treasure to the world, "the freedom to love truth."

Chinese National Character explained Chinese behavior for an American audience. From its front notes, it was clear that Zi Ming had worked with a literary agent to help him place the book with publishers in New York. It is not clear why it was never published. Perhaps its message went too far against the grain of what the CIA wanted to hear.

The MKULTRA project has since been widely discredited for its unethical use of human subjects and its advocacy of torture which resulted in psychotic breakdowns and suicides for the people who participated in brainwashing sessions. Rather than control minds, it destroyed minds.

Like *Confessions*, *Chinese National Character* provided selective autobiographical information. And again, nothing at all about Katherine. I did find one mention of Andrew in a section on how the Chinese were insensitive to people's suffering. Zi Ming described that in "1945 when my wife and I with one 6-year-old boy and a few months old baby in arms crossed an upper Yangtze rapid in a wooden junk," he had witnessed passengers drowning, their luggage and belongings capsized. Other boaters rescued the goods and let the people drown.

By 1945, Katherine had been dead for probably less than one year. In the boat were his six-year-old son by Katherine, Andrew, his infant grandson, and his third wife, Julia. It was not clear if World War II had ended and if they were relocating to Shanghai. Within one sentence, he has transformed these four individuals into a family, giving the impression of a journey with a husband, wife and their two children. The sentence was ambiguous, neither claiming the children as "ours" or "hers," but asserting his new "wife." This rare reference reinforced how easily Katherine could disappear from the record, and a new family could as easily be invented.

The question remained: Why such thorough evisceration of Katherine?

Interlude: Document No. 10

I am grateful for this opportunity to describe how I experienced what happened to my sister, Qui Fang, English name Katherine, name of endearment Kitty, road name unknown, a hungry ghost, and how our relationship changed before, during, and after the last war with Japan. It is not often we have the chance to write down exactly what we believe to be true. This is not a political confession. This document has not been coerced, and no one has pressured me in any way to compose it. I realize some of you will find my account unnecessarily harsh. So be it. Those were the times.

Last year, a young patient walked into my sparse examining room at the Dazhuangzi Mine, her eyes searching for answers, and I saw Qui Fang, my younger sister, standing in front of me. One more day, I said to myself, I wanted one more day with her, and then her face disappeared beneath the coughing spasms of a woman worker. At night, alone in my apartment, I tried to conjure her up, but I couldn't. She only came uninvited. A hungry ghost with a taste for surprise. She came when I was distracted listening to the beat of a heart or filling out reports, exhausted by endless work.

She won't let me forget her. And I have tried. For years, I condemned her, even executed her in my mental theater. I made her appear on a deserted stage and flung accusations at her pathetic, tearing face, blaming her for what happened to

China during the war. She had to be punished. She deserved to die. For years, I made her into a shadow puppet waiting for her sentence. I became my sister's assassin. Not like Dai Li's assassins, the Generalissimo's secret unit, who gunned down liberal and communist dissenters to his Party, the Kuomintang, the KMT. They killed viciously, men, women, and children at hotels, restaurants, and funerals, sensational slaughter broadcast daily in the *Shanghai News*. Their killings were warnings to comply or die, their targets broad, military resisters like Zi Ming Jingyao and Ji Hongchang, or leftists like Yang Xingfo and Deng Yanda. My assassination had only one target, my sister. My work was private, intimate, repetitive, and at the end ineffective.

If I could have one more day, I could tell her why our lives were broken. But she won't give me that day. She reappeared without warning and vanished without granting me time. I saw her once across the street from the market where I bought freshwater spinach and young ginger. Once on the television, I thought I glimpsed her amid a crowd gathering to gawk at a car accident. She always hid in shadows, waiting for an auspicious moment to appear. Sometimes she slipped around corners, down alleyways, and into the stucco surface of a white wall.

The war years are long gone. Instead of fighting, the Japanese watched the latest Godzilla movies and relived their atomic contamination with the flaming breath of a lumbering monster. Most Chinese worked hard, their heads down, trying not to think about their bitter revolution, their resistance reduced to telling silly jokes and inventing puns on the names of our leaders. Others retired into complacent cynicism, a shell impervious to the television news.

It's not the pain of those forgotten years I wanted to record. It's that what I want to tell you, you will not believe. And I hope you never have to believe it.

Don't try to understand what I am saying as a heart-rending confession. It's not. I have already made public confessions twice, first in 1943 to fascists in a KMT concentration camp, next in 1958 to communists in Tilanqiao, renamed Shanghai People's Prison. In a confined cell, I learned how not to be a martyr. I learned what was expected of me, the necessary admissions of guilt, the tear-stained words spoken with sincerity, the predictable process of accommodation to the interrogator.

On the contrary, what I am doing in this document has nothing to do with a confession. You see, I admit nothing because I believe nothing.

When Qui Fang was still in high school, I became a communist. For my circle of friends at Nanjing Central University, the Party was an explosion that tore us from our families and everything we were brought up to believe. Catastrophic. Deafening. We were overcome, mesmerized, intoxicated, and starved for not only a truth, but a way to live. The communists gave us words that we grabbed with greedy minds to craft into holy weapons. Their words transformed the stinking poor outside the university gates into seething masses struggling to be free. When we protested against the government's corruption and its unwillingness to fight Japan, my roommate was mowed down by three bullets in her back. Right then, I committed to finishing my medical degree and practicing among the poor in Shanghai, showing how a communist who grew up in a scholar's home and benefited from a university education could help the people, both peasant and worker. In 1937 when the war of resistance against the Japanese fascists started, I helped to organize clandestine cells of silk factory workers to fight against the government who never stopped imprisoning our cadres even in the middle of war.

A document must have dates. Timelines are necessary to clarify actions. Without them everything we have done in the past evaporates like mist. Rather, records with dates are necessary. They compel us to establish sequence and determine not only what happened but why it happened. For instance, I can precisely pinpoint when my life began to separate from my younger sister's, the first crack in our shared childhood. On September 14th, 1924, the 16th day of the 8th month, or the Mid-Autumn Festival (that's why I remember it so clearly), Meifang, my roommate, had read Qu Quibai's poem in a local pamphlet and dutifully copied the lines into her notebook. We sat on my bed reading the poem out loud. It was the first time that poetry made sense to me. *Nobody here is waving a feather fan, engaged in a stately dance. Here what you see are calluses—and strength.* Inspired, Meifang and I called ourselves the Iron Flowers, young Chinese women committed to worker's rights who had thrown aside the frivolities of the elite. We were strong. We would fight.

Two weeks later, on September 28th, I visited my younger sister at Suzhou Girls' High School eager to share with her Qu's poem. We were sitting across from each other in the school cafeteria eating diluted soup and chatting about the bad school food. As if handling a sacred object, I took the poem out of my satchel and slid it over to her. Setting down her bowl, she skimmed it quickly and set it aside.

She asked no questions, not a hint of curiosity. The poem might as well have been a piece of newsprint for wrapping fish. I tried to hide my reaction, but I could tell from the tilt of her head that she did not approve of the poem and worse, she knew she had hurt me. In a polite, muted voice, she told me she had to hurry to class. Later, when I lent her a copy of *Women's Voice* and encouraged her to read Ding Ling's story, she refused to read it.

My sister gradually became someone I did not know and then someone I did not want to know until she became my enemy.

After my sister followed me to National Central University, Qui Fang ignored what I was doing, even though we both studied biology and zoology. She worked long hours in the physiology laboratory, complaining that medical students were sloppy scientists. I can still see her dressed in a white coat over her pale blue cotton cheongsam, her hair pulled back, her hand delicately pouring liquid down a tall beaker in the laboratory. When I visited her and teased her about her devotion to test tubes, she only smiled, opening her notebook, unable to even carry on a conversation. She would barely look at me, her eyes obsessively drawn to the dyed slides she scrutinized under her microscope. If she said anything, it was about adenosine triphosphate or the latest article on enzymes and proteins by John N. Northrop at the Rockefeller Institute.

Qui Fang had no interest in me or the practice of medicine. No interest in the hours I spent learning how to amputate mangled limbs from accidents in our satanic mills. No interest in how I treated the wounds of coolies beaten by the canes of American businessmen and the batons of KMT soldiers.

How could two sisters raised so closely feel such gnawing resentment? Part of the answer was in books. From our father, we both had learned about George Washington and Thomas Jefferson as the founders of American democracy. A classically trained scholar, he was drawn to republican political thought. He believed that China could learn from the revolution in the United States. A devoted daughter, Qui Fang was persuaded by his arguments. I too loved father, but in college I began to judge his beliefs as naive, even impetuous, unable to account for the unrest in China. In my Marx study groups, I learned that the men who had revolted against the English king to build a republic embraced the plans of greedy bankers.

Qui Fang and I both read *The Declaration of Independence,* and its stirring words, *all men are created equal.* But only a white, male elite was freed from the chains of the king; the rest were slaves. Jefferson's words of equality depended on a forced slave system America's founders built and the wage slavery they exploited, pitting white poor against black poor. American capitalism, the heart of the American Republic, worked to divide the working class and reward the factory owners, the wealthy landlords, and the reactionary businessmen who bled the people dry. Our communist revolution freed all men and women from a *feudal-patriarchal ideology and system.* And women were essential to the grand march of labor and revolution. Where were the women in the American revolution?

To this document, I have attached a list of books my sister and I read in high school and college with corresponding dates. Our emotional logic and alienation can be reconstructed from the titles alone. Take one parallel entry: John Dewey's *On Democracy* and Li Da's *Elements of Sociology*. I could have been killed for reading Li Da. Meanwhile, my sister was applauded for reading John Dewey. My books were labeled subversive, hers enlightening. Censorship was the glue of the Generalissimo's regime. What we were reading on the streetcar or what newspaper we carried in our school satchel or what pamphlet we had tucked in our biology textbook could be our death sentence. The schools had KMT spies who seized and executed my friends for what books they bought and where they bought their books. Bookstores were filled with government undercover agents masquerading as college students. The government even established its own bookstores to lure potential subversives into its trap.

Oblivious, my sister attended the college lectures of Hu Shih, the Chinese philosopher and supporter of John Dewey preaching his version of the independence of women. How starry-eyed she was about his encouragement for girls to study science and not succumb to radical ideas. His "save-the-nation-through-study" slogan became her mantra as she worked long hours in the laboratory. Her philosopher-king was educated in the United States at Columbia University where he was infected by the virus of reform. After we won the revolution, he fled China, preferring to criticize our revolution from the safety of Taiwan. A coward and traitor.

Qui Fang also took time out from her science studies to attend Pearl Buck's lectures on American literature. Later, Buck would win the Nobel Prize in Literature for her novel on Chinese peasants, *The Good Earth*, that she drafted at our university. Born in China, a missionary from birth, what did Pearl Buck know of the people? Her scenes of poverty only brought more American money into Chinese mission schools and hospitals, spreading their vicious lies and sickly nostalgia about our peasants. American money turned Chinese away from our revolution and made them fit only to live in the United States. The communist revolution forced the missionaries to flee and take their Jesus with them and his belief in an afterlife, the only guaranteed place where injustices were punished.

Neither Hu Shih nor Pearl Buck could foresee the *colossal event*, the *hurricane, the mighty storm* of the peasants that our prophet Mao Tse Tung saw. How fervently I believed that *we should go to the masses and learn from them, synthesize their experiences into better, articulated principles and methods.* Revolution required a great cleansing of our institutions, our families, our way of thinking.

My anger festered. Qui Fang, my dearest sister, my childhood playmate, had betrayed our love and our country's destiny. How simple it was when I was young. To believe or not to believe. To condemn or pardon. Life reduced to yes and no. And how deeply I believed. I raged at her because she could have done so much to educate the masses and spark a revolution in science among the poorest of villagers.

I forced her to appear in my nightly assassination theater. I would yell at her drooping figure, standing with her hands at her sides, her head down, her perfectly white lab coat smeared with blood. The more outraged I became the more severe her torments became, enduring hours of taunting as she knelt in center stage with a jeering audience of farmers.

Writing this document, I can clearly see the trajectory of our lives. In the end it was not only books that altered our fate. More than books, it was love, and her lover was the embodiment of the books she chose to read.

Her beloved mentor, Professor Zi Ming posed as the grand god of western science and American democracy. What deceits did he whisper to make her his mistress? In their secret liaison, they must have seen themselves as rebels, defying the antiquated feudal strictures about marriage to become the ideal modern Chinese couple except for the minor inconvenience of his arranged-marriage wife and their five children. Professor Zi Ming in his stylish western suit with his American PhD and Qui Fang in a lovely peony cheongsam with her radiant face, brilliant mind, and perfectly bobbed hair embodied the educated offspring of China's elite ready to use science as the springboard of progress. Their photos could have appeared in Shanghai's popular magazines with romantic tales about their revolutionary love.

Of course, she told my mother that Professor Zi Ming had divorced his wife and married her. Even now, I can't decide if she lied or fooled herself into believing his lies. She left the university before graduation and followed him to live in Hangzhou as his research assistant where his wife and children moved into a West Lake villa. At Zhejiang University, the professor climbed the ladder of success, first as a distinguished research scientist, then as its president.

What arrogance. Qui Fang dutifully worked in his laboratory while he set about reforming the university in his image. When he looked at China, he saw a scientific problem that needed to be solved. He did not see people suffering. He did not see the threat of Japan or the Nationalist government. He saw himself in control with the Generalissimo's generous support of his educational experiment in rational organization. When he looked at my sister, did he see only a beautiful Chinese devotee ready to do his bidding?

On December 20th, 1935, the crack between my sister and me widened beyond repair. I marched as a member of the National Liberation Vanguard, a feared communist agitator, along with the students at Zhejiang University, against her lover. When he lectured the students at the university, urging them to return to their classrooms and forget the suffering happening outside its gates, we stormed his classroom and threatened his life. When he told us to forget the Japanese Imperial Army threatening the sovereignty of China, forget the misery of millions, keep your heads down and study, we screamed back, *Strike!* We rose against him. Even when the Generalissimo came to talk with us, claiming to have read our petitions, we did not stop the protests. The fires of youth burned throughout China that December. Universities in Beijing (then called Peiping), Shanghai, and Nanjing joined the fury. Only police batons, the prison cells, and the torturer's lash stopped our movement.

In less than a month, my sister fled with Professor Zi Ming to the United States. There, he invented a new life, a new lie, with my sister at his side. From her safety in the United States, she worried and cried about us, her guilty letters to my mother a mixture of anxiety and anecdotes about her American friends and how they admired her English, her training in zoology, and her distinguished husband.

One letter appalled me. When she was living in New Haven, she was so pleased with the intimate gathering she hosted with her Yale friends on October 10th to celebrate the Chinese Republic's founding. Did she choose to ignore what the Generalissimo was doing to his fellow Chinese? His repression, death squads, purging of communists and liberals? How I despised her *tea* party with its sandwiches that she served with the help of her beloved Mrs. Withington, who was teaching her the proper use of English and who had renamed my sister Katherine and, worse, had given her a pet name, Kitty. Qui Fang is not Katherine. Qui Fang is not Kitty.

In another letter, my sister described the special Chinese dinner she hosted for her Yale friends, *xiaolongbao*, steamed buns, followed by mandarin fish and sautéed greens. Did she teach her guests how to use chopsticks? Did she wear the peacock blue embroidered jacket mother had made for her? I hated her and her supposed friends, especially Sidney Withington and his wife, Dorothea, who were fervent supporters of the Yale-in-China Association. Could my sister have ever predicted its future? What a fool she was. After we won the civil war and destroyed the

Republic of China, her precious Yale-in-China organization in Changsha was seized and renamed "Liberation Middle School."

Could she not see anything? These are the reasons I needed to assassinate her. I had proof of her treason. I kept her letter of October 20th, 1937, as a constant reminder of her treachery. I would make her read it before she was given her nightly punishment. Once, she cried in midsentence, pleading with me to stop. That night her sentence was severe.

In the middle of the war with Japan, her so-called husband returned to China with my sister and their 9-month-old baby (did I mention she had a son? I try not to think of her as a mother). The Generalissimo had called him back to Chongqing, the wartime capital, a miserable place of KMT corruption. They stayed in the interior for barely a year. Then her lover, the *favored man* of the Generalissimo, was sent on an extended mission abroad to the United States and England. While he was gone, she left the miseries of Chongqing and traveled back to Shanghai, her lover's money paying for a China National Aviation Corporation 14-passenger DC-2 flight to Hong Kong, then a ship up the coast to Shanghai. Even during war, she managed to escape the worst sufferings of ordinary people.

When she first moved in with her two-year-old boy, I was amazed by how much she had changed, her once glowing, round face now puffy and sallow, her flashing eyes dull and darkened. At first, I thought it was caused by her difficult pregnancy or the conditions in Chongqing, the dirt, the damp chill, the lack of fresh vegetables, the lack of milk for her child. The complaints in her letters to mother were endless. Did she not register the war? Then I perceived a penetrating loneliness in her actions, the way she clung to her child, the hesitancy of her speech, her listlessness.

A few times when we walked the streets of Shanghai, thousands of dead children discarded on the sidewalks [in 1941 alone, 20,720 dead], their tiny arms shriveled into sticks, she whispered under her breath that with the help of the West the Generalissimo would save them. Ironically, she suffered more than I did because she believed in the Republic of China. She remained committed to her belief that the KMT would defeat the Japanese and make a grand alliance with the United States. The future of China was in the hands of American guns, planes, and generals. She truly believed in the Republic, despite its rot and corruption, its corrupt warlord generals and American military experts, its General Joseph Stilwell and Major General Claire Lee Chennault, its Flying Tigers and the Burma Road.

Fed up, I no longer could tolerate her delusional beliefs. I stayed away at the clinic for weeks and only came home to check on mother. Qui Fang and I had little to say to each other except icy greetings of hello and goodbye. I had no sympathy for her problems and her son.

My sister never ventured into the warehouses packed with dying workers, many of whom were children fleeing starvation in the countryside. She did not smuggle food out of our kitchen for sick babies. Her world seemed to revolve around her child. And even that love was not spared.

On July 3rd, 1941, shortly after she returned with her baby boy dressed in his Su embroidered jacket and hat, a kitchen servant tempted the toddler outside the front gate with pear candy. We never discovered who paid the servant to kidnap the child, for the woman's body was later dumped in the Whampoa River. The war had ruined Shanghai's economy; extortion rackets replaced law. In the pay of either the Japanese, the Generalissimo and his Green Gang, or the puppet president in Nanjing, violent thugs ruled our city. They kidnapped for money. They kidnapped to punish the rich who hoarded their money. They kidnapped to terrorize the city's inhabitants. After six weeks, the exorbitant ransom paid (money that could have gone to my work in the clinic), her son was returned, starving, his left thigh scalded, a red bubbling scar covering his leg.

I was home the day he was returned in a crate left at the front gate. I watched Qui Fang collapse in tears, how tightly she held him, how she refused to let him go even when he struggled against her. I was not moved by her tears. I knew that she could not weep for the thousands of children dying in the city. I hardened against her. Built a wall against her pain. Cast her out.

The war against the Japanese and the Nationalists was the same. Both enemies would not free the masses. Both enemies would not feed the masses. She did not see *the mighty storm coming*. She did not understand that *our duty is to hold ourselves responsible to the people.*

Fact: the people were starving.

Fact: the people needed food and land.

Fact: the people needed guns.

Fact: the people needed revolution.

With the noose tightening against foreigners and Chinese in league with the Allies, Qui Fang feared seizure and even separation from her son. After a long argument with our mother, she decided to flee west through northern China to rejoin her lover 1,000 miles away in Chongqing. He had returned after working frantically in the United States on postwar reconstruction plans, traveling from coast to coast to gain support for rebuilding the wreckage of China's universities that the Japanese had destroyed. He succeeded in getting commitments from eighty American universities, promising to help. He returned triumphant, submitting his reports to the Generalissimo.

He was a fool.

China's children could not read or write. But they could die in the millions from starvation. Did his grand schemes even once consider that?

On a balmy night in spring before Qui Fang left with her son on one of the rare times when I slept at home, I had a technicolor dream: my sister and myself on stage in a peasant folk opera, arms linked, bowing to thunderous applause, singing:

The east is red, the sun is rising.
From China, appears Mao Zedong.
He strives for the people's happiness.
Hurrah, he is the people's savior!

I woke up in the middle of the opera, laughing at how absurd our minds are, tricksters, setting traps to undermine reality. My sister could never be my friend, my comrade, my fellow-in-arms. I stayed awake the rest of the night, scripting more humiliations, honing my skills as her assassin. I never saw her leave.

My mother and I were soon forced to flee the French Concession. Mother cried when she left our home, taking only a small bundle of clothes for her journey. She cried for Qui Fang and for her child. She cried for the world of her ancestors that had crumbled before her eyes. I tried to comfort her and remind her that she had wrapped the golden shawl around Qui Fang's waist to keep her safe on her journey and bring her home again. It would be her prayer bead, her rosary, her good luck charm. I was a total hypocrite. And my mother sensed my duplicity. With a quick goodbye, we fled the next day, going our separate ways. Mother to live in a fishing village on the coast, hiding with a relative of a servant. In eight years, she would be denounced by her protectors and placed in a reeducation camp for landlords and reactionaries, dying soon after. At the time I accepted that sacrifice. I believed that blood was necessary to build a new nation. *Wherever there is struggle there is sacrifice, and death is a common occurrence.*

My goal was to escape north past the Japanese lines and the Nationalist barriers to reach the headquarters of the Communist Party in Yan'an, north of Xi'an, and help *win a country-wide victory in the long, revolutionary march of ten thousand li.* Chairman Mao's words became my words. I would have to wait five more years until 1949, spending three years in a squalid Nationalist concentration camp, before I could savor this victory that would expel every American businessman, intellectual, soldier, and missionary from our country and witness the end of foreign intervention. The end of Standard Oil. The end of the Nationalist government. The end of the Generalissimo.

Close to Nanjing, I was captured, shackled and transported by Dai Li's agents, who would rather round up communists than fight the Japanese, and sent on a train to a secret concentration camp where I underwent a thorough interrogation. I was not killed immediately because I was seen administering to the wounds of some of my fellow prisoners. Doctors were in short supply. While I was incarcerated, the camp underwent a complete propaganda overhaul. Euphemisms were attached to acts of sustained and systemic violence. The camp became a *school*, the prisoners became *self-cultivators*, and when we were released, we were given certificates that said we had *graduated*. We were *biye*. Henceforth, we were to experience mental brutality not physical brutality, except when it was deemed necessary.

The surveillance system in the camp permeated every cell, mess hall, and work room, creating an atmosphere of strained, comic and bizarre dialogue. We were asked to inform on each other, record conversations, odd behavior, even dreams. All of us figured out quickly how to say nothing while talking. Since silence was subversive and indicated resistance to the social well-being of the *school*, we carried on like insane students in a mad house. Early on, I was enlisted to teach first aid and help with basic science classes that rarely met, since interrogation—or should I say persuasion sessions—always trumped learning. The premise of our founders, the secret service of the Generalissimo, was that our communist activities were "muddle-headed." We simply were not thinking clearly and had let our youthful emotions about poverty and injustice hamper our ability to see the truth.

In the Nationalist *school*, I invented more gruesome assassination techniques to punish Qui Fang for her loyalty to the KMT. Some were quite imaginative. Instead of a long interrogation on my bloodied stage, I imagined my sister walking west on the northern road to Chongqing surrounded by illiterate peasants, the *mighty stream* of history. Did she realize that the farmers would soon swarm over the countryside, taking what they firmly believed was theirs, my comrades helping them to execute, humiliate, and torture landlords? Those who could not escape would feel the hands of the soil on their necks. Land reform came and swept away the past.

I went further in my analysis of her character. Did my sister speak her beloved English on the northern road? How did she learn to speak to the peasants? Did the peasants help her or beat her?

For my sister, history was bourgeois an ever-ascending timeline of democratic reform and scientific progress. I wondered if those beliefs sustained her in the dark caves where she hid with the peasants. Or, did these ideas fall away like useless baggage? Did she only want to survive and protect her son, survive long enough to reunite with her husband?

Before my capture, I read reports of what happened to the villages south of the Yellow River, the mad dog violence of the Japanese soldiers, the desperate brutality of the Nationalist troops. Qui Fang must have walked through this disaster and somehow survived. The roads were clogged with coolies, teachers, farmers, and factory workers who hid in caves at night desperate to find a fraction of space, hoping to find shelter from the Japanese artillery and bombs. Did the journey across China change her when she met its starving peasants and saw its destroyed farms?

My curiosity delayed her inevitable humiliation and punishment, sometimes for days, then weeks. A pensive assassin, I became more her playwright, crafting long dialogues between Qui Fang and a series of women peasants. My favorite setting were her days and nights inside a cave, not far from Chairman Mao who was protected by a parallel cave in Yan'an, north of her route, writing the laws of revolutionary war, the need for fluid battle lines and mobile warfare, the need to oppose bandit ways and uphold strict political discipline, and the need to understand strategic retreat.

I revised the dialogue incessantly since we had both grown up in a Chinese paradise of canals and moon bridges, the Venice of the East, and of exquisite Su embroidery, dragon robes, longevity screens, and peacock vests, inspired by the magic needle of Shen Shou and worn by emperors. Together we had played in our family garden where ancient trees were revered, the curves of their trunks beaten by wind and rain, proof that the ancestors were suspended in a living past that we could see, smell, and touch. Even after the Qing dynasty was destroyed, our family's speech, clothing, and manner expressed elegance and grace. As soon as we spoke, our ancestors appeared.

On the road west, my sister must have struggled to communicate with workers and farmers. In the beginning of the revolution, I practiced day and night the dialects of factory workers pouring into Shanghai from the surrounding countryside. I had to rid my speech of its artifice. To work with the people, I had to speak like a worker. Every day, I stood in front of a mirror, purging from my tongue every hint of my decadent ancestry.

You must understand. I had to destroy the past that had caused such suffering. Our revolution did not need the past, only the future. The ancestors and their gods needed to be smashed.

When my ears opened to the people's speech, I came to accept how much violence was necessary to eliminate the reactionary elements standing in the way to liberation. The Communists needed to destroy the KMT, the landlord class, and the intellectuals spawned from its gentry. Galloping history was my god. I accepted unspeakable horrors.

Sometimes, I would shift the setting of my play to the road, where she trudged alone in the freezing cold, having lost everything except her son. A favorite dialogue topic was her growing doubts about her husband and his grand belief in science. She became pitiful. I even tried to make her cry out for me. I became pitiful and then bored with her plight and returned to the simplicity of the spotlight in stage center. She would barely step into the glaring circle and I would condemn her to death, usually by hanging. Quick and easy.

At one point in the KMT's *school,* I was classified as belonging to a group of educated women who were about to be condemned to death for their *dangerous* thoughts—that is, communist beliefs and defective social upbringing. In fact, I was at the point of being transferred from my propaganda classroom to the execution grounds when I converted to the Generalissimo's way of thinking. You may wonder how that could happen? Faced with death, the human heart becomes devious, cunning, a spinner of lies. Collapsing to my knees, I grabbed the legs of my guard and pleaded, not for mercy, but for my damaged mind that had not realized the errors of my way. In a dazzling performance, I became a rabid anti-communist. You are surprised? It wasn't that difficult since I had watched my fellow communist inmates slowly transform. Most were quickly killed but the rest succumbed to the torturer's persuasion, mimicking the words of their interrogators in clever, disguised tones of respect and submission.

At first, their duplicity revolted me, but then I came to admire their tenacity. Of course, most were not believed, and became gutted, empty shells, but a few thrived, learning to turn their guards into trusted friends.

A brilliant charade, you must admit. Worthy of the best magician.

In this way, I too survived. Once I was released to continue the good work as a loyal and patriotic field doctor with Nationalist troops, I melted into the extensive network of communist spies and agents surrounding the countryside. I had learned many valuable lessons at *school* and was able to convey what I had learned, interrogation techniques, shifts in personnel, numbers of prisoners, even food allocations, to my compatriots fighting for Chairman Mao.

After the Japanese defeat, if the Nationalists had won our civil war, my sister and I could have easily exchanged places and she could have watched as American businesses spread throughout China, not our productive work co-ops and collective farms. She could have become the wife of the Minister of Education, and I could have been executed in a basement cell of the Republic of China, probably by one of my former jailers who had mistakenly thought he had purged me of my muddled ways. You see where my thinking takes me? Endless possibilities that never happened. History becomes a game of odds, strewn with corpses. Should I stay, or should I leave? When does a country strip you bare and burn your body? When do you have no choices left?

Can I tell you a secret? When my sister left our Shanghai apartment with her son, I whispered to her, *You will never find your lover. He will forget you.* I desperately wanted to punish her. Even now my lack of sympathy reveals much about the human heart.

Was the father of her child as vicious?

Before we won our civil war, he left our country with a whore, his daughter-in-law. What more needs saying? Qui Fang's fate entangled with a treacherous man, a traitor, a murderer some say, and a coward. A favorite of the Generalissimo, he could not have loved anyone or anything, except his bestial desires, an endless pursuit of ambition, lust, and glory stretching into his imagined future.

I once believed in Mao's future. And anyone who did not violated the truth. Be wary of what future you want. It will kill the ones you love.

You see Mao forgot to tell us that death waited at the end of history.

All stories about the future were lies, history a mere narrative covering our fears. He fooled us with his talk of an earthly paradise. He committed the worst sin. He made us believe in his future. Purge the land of the decadent past, work hard in the present, and future prosperity was guaranteed. What a bitter delusion. The party was still wrapped in these lies, locking up anyone who refused to believe in their version of history, their absurd attempts to shackle time.

After my loyalty to the Party, my years of fighting against injustice, and my torment in the Nationalist *school*, I had a crisis of faith in 1957 when I was labeled a Rightist because of my Western medical training, a training I had used to relieve the sufferings of silk factory workers in Shanghai thoughout the war with Japan.

The poor knew what I could do. They saw the results of my daily work. What did knowledge of anatomy and physiology have to do with reactionary thinking? For the first time, I saw how Mao could err. My years of reading books were labeled Rightist, my years of listening to lectures were Rightist, my reliance on Western textbooks was Rightist, my training at Zhejiang Medical University was Rightist. Dismayed, I wrote a letter to the Ministry of Health objecting to the criticisms hurled against me by the political cadre of my work unit.

At that time, I was assigned to work with the gold miners in Qingdao, Shandong, men whose lungs collapsed from cancer, silicosis, and pulmonary tuberculosis. I never wavered in my duties. I treated their wives and children whose chronic coughs and fatigue were each day made worse by the spirits their husbands drank to ease their pain. I nursed their wounds. I listened to their stories. I gave them medicine and hope.

After the authorities read my complaint, a detailed summary of my activities, my necessary background training, and careful observations about the current direction of the Party, I was immediately accused of historical nihilism and imprisoned. I, who sacrificed everything for the Party, imprisoned. I felt like I had been tricked, falsely accused by jealous colleagues. I was not a reactionary that held up Western democracy to shame our revolution.

The regional political committee did not listen. They stamped me a Rightist in need of rehabilitation. I spent four years in a communist reeducation camp where I was made to confess my crimes against the Party and listen, endlessly listen, to criticisms hurled at me by my fellow prisoners as a stood at the middle of a circle of gawking guards and smug cadres. I mentally recorded the incorrect statements about the past that were invented by our political leaders, statements on specific days that injured me and my colleagues and altered the future. I saw the warping of time present, past, and future as cadres revised for their own greed what had happened and what was to happen. They demeaned my medical education and erased my medical service to redirect the trajectory of our revolution.

On the prison courtyard wall was plastered a poster with large red characters, "The Party rules the earth and sky." It was there that I learned there were no comforting stories about the future. And anyone who claimed to have a shape for time was insane. Whether it's the Generalissimo's Blue Shirts in the Nanjing *school* or the eager political cadres of the CCP in the reeducation camp, it simply didn't matter. The people who insisted on a narrative, a beginning, middle, and end, were dangerous to humanity. I rejected all myths of progress, scientific, technical, or biblical. I no longer believed in Marx's future or even less in Marxism with Chinese characteristics. I no longer believed in slogans about history based on beliefs in the Republic, the Emperor, Buddha, Mao or God. I no longer believed the future was a better place than the past or the present. Nor was it a worse place. Whatever the future brings will be momentary, chaotic, unpredictable, here today, gone tomorrow, conveying an idea that dissolved as soon as it formed.

I completely erased the meaning of history.

Released from the CCP's camp, I was assigned to a new clinical practice at the Duzhuangzi Mine. I thought about my sister more every day. What she must have gone through in her mountain cave and on the road. What she faced when she returned to the hellish Chongqing to rejoin the devil, Zi Ming. Had she too learned that the future was a product of chance, hatred and greed, the pure force of circumstance that changed every second? If we ever met again, would we see the world the same?

Every day for twelve hours, I worked in the miner's clinic repairing broken bones, treating lacerations, giving inoculations, and writing reports. What time is there to think or talk? I simply repeated the words I was given by my political officer, knowing the emptiness in each phrase. My patients' pain spoke louder, the rest was noise, claptrap that came from directives formulated in committees that became collective speech. Work rescued me from these social pitfalls.

Only one problem remained: I have found it impossible to erase my sister. I stopped being her assassin years ago.

I made my peace with what happened, the deaths, the confiscation of my family's lands and wealth, the destruction of our childhood garden, the pond choked on weeds, the carp long dead, and the trees withered. Even my years in KMT and CCP prisons. The past cannot be altered.

I no longer believe in punishment. What purpose could there possibly be? Certainly not to create better citizens for the future state. Not to affirm my beliefs in the righteousness of my cause. The theater of the assassin was as empty as my heart. No one came anymore. Not my sister, not the interrogator, not the executioner.

Only in my heart did my sister remain, a shapeshifter, a tempestuous child, a conflicted student, an eager scientist, and a woman in love walking through our Suzhou villa's garden aglow with pear and loquat blossoms. I turned away from her when she needed me the most, and I kept trying to discard her, but she kept returning, her laughter when she made mistakes playing the pipa, her penetrating eyes when she questioned my unblinking intensity, her shadow walking down the hall ahead of me, just a few seconds ahead of me, in the miners' clinic.

Once our Suzhou garden resounded with the laughter of two young girls who were unable to see their future. There, we watched the flickering shadows on the leaves change their shade of green from chartreuse to deep olive until our mother called us back inside to embroider on a square screen. Each silk thread separated into tiny filaments as our fingers gently rubbed the wispy strands that lifted in the slightest breeze. We learned to sit quietly, coaxing the silk into the needle's point, working slowly to build layers of stitches, flat, pointed, reversed, even ones hidden underneath to create hues of green.

At night, I recreated this scene, each gesture of our hands, each color of every stitch, raven black, lotus green, grass green, azure, moonlight blue, persimmon, tangerine orange, rose purple, jade white, silver gray, silver, and gold, picturing the slightest variation in hue as if together we held the thread and needle.

I have gone beyond hatred. Beyond history. Beyond lies.

I wait for Qui Fang near the garden gate.

18

As Good as Dead

Every spring, Andrew and I continued to fly across the Pacific and teach a graduate seminar in Beijing. Interest in his father had escalated even more. We had meetings, luncheons, and banquets with historians of science, psychologists, and publishers seeking permission to republish his father's works, enlist our help in finding additional biographical information, or present a new tribute in the ongoing restoration of Zi Ming's reputation. With such attention to his father's life, I even entertained the idea of editing *Confessions* and *Chinese National Character* for publication.

I still went through the ritual of giving Katherine's Chinese name to our colleagues who would politely respond that they would try again. But no information ever materialized. We never stayed long enough in China for sustained investigation aided by a translator. I was at a loss for how to proceed. What was there left to do?

Despite these frustrations, Katherine's presence persisted. At home, I'd wake up in the middle of the night, feeling like I was back in Beijing, walking on a busy street, her shadow alongside, sticking to my movements, mocking my steps. I couldn't shake her.

There were no more packages from Katherine's elderly friends. The people who could have provided firsthand information were gone. Julia died in March 2009 and Ida in April

2016, taking their secrets to the grave. Even Ida's former husband refused to answer my queries about Andrew's father and mother. Andrew's nephew, Peter, would not respond to letters, phone calls, or emails. Katherine's past was once again sealed behind an impenetrable wall.

Ghosts, however, can go through walls.

In the spring of 2018, Andrew was sent another article on Zi Ming. The writer had uncovered new primary materials in China on Zi Ming's years as president of Zhejiang University, where he and Katherine had lived on West Lake outside Hangzhou. It claimed that the student uprisings of 1936 had forced Zi Ming out of the presidency. The researcher, Beverley G., had interviewed prominent student activists and, according to them, Zi Ming was violently anti-communist and had used the police to imprison students and silence their demands. Locking them up for days or longer, he perpetuated a climate of repression.

Not the man in the middle as he claimed in his *Confessions*, Zi Ming was supported by Chiang Kai-shek, who directly appointed him university president. Chiang Kai-shek had even traveled in 1936 from Nanjing the capital of the ROC to the Zhejiang University to quell the student uprising. It didn't work. Zi Ming was forced to resign.

In the Chinese documents Beverley uncovered, Zi Ming was labeled "a fascist running dog," an insult continually used by communists to condemn their enemies. An "expel the president" petition circulated in 1936 that accused Zi Ming of a list of transgressions. Besides police, he had used spies to weed out leftists and communists. The petition charged that he was involved in shady business dealings with contractors for the university and had seduced his female students, taking one as his concubine. Was this Katherine?

A common tactic of communists was to smear their enemies with false charges, muddying the truth. This technique was also used by the Nationalists. In this overheated political period, the truth of accusations was difficult to discern unless hard evidence could stop slander. With Nationalists shutting down newspapers and locking up anyone criticizing the government, the truth was often impossible to know.

In her article, Beverley described the intense political atmosphere at Zhejiang University and concluded that Zi Ming was less the man-in-the-middle than a man blocked in his attempts to reorganize Chinese higher education. He had no compunction about silencing dissent. In his strategic planning, communism had no role, but highly organized and monitored student life did. Like Mao and Chiang Kai-shek, he also had a totalizing vision of how to remake China. Higher education was the key, not a peasant revolution. Its institutions would train both the body and the mind of a select group of young Chinese, the future leaders of the nation, requiring military exercises, challenging academic subjects, especially science, and complete loyalty to their country. Unlike Mao, Zi Ming had no role for peasants in the making of modern China. His vision was top down.

When Zi Ming left Hangzhou with Katherine in 1936, he was running away from political chaos. Had Katherine and Zi Ming legally married? All I knew for certain was that ftom when the couple docked in San Francisco until they departed Victoria, B.C., three years later, Zi Ming called Katherine his wife and Katherine called herself his wife. Moreover, their social circle in the United States considered the couple married.

I knew that traditional Chinese marriage customs for the wealthy were not monogamous. When the last dynasty, the Qing, began their reign in 1644, the United States was barely a colonial outpost of the British Empire. As in previous Chinese dynasties, the rulers and wealthy had multiple wives and concubines. They also visited pleasure houses. Their wives were carefully ranked as were their concubines, and the patriarch had legal responsibility for each woman and the children of these unions. Depending upon which wife or concubine could produce a male heir or heirs, power shifted between the women. Dynastic families were governed by exhausting rituals and codes prescribing behavior and cementing hierarchy, not unlike the elaborate rules for primogeniture in European and British royal dynasties.

In this system, matriarchs could assume far-reaching powers to run their households and their children's lives. The Empress Dowager Cixi, a concubine of the Xianfeng Emperor, in effect ruled China for 47 years until 1908 when she died. Jung Chang in her 2013 biography of Cixi reappraises her remarkable achievements in modernizing China. In clan structures, matriarchs presided over the running of households with hundreds of people. They were not mere decorations or pawns in the hands of men.

It was equally the case that most women never achieved this status, remaining restricted in their marriages. Many were simply slaves.

When the Republic of China succeeded the Qing Dynasty in 1911, the government began to revise the marriage codes, making divorce possible and promoting monogamy. For many Chinese, these traditional customs were slow to change. Only under the Chinese Communist Party, was there a concerted push to enforce monogamy. To get around the tricky legal problems of monogamy, the ROC devised a middle term, "household member," to protect second wives and concubines with or without children from complete loss of status and income. In court, women who were not first wives had some legal means to receive alimony.

Christian-inspired or communist monogamy was often a grim solution to traditional marital systems, even though it was presented as liberating to women. Concepts like "fidelity" and "chastity" rang true in one culture and barely sounded in another. Even societies that affirmed monogamy through religion and law had a high percentage of husbands that led separate lives outside the home with mistresses and prostitutes.

I had often wondered about Zi Ming's first wife, whose name was unknown. Who was she? I assumed she was from a place near Zi Ming's clan village in southern China. What happened to her when Zi Ming and Katherine left for America in 1936? More unanswered questions. Family history was a receding line of specters without names or faces. As the Tang Dynasty poet Cold Mountain wrote in the ninth century, "Our fragile dreamlike bodies disappear like smoke."

Once I dared to ask Ida about her mother. She seemed surprised I would want to know. At first, she refused to say anything, but then added, "She was stupid." That was all I knew about the mother of Zi Ming's five children, one devastating comment summing up an entire life, a woman whose life was ruined by war, dislocation, and divorce. How easily the past is reduced and discarded.

Rereading Beverly's article, I found a way that might uncover more information about Katherine. In her footnotes, she quoted from correspondence between Zi Ming and several American psychologists. There was no personal information included in her essay, but there might be in the letters. When I emailed Beverly about references to Zi Ming's wife, Katherine, she responded that there were comments about family throughout the correspondence, but she hadn't paid any attention.

I resolved to do one last thing. It was a long shot. In the winter of 2018, I traveled to a private library in Philadelphia to read Zi Ming's correspondence. I owed Katherine one last chance. His unpublished manuscripts had worn me out, buried me beneath the myth of the great man. Maybe his letters would revive his second wife.

Philadelphia was freezing, the library a few blocks away from my hotel. I regretted coming as soon as I managed to trudge through the snow my first day to the reading room. I was used to the peculiarities of archivists, their protectiveness about the documents in their charge, their odd demands on researchers, their hovering. What I resented was another immersion in the great man's world. I had to wade through decades of his letters to try and find scraps of information about Katherine.

Her letters were saved by a fluke, finding their way to her son by a series of improbable events. Zi Ming's were carefully preserved in folders, each catalogued precisely and kept safe under carefully controlled atmospheric conditions. It was clear whose life had value. Whose life was worth recording.

The letters I read started in 1936 and ended in 1971 after Zi Ming's death in 1970. Mainly they confirmed the facts I already knew.

Indeed, Andrew was kidnapped in the summer of 1941. What I didn't know was that he was returned six weeks later, a considerable length of time. I found out from my readings about 1940s Shanghai that this was not unusual. Kidnappers expected to negotiate with the wealthy family for return of their relative. Often, members of the criminal underground became go-betweens in these negotiations.

The Green Gang, notorious for their control of opium, prostitution, and gambling in Shanghai, had links to businessmen, bankers, policemen, and even Chiang Kai-shek. The Green Gang's profits supported the ROC's government and military. Since Zi Ming's uncle was a dominant force in Shanghai opium smuggling, it is likely Andrew's family turned to the Green Gang to negotiate the ransom amount. According to Julia, the ransom was large enough to cause considerable damage to the family's resources. But Andrew survived. Many victims did not.

I worried that my husband's nightmares came from this horrible experience. He was extremely uncomfortable around knives, insisting I come nowhere near him when he was cutting vegetables. He also had a large scar on his leg. He believed it happened when he was kidnapped. The kitchen was a place of danger. Also, Andrew never closed his study door or our bedroom door. He avoided shuttered interior spaces. Was he locked away in his captivity?

In the woods, on the islands of Hong Kong, throughout remote mountains, he felt at home. Bears, no problem. Snakes, no problem. Winter camping in freezing cold, no problem. Jumping out of an airplane into a forest fire, no problem. The outside provided freedom and safety. The inside could kill.

Writing to his American friends about his son's kidnapping, Zi Ming offered few details. Since he was in the United States when it happened, Katherine had faced this crisis without him. In the archival letters, his American friends consoled Zi Ming with reassurances that his son would be fine because children given proper care can heal.

There was also a significant contradiction in the letters. As Beverly argued in her article, Zi Ming was not the man in the middle. His postwar reconstruction efforts between 1941 and 1943 in the United States and England had the full support of the ROC. In one letter, he claimed to have direct backing from Chiang Kai-shek, the opposite of what he wrote in *Confessions*. Ambitious, Zi Ming wanted influence in the government, exactly as he had expressed in his letter to Mrs. Withington. Despite Katherine's fierce objections to returning to China, he worried more that if he did not return in 1939, he would pass up his opportunity to play a leadership role in the government and Chinese institutions of higher education. The letters described offers for university presidencies and ministerial positions from Chiang Kai-shek and his close advisor, Chen Li-fu, that he had already turned down in order to focus on his far-reaching reconstruction plans. He was a big man with big plans.

The letters that he wrote between 1941 and 1943 when he was traveling in the United States and England did mention Katherine. He was anxious about his wife, losing contact with her for months at a time. In February 1943, he wrote from the United States about his slight hope that his wife with help from his private secretary would be able join him in Chongqing once he returned. In fall 1943, he did return to the interior capital after completing his reconstruction alliances.

These references to Katherine convinced me I would finally find out when and how she died. Excited, I skimmed through piles of letters to find details of Katherine's return with Andrew later that fall or in early 1944. The couple had been apart for two and a half years.

In the silence of the library, sitting at a long table with only three other researchers, I could feel my heart beating faster.

What had started in 1989 with the arrival of her dress might find resolution almost thirty years later in Zi Ming's correspondence. At last, I would find out what happened to her.

Then I fell into a black hole.

There were no letters between February 1943 and March 1945 in any file. This entire period was silent. Not one letter from 1944. The year Katherine had probably died.

I had spent days in the archives sorting and reading in sequential order letters about Zi Ming's professional life, his lectures, his concerns about Katherine, and then nothing. I had been moving toward a revelation and instead discovered only a giant gap in the narrative.

Had there been no letters? Had the letters been destroyed? If so, who would have destroyed them?

The next letter was written on April 21, 1945, two years before Zi Ming left China for Hong Kong. He was probably in Shanghai or still in Chongqing getting ready to leave for Shanghai. In the letter, he claimed that he had sent letters to his American psychologist colleague, LC, for over a year. He had heard nothing back. He asked LC if he had received them.

In this letter he informed LC about "Katherine's sudden death." There was no mention of a lingering illness from tuberculosis and many trips to the hospital. Julia's account was contradicted by three words. Sitting in the hushed quiet of the library, I was stunned.

I could hear Andrew's voice, "white arsenic powder." Had Julia really killed his mother? What could cause a "sudden death" in a young woman in her thirties? Scenarios raced through my mind: suicide, stroke, heart attack, a terrible accident, poisoning, or murder? I started asking these questions out loud. An older scholar, submerged in his documents across from me, sensed my agitation. I got up and left.

The streets were covered in snow. I trudged over to the commercial district and found a hole-in-the-wall Indian restaurant. I wasn't hungry. I wanted to get away, far away. After a few drinks, I went back.

Over the years, I had compiled a list of reasons for Katherine's death. Some easily dismissed, others more convincing. Because of Mrs. Loring and Julia, I had always trusted their account of tuberculosis and doubted Andrew's accusations. Had Mrs. Loring been fed a lie by Julia? Had I fallen for the same lie?

One technique I had followed methodically for thirty years while trying to find Andrew's mother was to construct a chronology of events for both Zi Ming and Katherine. It was my anchor. Each time I revised my timeline, it was because I had found new confirmation of what events occurred when. Since there were so many lies and deceptions, I felt that at least I could try and establish a sequence. I insisted on several corroborating accounts before an event was added, a technique that biographers used when shifting through archives. For Katherine, I had typed "death from tuberculosis" after the entry for the year 1944.

Julia had said this. Mrs. Loring had said this.

Zi Ming had contradicted this. If Katherine had died from tuberculosis, what possible reason would he have to cover this fact up? And since he wrote the letter close to Katherine's death, it had the authenticity of time.

What could a "sudden death" imply? Had Julia invented elaborate stories to cover her tracks, lying forty years after the fact? Was Zi Ming an accomplice? He must have known what his third wife had done. Or, another possibility, had Katherine committed suicide? Was that the unspeakable death? If that was true, why would she commit suicide, especially after her arduous journey from Shanghai to Chongqing to rejoin her husband?

I crossed out tuberculosis from Katherine's timeline and wrote, "sudden death."

The next day I had to force myself to return to the library.

I had to believe there would be more references to Katherine after 1945 that would shed light on how she died. Only two documents remained in the 1945 file, a cable from LC informing Zi

Ming of a university professorship in America, and a personal letter from LC expressing his and his wife's sadness at the death of Zi Ming's "brilliant, able, and charming wife."

Nothing in 1946. Then, in April 1947, there was a letter to LC about his new life in Hong Kong with his wife, Julia, and their new baby. There was no child born in that year that survived as far as I knew. Was this baby supposed to be Peter with a later birth date to confuse LC? Years later, Zi Ming had described in *Chinese National Character* his disturbing boat trip with his wife, a baby and 6-year-old-son. Was this baby Peter? The baby in the boat in war-torn China and the baby born in Hong Kong two year later must be one and the same. Attempts to make Peter appear as Zi Ming's son, not grandson, to his American friends started three weeks after the newly constituted family left China.

In the letter, Zi Ming asked LC if he thought he had been dead? He admitted that "socially and publicly" he was. Worse, "outside my home, I am just as good as dead."

Leaving China in 1947, before the end of the civil war, and fleeing to a British Crown colony had ended his life. Isolated, depressed, and restless, Zi Ming became the father Andrew remembered growing up. He rarely talked. He rarely went out. He paced in his bedroom and living room.

Zi Ming urged LC never to reveal to anyone his presence in Hong Kong, especially to any Chinese colleagues. No matter what the Chinese newspapers were saying about his movements, LC must promise to keep his location secret. The newspaper reports that he had moved to America were fine with him. Let the Chinese believe the rumor.

The letter also confirmed that Zi Ming's finances were in disarray. Inflation had reduced what funds he had managed to bring out of China. He entreated LC not to give up trying to find him a university job in America. He also described his brilliant new wife's abilities as a physician who had excellent command of written and spoken English. Julia became the star. Katherine was never mentioned again.

In later letters, every scheme to relocate to the United States fell through, often because he could not find a way to bring Julia. Eventually, she found steady work as a physician in Hong Kong and then a hospital administrator, supporting the family. Zi Ming settled into the inglorious task of writing his *Confessions,* a grim existence compared to his previous professional glory, when he had traveled throughout the United States and England making plans for postwar reconstruction with presidents of universities like Yale and Columbia, and working closely with major figures in the ROC, including Chiang Kai-shek.

Zi Ming defended his move to the British Crown colony by insisting he no longer wanted anything to do with China or the Chinese whether they lived under Mao or under Chiang Kai-shek in Taiwan. His sole desire was focused on a return to a research laboratory in America and to forget his homeland had ever existed. That never happened. His life upended, his profession obliterated, his family scattered, he endured years of self-exile.

As I continued to read, the letters traced how Zi Ming emerged from his shell twelve years later. In 1959, he started working for the CIA with the support of the Human Ecology Fund and a paid staff, interviewing more than one thousand persons coming from the mainland. These refugees ranged in age from 5 to 60 years old and had education levels from illiterates to college professors. Their political beliefs varied from devoted party cadres to violent anti-communists. He recorded their satirical songs and jokes about Mao and kept track of their diseases and medical care under the communists. He read communist newspapers, magazines, and books. He relied on his lengthy correspondence with contacts inside China, and he administered impromptu and short psychological tests to selected subjects. He submitted reports, attended meetings, and, in 1963 when he came to the United States to visit an American psychologist in North Carolina, he made a side trip to Washington, D.C., working incognito for his old friend Uncle Sam.

In his letters, he described his relationship to the CIA, his eventual disgruntlement with how they paid him, his refusal by 1964 to take a "single cent" more, and the enticements they used to persuade him to continue, including an offer to help him find a publisher for his two manuscripts, *Confessions* and *Chinese National Character*. Once again, he presented himself as too independent to work for the "gang" and had chosen to gather materials for them at his own expense. Since he thought his research essential, he would continue unofficially to submit his reports.

After cutting ties with the CIA, Zi Ming faced a new, dangerous challenge. In 1964, his letters started to criticize and demean Andrew. Previously, Zi Ming had praised Andrew's intelligence even if he couldn't always understand his son's school activities like soccer or track and field. He was also puzzled by Andrew's stamp collecting. In secondary school, Andrew was expected to study mathematics and science, excel at the piano, and complete his weekend lessons in calligraphy and Chinese because his academic excellence would guarantee his son a ticket back to the United States to complete his education, hopefully at Yale University. When Andrew turned down Yale for a small liberal arts school's creative writing program, Zi Ming was disappointed in his son's turn away from science, but he insisted to LC that he was not a traditional Chinese father and must adapt to the modern ways of American society. He was generous and flexible.

That attitude changed abruptly in 1964. In a letter to an American confidant, CM, Zi Ming fumed:

> *Out of the clear sky, we got a most ugly (or rather amusing, I say "amusing" because I still can keep my sense of humor so to avoid another ulcer bleeding) from Andrew in which he asked a number of questions about the relation between Julia and me 20 years ago and by implications we both must be very immoral. He wants me to answer this letter*

by return mail. I have answered him by saying that I am putting two long chapters in my autobiography which will be published after my other books are out—and in these chapters I shall put in all the details about my family life before Andrew was born and when he was a small boy.

He then informed CM that he wanted his wife, Julia, and Ida to have no contact with Andrew. No letters. No visits. Nothing. Ida was then living in the United States, and I assume he had written her about this request for the absolute separation of his two children.

He followed this request with an assertion that his two children still living in China loved him intensely. They would be upset by such an accusation. He also questioned whether Andrew's ex-wife was conspiring with his son to accuse him and asked CM to watch carefully their behavior. He was particularly worried that Peter might hear about Andrew's accusation since Peter was also living in the United States.

"To Peter his father is his God and if he hears someone say ugly things about his father, he could become very violent and dangerous. I am really worried." He urged CM not to let Peter have any contact with Andrew or his ex-wife. Zi Ming was terrified Peter would find out that he was his grandson and that his real father, Yaoming, was alive in China. Andrew's questions about 1944 had exploded the calm in the Observatory Road household.

Zi Ming included in this letter an excerpt from a letter he claimed to have sent Andrew, responding to the accusation.

I am glad you have raised these questions. These were among the many things I wished to tell you when I asked you to come meet me in Chicago last year, as I thought you are now old enough to know them. I was disappointed when you refused to come and I had to spend 6 hours at the Chicago airport reading detective stories.

Fortunately, I am planning to go to the States again next summer. Then, we shall have plenty of time to talk together and tell everything you ought to know. The story is very long, too long to tell by letters.

He repeated that he was in the process of writing two long chapters to insert in his autobiography, i.e., *Confessions*, then added: "I do not believe that whatever your father was or did before you were born or when you were a little child should have anything to do with your present or your future."

After reading these letters, I called Andrew that night from my dreary hotel room and asked him about what had happened in 1964. He had never mentioned this confrontation.

"Oh, God. I forgot about that," he replied. He had written his father because his ex-wife had heard gossip about Zi Ming from a group of Chinese graduate students from Taiwan studying in Pittsburgh. Some big scandal. Andrew was on friendly terms with his ex, and they had tried to figure out what it was. Something big. Something immoral. He always knew his family had secrets, and after he spent the summer living in a look-out tower in Idaho and working for the Forest Service, reading William Faulkner's *Absalom, Absalom!*, with its contorted family relationships, he had to write that letter.

He insisted that he had never received a letter back from his father. There was no "I am glad you raised these questions." And he hadn't refused to meet his father at the Chicago airport in 1963. He was living twelve hours away from O'Hare, had a dicey car, and had to work that day. He had explained the reasons to his father in detail. "More lies," he said.

Relations with his father stopped after 1964. He never went to Hong Kong for his funeral in 1970.

Zi Ming worked behind the scenes to assassinate his son's character with his American friends, claiming that Andrew was irresponsible, stupid, without scruples, a second-rate poet, and a failed husband. He used every opportunity to blacken his son's name.

I chose not to tell Andrew on the phone the upsetting details about what his father had done. I was barely able to grasp Zi Ming's ferocity. His father announced that he would have nothing more to do with Andrew and wanted everyone else in the family to reject him.

What choice did Zi Ming have? He was Peter's grandfather, not his father. Zi Ming sacrificed his son with Katherine to maintain his family with Julia and her son, Peter. Ida would have to play her part. She was required to stay loyal to her father.

For a while, I tried to find the two supposedly missing chapters of his *Confessions*. Searching through online archives, I finally gave up. They could have been destroyed, but I doubt they ever existed. Zi Ming had composed a fake letter to Andrew, inserting it in a letter to his friend, CM. He was terrified the truth that he was not Peter's father would come out. Let alone that Julia had been his daughter-in-law.

I may not have found an explanation of Katherine's death, but I had uncovered the ruthless actions of a man who was threatened by what happened in 1944. I also read in a smattering of letters his urgent requests to his American friends to disregard gossip about him when he lived in China. He insisted that both the communists and the Nationalists were up to their old tricks, slandering him. Zi Ming warned LC's wife that the Nationalists in Taiwan created ugly rumors about him as they had done many times before whenever he refused to go along with them.

The truth of these rumors had been behind the bamboo curtain or kept on the island of Taiwan until lurid whispers found their way to Pittsburgh via Chinese students. Hong Kong, Mainland China, and Taiwan were no longer discrete, air-tight spaces. They were leaking information to the United States and not only by way of professional spies. Once again, students threatened the best laid plans of Zi Ming.

In a poignant letter he wrote to LC's wife in 1960, Zi Ming said he had learned that an enemy was spreading the lie that

Andrew had died with his mother. Since she knew this was not true having met Andrew several times in the United States after he had returned for school, he tried to persuade her that the rest of the rumors must be fake, meant to punish him for not joining up with either the communists or Nationalists. He was the man caught in the middle, standing defiantly against Red China and Nationalist Taiwan. He would never cave into their demands. He didn't want his American friends to cave in either and swallow their malicious propaganda.

In 1967, three years before his death, Zi Ming wrote about the Hong Kong riots that pitted the police against communist sympathizers and pro-communist unions, and his fear that Red China would soon overrun Hong Kong. Never secure, he watched as the Cultural Revolution swept across the mainland. There was no word from his two children left behind in China. He feared for their lives. They were tainted, descended from the landlord class.

His fears were not in vain. His daughter, Ifong, would die from starvation during this period and his son, Billie, would barely survive, having discarded his career as a businessman for that of a surgeon working in a miner's clinic.

In 1968, Zi Ming lashed out at Andrew for his support of civil rights and the Black students at the University of Wisconsin-Oshkosh where he taught, accusing his son of being duped by communists. How could someone who had lived through the terrors of the civil war turn on their country and actively participate in the actions of students clearly in league with communists? In response, Andrew wrote a telegram officially disowning Zi Ming.

Increasingly paranoid, Zi Ming died in 1970, never reconciled with his son and loyal to Julia, never revealing the truth of what happened in 1944.

19

Hungry Ghosts

Before Zi Ming and Katherine sailed to the United States for their three-year sojourn, a play called "Summoning of the Spirits" began at sunset near their home on West Lake. Fantastically decorated with colorful hats for specific gods and ghosts to wear, the stage awaited its otherworldly guests, hungry ghosts that roamed courtyards, riverbanks, temples, and crossroads.

The audience feared these dangerous, supernatural beings. To calm them, local children were enlisted as ghostly soldiers serving a ghostly king whose blue face was streaked with scaly lines. On horseback, the children galloped off to visit deserted graves nearby. After lunging at the graves with prongs, they raced back to the stage, their work done. From that point on the audience understood that they could watch the play with ghosts in their midst. For one night, the hungry ghosts promised not to harm them.

On stage the human actors were shadowed by ghosts who had been burnt to death, eaten by tigers, drowned, or murdered. These ghosts, however, were merely a warm-up to the major event of the evening, two Hanging Ghost Dances. In the first dance, a Man Hanging Ghost swung acrobatically in and out of a noose suspended above the stage. He would dangle from different parts of his body: waist, thighs, elbows, knees, plus forty-five additional points, making a total of forty-nine or seven times seven. He played with his death.

Then came the Hanging Woman Dance, awaited with mounting dread. A female ghost dressed in a red jacket and a long black sleeveless coat, her long hair disheveled, strings of paper coins hanging from her neck, wound her way around the stage, tracing the Chinese character for heart, her face hidden from the audience. Tense and fearful, the crowd would cringe the moment she lifted her head and exposed a round chalk-white face with bushy black eyebrows, black eyelids, and crimson lips to sing her haunting lament about how she was forced to hang herself because she was so cruelly abused in her marriage.

Responding to her song, a woman actor who had suffered similar marital torment shouted that she too wanted to commit suicide. The horrifying power of Hanging Woman was her ability to lure other tormented married women into committing suicide. And she did it selfishly. The woman had fallen into the Hanging Woman Ghost's trap since the ghost wanted a substitute for herself in the land of the dead.

Hungry Ghosts were wily and full of tricks. They sought revenge and replacements. They were restless, preying on humans. They demanded tribute. Held in late summer in China and Hong Kong, the Ghost Festival offered paper food, goods, and even ritual wives or husbands to suffering ghosts who had not forgotten what happened to them in life. They lived on, bothering their descendants and unlucky humans straying in their path. Their pain and sorrow demanded recognition and offerings. Many Chinese ghosts were not dangerous, more like spirit guides, but unnatural deaths created dangerous ghosts that called for public appeasement through ritual, song, or story. They demanded sustenance and sympathy, or else humans beware.

For thirty years I couldn't tell the difference between summoning the ghost of Katherine and Katherine summoning me. I was suspended in that dangerous liminal territory, living a double life, searching the past for traces of my mother-in-law's life, and trying to live my life in the present with her son. Often, if truth be told, I felt more alive in her past. Like her dress that I had slid over my body, her life fit. She had never stopped looking at me from her oil portrait on the hallway wall, questioning my actions and prodding me to act. Restless, I felt compelled to keep digging for information. She urged me forward or, more precisely, backwards to unpack her packages, read her letters, scan her photographs, search for her records, or interrogate her son's memories.

Except for the details of her death, she had partly materialized. I had helped to save her from the efforts of Andrew's family to erase her life. Yet, despite my success in snatching her from oblivion, I worried that I hadn't done enough. She wanted more.

I still regularly emailed archives hunting for more of Zi Ming's letters, hoping for some additional facts to enter into my timeline about her life between 1936 and 1944. No matter how hard I searched, I located only trivia, business correspondence and comments on psychological research.

At the end of the summer of 2019, I tried to convince myself that, through a series of odd events, random occurrences and dogged research, Katherine had been restored. Like Zi Ming, Katherine had been rehabilitated.

After frustrating months of no results, I thought about packing up my China files, dismantling the large corkboard in my study stuck with photographs, maps, and notes, and admitting the end of what Andrew had called "my project." I dreaded this step. It was a betrayal. I was also afraid to admit defeat. The warnings of Louise's *Popo* still rang in the back of my mind. Katherine's ghost might be dangerous. If not appeased, she might bring disaster. Unease, that's what I felt, not satisfaction at what I had accomplished, but unease at what I hadn't.

I was a rational person, I told myself. Hadn't I made timelines and searched for evidence? I wasn't some fortune teller at a Taoist temple or my Polish grandmother who told me stories about how the scent of gladiolas always permeated her bedroom when a relative died.

I decided to postpone my decision. Instead, Andrew and I took one last trip to Beijing.

By October 2019, Andrew was eighty, barely able to endure the long flight and demanding work schedule in Beijing, and I was seventy-three, dreading the pollution and crowds in Haidian, the university district. Over the last three years, we had watched the CCP government retrench, limit academic freedom, and insert President Xi's thought into university courses. "Foreign experts," especially from the United States, were no longer needed.

Our students had cooled, their normal openness replaced by suspicion. This last trip was meant to be a good-bye to colleagues more than an exchange of ideas between teachers and students. The luster of American expertise had dulled. What could we possibly offer modern, technologically advanced China? We thought we would be tolerated at best.

It was surprising then when both our classes succeeded beyond our expectations. Students asked questions, read critically, and visited our offices for more conversation, not less. They were funny, outspoken, even affectionate.

It was our faculty friends who had changed. In the past, we had been taken aback by their frank dislike and even ridicule of the government, and we were worried when they were so outspoken at restaurants and coffee houses. In public places, they spoke openly of their anxiety, even horror, at what the future might hold as surveillance, restrictions, and political requirements strangled their daily faculty duties. One friend was panicky, fearful about her child, her future, and the "shameless" way the media had succumbed to publishing propaganda about President Xi.

During this visit, when we met with colleagues, the old camaraderie was gone. They were reserved, polite, and silent about the latest political events. A chilly breeze had swept across our friendships. We had the eerie feeling we had been downgraded to acquaintances.

People we had known, some going back forty years, had retreated behind an invisible barrier. Their decision to recede from their American friends was clear. I could get on a plane and go home. They were home. They had to find a way for themselves, their parents, spouses and children to go forward and survive. Caution was their new mantra.

Every morning at breakfast at our hotel, Andrew and I would pick up *The People's Daily* and *Global Times*, trying to guess how many frontpage articles would be about President Xi. He was always the subject of the main headline with a photograph of him, glowing from his latest triumph.

Filled with propaganda, the Chinese press was reduced to a rag, easily parodied. Less funny were the tall stacks of Xi's latest book, *The Governance of China,* translated into twenty-four languages at the entrance to the Foreign Language Bookstore, a favorite haunt for finding British editions of Chinese literature and history. The store stacked his books ten feet high, front and center. Worse, the holdings of the bookstore had been emptied of anything but light, fluffy books and magazines. President Xi's writings had become the essential *book* to read.

One evening when we left our campus office late, we had to walk to the elevator bypassing a large meeting of the faculty. On a raised platform in front of a wall-size video screen was a middle-aged female political officer lecturing the faculty. On the screen dozens of Chinese flags waved with intermittent blasts of patriotic music. Our older colleagues sat in the front rows, their faces blank, the younger faculty sat behind them, checking their cellphones or correcting assignments. The political officer harangued her audience, her hands gesturing wildly back and forth at the screen and at them. The room reeked of blatant cynicism and unbearable boredom. It felt like a cartoon I saw in Warsaw about communist Poland. An empty chair stood in front of a TV set featuring a communist speaker with flags waving behind the podium. No one was listening.

The weight of that moment was crushing. We exited the campus depressed and claustrophobic. The culture had changed, our friends' lives had changed. We had no future in the new, improved China.

Despite these changes, when we weren't teaching, we repeated familiar off-campus activities, the same lunches at our local restaurant, the same walks around the neighborhood, the same evenings at our hotel, watching the sun set over Tsinghua University. We settled into our old routine complete with two trips to the art district, 798, which each year was becoming more commercial, filling up with tourists, tacky art galleries, and boutique clothing stores.

By 2019, it had deteriorated further. Cutting edge, contemporary Chinese art had fled to smaller galleries in corners of Beijing, Shanghai or abroad to New York or Paris. Kitsch had descended as pablum for the hungry middle classes looking to decorate the walls of their new apartments. Affluence had not made Chinese eager for art. As in the United States, the middle class had a familiar aversion to what disturbed or perplexed their minds. The rich wanted it solely as an investment.

Two nights before we were scheduled to leave Beijing, Andrew had another request for a copy of Zi Ming's *Confessions*. An historian of science, Chen, who had been emailing Andrew about his father, wanted to meet us for dinner with his translator and talk over the possibility of receiving a copy of the manuscript. He felt that Zi Ming's early laboratory techniques needed more explanation, especially his methods to observe embryos accurately over time. This document was certain to settle some debates.

We agreed to meet downstairs in our hotel's restaurant.

The young translator introduced himself with his business card, listing his PhD in the history of science and his appointment at Tsinghua University. Tall and impeccably groomed, he spoke American English without an accent and easily ate, translated, and contributed effortlessly to the dinner conversation. Having studied in England and the United States, he had roamed freely across national borders to acquire his education.

Chen was his opposite. In his fifties, short, nervous, dressed in a dated blue suit, he sat down abruptly, anxious to get an answer from Andrew to his query. He seemed desperate, as if this meeting was his last chance to claim a document that would advance his career.

Instead of answering, Andrew acted completely out of character. He told Chen that there was a gaping hole in the Chinese history of science. He should be researching the role of Chinese women in the development of science. Zi Ming's second wife, Katherine (Lin Qui Fang), his mother, was a case in point. A committed scientist, she had started on a similar trajectory to Chinese women like Madame Wu, the famous physicist who was the first female president of the American Physical Society and winner of the Comstock Prize in Physics from the National Academy of Science.

Madame Wu and Katherine had both attended Suzhou Girls' High School and Nanjing Central University. Their paths continued to cross at Zhejiang University where both worked in research labs. Wu's life had been rediscovered. She was a celebrity woman scientist in the United States. Why not do something similar with Chinese women scientists? Chen could start with Katherine and go from there.

Surprised at the turn in the conversation, Chen didn't know what to say. He sat silent. But I think he had the distinct impression that he had been offered a quid pro quo: research Katherine or you will not receive the *Confessions*. At the end of the meal, he literally raced out of the dining room, the translator rushing to catch up to him.

After his abrupt departure, we went upstairs to our hotel room. Up until now Andrew had let me do the research on Katherine. I kept him informed about what I had found, but it was clearly my project. What had made him change?

"Why not?" my husband said, plopping down on the bed. "Why not?" he repeated. "We're leaving tomorrow. One last fucking chance."

For two months we heard nothing from Chen and weren't surprised. As the pro-democracy moment in Hong Kong heated up, the Chinese government bared its claws. President Xi announced in the *People's Daily* that he would grind the bones of the rioters into dust if they pushed for sovereignty. He meant it. We didn't hear much from our Chinese colleagues and felt an entire chapter of our lives had closed. Once again, Katherine was submerged beneath political power struggles.

A few days before Christmas we drove over to our niece's home in eastern Washington and spent the holidays with her and her eight-year-old son. We cooked, ate, played Legos, and watched children's movies. On Christmas morning before I joined everyone, I checked my phone for texts from my Chicago family. Some were hilarious with talking elves and singing Christmas trees. I noticed an email message from Chen. I was surprised because he always emailed my husband. Not me.

The email was brief. Andrew's mother had died on July 12, 1944.

Excited finally to have an exact date, I emailed back right away to thank him. Then I thought for a moment. How did he know the precise date? I emailed him again asking about the source of the information. Was it a death certificate, a notice in the newspaper, a reference in a scientific note?

Soon, another email appeared.

Chen wrote that he had found "something" and did not want Andrew to be angry. In his strained English, he added that since Andrew was 80, he wanted me to decide what to do with the information. He would not be the messenger. If I decided to pass on the information, then "you can tell him and tell him keep emotion stability."

Through an online search with Katherine's Chinese name, he had discovered a Shanghai newspaper published on November 22, 1946, that created "a great sensation." It was "extremely negative" about Zi Ming. Its headline went across the top of the front page in large, bold, Chinese characters.

郭任遠亂倫姦媳逐子

Roughly translated it said: 'Guo Committed Incest with Daughter-in-law and Drove Out Son.' The article described how in February 1944 when Zi Ming was in a Chongqing hospital for a flare up of a gastric ulcer, he had been treated by a woman doctor, Liu Daiyu (Julia's Chinese name). They soon started a secret affair. A few months later Lin Qui Fang (Katherine) arrived in Chongqing from Shanghai, traveling with their son, Andrew, intending to rejoin Zi Ming. Within a few days Zi Ming announced that Qui Fang had died from a heart attack. "She was found dead in the morning 12 July 1944."

Chen ended his email with the sentence, "I really worry that Andrew would be angry with that information, and he would not continue to help me on my research."

Clearly, Chen thought that Andrew would be furious to find out that his father had an affair with a woman doctor before his mother had rejoined his father in Chongqing. Chen didn't know that Liu Daiyu was Julia, the woman who was Andrew's sister-in-law and had raised him as his stepmother.

Worse, Julia's elaborate lie about how Katherine suffered from tuberculosis over a protracted period was refuted by Chen's information. I saw no reason to tell Chen that invented explanation for Katherine's death and only replied that I was grateful to have the exact date of her death and confirmation that she had died suddenly and why. I reassured Chen that my husband already knew about Dr. Liu, but I left out that Julia had insisted her relationship with Zi Ming had started after Katherine had died and her own husband, Yaoming, had fled their villa in Chongqing. According to her story, she and Zi Ming were the "only ones left."

I was still puzzled, however. If Zi Ming and Julia knew exactly when and how Katherine had died, why did they need to keep it quiet, never telling Andrew? A heart attack was not a motive for secrecy. Was this part of the mysterious information that was to be included in the two missing chapters of *Confessions*?

Reading the email over again, I sensed that Chen had omitted crucial information from his summary of the 1946 article. For one, I wondered who would write such an article for a Shanghai newspaper. It made no sense. Why was this news? Something was wrong. I had to receive a translation of the entire article and a copy of the original Chinese newspaper article. Chen was clearly upset that the article might jeopardize his career. What else had he left out because Andrew might be angry?

I was at Chen's mercy. He might never email me back or agree to cooperate. How far could I push him?

I decided to email Chen right away and reassure him in several different ways that Andrew had known for years about Dr. Liu. More importantly, Andrew was very grateful that the date and reason for his mother's death was finally known. I thanked him profusely for his help. I urged him to send a scan of the original Chinese article and, if possible, a complete translation. Assuming this request would take some time, I went to help fix the Christmas dinner.

Cutting up cucumbers for the salad, I keep thinking how important it was that I get a copy of the Chinese newspaper article. I needed it because I was convinced that Chen had held back information. He was censoring his translation. We had several Chinese friends who we knew would be eager to help, and they were excellent translators. If I could only receive a scan of the newspaper article, I could pursue my own translation.

Sitting at the dinner table eating a piece of pecan pie, my stomach was doing flips.

Oblivious, Andrew was making faces with our niece's eight-year-old son, laughing as each stretched mouth, bulging eyes and contorted tongue created another monster. Rarely spontaneous around children, Andrew seemed free of his past at last. I told myself to savor the moment. Isn't this enough? I could hear my mother saying to me, "Be careful what you wish for, you might get it."

When my phone beeped, I jumped.

"Are you okay?" my niece asked.

"A little woozy," I replied. "Maybe I'll take a little rest."

I glanced quickly at my phone and checked to see if Chen had sent me anything.

He had been playing his own game with me like I had with him.

He had fed me a piece of the article to see how I would react. Based on my response, he sent another email with several attachments, a scan of the newspaper article, a Chinese transcription of the text, and a translation of the article.

I hadn't expected it so soon. I needed time to read what he had sent. After finishing my pie and helping with the dishes, I told Andrew and my niece that I was going to lie down for a half hour or so. Closing the door to the guestroom, my hands started to shake. Had these years of looking for Katherine come down to this moment?

The scan reproduced a long article punctuated by photographs of three women. From the poor reproduction, I could not tell who they were.

The source of the news about Zi Ming and Julia was her husband, Yaoming. The Shanghai newspaper had reprinted a letter that Yaoming had sent to his extended family in Shanghai. In it he accused his father of horrible crimes. He accused his father of stealing his wife, Julia, thereby committing incest, and having hidden this relationship from him for two years. When Yaoming discovered the truth, he agonized over what had happened since he claimed he truly loved his wife. But when he found out that his father and wife were planning to escape to the United States with his son, he made the decision to expose his father to his Shanghai relatives and shame the couple. Zi Ming's private life had been paraded in a newspaper complete with photographs of his first wife, Katherine, and Julia.

There was more. Not only did Yaoming accuse his father of incest, he also accused him of embezzling public funds from the Institute of Psychology and Physiology of China in Chongqing that Zi Ming headed when he returned to China in 1940 with Katherine and Andrew. Trusted scholars and senior government officials were named to collaborate these charges.

Then came the worst accusation. Yaoming denounced his father as a murderer. Katherine had been rejected by Zi Ming when she returned to Chongqing with Andrew since his father "had already committed adultery at that time and had abandoned the old and fell in love with the new." The day after Katherine's arrival, she and Zi Ming became "enemies." Their relationship destroyed, there was not "one moment of peace."

On the morning of July 12, 1944, Katherine's body was found, and horrified friends came to Zi Ming's home to ask what happened. To some Zi Ming explained that Katherine had been "unfaithful and committed suicide because she could not bear the reproach of her conscience." To others, he said, "her heart was so bad she could not be saved." Once they compared notes, Yaoming and family friends did not believe what Zi Ming said. They felt Zi Ming had murdered Katherine. Also, Yaoming identified the family friends: Xu Yuanlong, Wu Nanxuan, and Zhu Yicheng. Together, they did not have enough evidence to go to the police, but they believed in Zi Ming's guilt.

The letter ended with a damning paragraph. Defending his decision to publicly accuse his father, Yaoming explained that his father had on several occasions threatened his life. He had caused agony to Andrew by killing his mother. He had embezzled funds. He had committed adultery. Yaoming had no choice but to write to his family denouncing his father's "bestiality." He also added that he needed to protect his young son, Peter, from possible harm.

How the letter made its way into the newspaper was not clear.

Numb, I sat down on the bed, staring at the email. I wished I had never read it. I wanted to delete it. I didn't want to tell my husband what was in it. I wanted to cover it up. I wanted to lie.

I had already chosen not to tell him about the demeaning comments his father had made about him after Andrew questioned what had happened between Zi Ming and Julia in 1944. He already believed in his heart that Julia had killed his mother. This secret fear carried by a child to adulthood now had a more frightening murderer, his father. How would this letter written by his half-brother, Yaoming, change his life? Do we really need to know the truth about our family? Aren't lies necessary?

I didn't know what to do. No one had ever protected Andrew. His family simply wanted to suppress the truth, flee from these accusations, and live out their lives in a parallel dimension without consequences, free of their crimes.

The scope of their deceit staggered me. I reread the translated article over and over again, each time recalibrating my conversations with Julia and Ida, remembering their evasions. I couldn't pry myself loose from the article. Now I understood Chen's warning. What would an 80-year-old do when he learned that his father was the prime suspect in the murder of his mother?

Sitting alone in the guest bedroom, I regretted my decision to unravel the mystery of Katherine's death. Why hadn't I left it alone? Why didn't we relax on our last trip to Beijing, say good-bye to friends and leave?

In self-defense, I started to question everything in the letter. What if Yaoming was lying? How could I be certain that what he was saying happened? Was he seeking revenge or justice? Or both?

Part of me didn't want to believe the article. But the stated names of family friends and government officials who had witnessed the events made Yaoming's account credible. Zi Ming's family was wealthy and connected to government leaders and the intelligentsia. Yaoming had listed public figures as witnesses to his account that could verify the accusations. And, more to the point, four months after Yaoming's letter appeared in print, Zi Ming fled Shanghai and relocated to Hong Kong, accompanied by Julia, his daughter-in-law, Peter, his grandson, and Andrew.

I decided not to decide. Not then, not yet. I would say nothing until we returned home after the holidays. I needed more time to think.

I went through the rest of our visit like a zombie, distracted, my equilibrium gone.

During my sleepless nights away from home, I realized that both Julia and Ida must have known about the letter as did all of Andrew's relatives in China, the grandparents, myriad aunts, uncles, and cousins that remained there. This letter had shaped Andrew's life.

The horrible deed that his brother, Yaoming, had committed was not to sleep with a servant in Chongqing but to write a *J'Accuse* letter that was reprinted in a Shanghai newspaper. By writing the letter, Yaoming had acted to save his son, Peter, but the opposite had occurred. Instead, when Zi Ming fled to Hong Kong, Yaoming lost his son. In the British Crown colony, Peter was folded into an invented family as Zi Ming's child. Not only had Zi Ming seduced his son's wife, he had stolen his son's child.

Yaoming wanted revenge, but when it came, it was bitter-sweet. His letter might have even precipitated his father's rash action to flee to Hong Kong in 1947 where Zi Ming hid below the radar from family and friends until the mid-1950s. War gave Zi Ming a buffer from his past, an excuse to flee China. And the Cold War with Red China had built a bamboo curtain between him and his accusers. Zi Ming could also claim that the stories carried from Taiwan to the United States by Chinese graduate students were malicious gossip. He was the victim, the man in between two enemies, the KMT and the CCP. He was innocent. Zi Ming was a master of lies.

In the middle of the night, listening to my husband's steady breathing while he was sound asleep after an evening of food, board games, and an eight-year-old's knock-knock jokes, I decided I had to get another translation of the letter. Could Chen's translation have left out other crucial information? That was my strategy. Wait. Buy some time. Wait for another translation from a trusted friend.

I couldn't face telling Andrew what I had read. One thing I felt for certain: at the end of her life, Katherine was no longer a devoted, compliant wife. In July of 1944, she became Zi Ming's enemy, her rage total.

She was a Hungry Ghost, summoning with the authority of the dead to expose the past and account for wrongs. I knew for certain Zi Ming betrayed her. But had he killed her? I was holding back from denouncing Andrew's father. I needed a trustworthy translation of Yaoming's letter before I would talk with my husband.

His mother could be a Hanging Woman, wronged in marriage who escaped through suicide. That exposure would shame Zi Ming as an abuser. Was that the truth she wanted told? Or was she murdered in mid-life by a scheming husband, her rage unappeased?

I had no answers. I simply couldn't tell Andrew. Not now. And maybe never.

20

February 8 – April 5, 1944

At a wide stretch near Suicheng, a crazed, Nanjing professor, dragging a cart of books, let Andrew ride on top of his trove of ancient treasures, the *Book of Changes*, *The Annotations to Spring and Autumn*, and *The Records of the Historian*. His wild hair hanging over his greasy face, he stopped to lecture in the middle of the road as if standing in front of a university auditorium packed with his students. Li Min kept walking. Climbing down from the cart, my boy stood transfixed, the freezing air frosting his tangled hair. I hated this man whose madness would destroy us; his ride necessary for my boy whose body was racked by cold. Drawing my son inside my jacket, we waited for the show to end. He was our last hope against the driving winds that swept across the road, unmerciful, malicious.

Taking an imaginary tablet from his overcoat, the scholar shouted to the gathering crowd, "Exhibit 1: the high schools and universities are destroyed.

Exhibit 2: Japanese soldiers break into our research laboratories, smashing every glass beaker and vial, firing at the burners, centrifuge and spectrometers, blowing to bits every machine."

Throwing his tablet on the ground, he stamped his feet, his arrogance growing like a storm inside him.

"Listen carefully," he commanded the gathering crowd.

"Conclusion: The Japanese are killing the Chinese reverence for education. The Japanese are crushing the foundation of the republic, slaughtering students, teachers and educational leaders."

He grabbed a young peasant who had stopped to gawk and shook him.

"Rejoice that the Generalissimo's soldiers hunt the Japanese. *Take No Prisoners! No Mercy! You in the front row, LOUDER!*"

My son laughed with the other children pointing at the funny man waving his hands and twisting his arms into snakes while his fingers hissed.

Crazed, the scholar swept his hair back and raised his voice, calling down the wrath of the gods to a row of farmers.

"*There is no united China!* Chinese communist ideas are infecting our students. Communist activists infiltrate our universities, causing riots and threatening faculty. Chinese communists seize Chinese factories, killing owners and managers. Communists publish propaganda and lies. Only the Generalissimo with foreign money can rebuild China and rid the country of Japanese dwarfs and communist vermin."

A ring of refugees stared, then laughed. Children mocked the dancing man. A one-person street fair on the edge of chaos.

One farmer strode forward and punched the professor in the mouth. The crowd grew silent. The man punched again harder, flinging the professor on a bank of rocks. Unfazed, the professor drew himself up, straightened his clothes, and from inside the lining of his tattered beret, pulled out a letter that he announced would be presented to the Generalissimo once he arrived at the fortified capital in Chongqing. In a falsetto voice, he read the letter out loud.

> *We are forced to defend our very existence and our way of life! Enemies are scattered and hidden in our own house ready to strike at any time under any circumstance. Servants and relatives betray us. They run to the communists or collaborate with the Japanese. The communists call*

themselves our saviors, killing our intellectuals and business leaders, their propaganda claiming the Generalissimo with the United States of America imposed **a fascist reign of terror. A lie!** *The Japanese call themselves our saviors, scrubbing clean decadent and dying China, cleansing the country of warlords, communists, and foreign imperialists until the country can emerge a partner of the Rising Sun, a new Asia taking its rightful place on the global stage!*
Insanity!
Kill them all!
Kill the communists!
Kill the Japanese!

His blackened fingers smearing the characters into a sooty mess, the agitated scholar waved the letter in his attacker's face. The angry farmer grabbed the letter, threw the professor on the ground, and kicked him in the face. A dull thud like kicking dough.

I grabbed my son's hand, shouting "Run."

The excited crowd drew near as the man kicked again, each thud burning my ears.

Close to Xi'an, we stopped at an abandoned village where rumors of war passed from mouth to mouth. In an empty threshing barn, farmers told how peasant women were jumping into wells when the Japanese came to seize grain and oxen. For centuries warlords and bandits had stolen their food, raping women, but Japanese soldiers came to dishonor and destroy their families, raping young women, old women, children, even the dead, ripping apart the shared bonds of the villagers. The Imperial Army soldiers scorched the earth, leaving nothing except people who wished they were dead.

The nightmare rumors about a massacre at Nanjing were retold at villages we hurried past. The fleeing peasants spoke of a place where the farmers shot their wives and daughters before the Japanese soldiers arrived, then grabbed their hoes and left to join the communist guerrillas. At night, stirring their fires, the peasants spoke only of revenge. When the Generalissimo's soldiers came for food, the farmers asked for guns. When the soldiers refused, they killed them and took their arms. They talked of nothing but revenge. *Kill the Japanese for defiling the village!*

I could sense how the stories made the farmers grow strong. Each telling made them more determined to kill. They told of villages where the communists gave them arms. They wanted revenge. Hate was an elixir, distilling their years of abuse beneath the tax collector's demands, the landlord's exploitation, the KMT's kidnapping of their sons, and the Japanese soldier's ferocious cruelty.

Along the road, Li Min listened, her eyes glimmering with excitement. The girl bartered with the farmers, trading the Mauser for rice and bean curd. Sitting close to their fire, she learned about the loess caves in the north stacked with weapons. Once, when she returned to where we sat, she asked, "tell me again. Why do you go to Chongqing?"

Once more, I told her about my husband who waited in a villa close to the Generalissimo. She asked if he had guns.

"He is surrounded by guns." He had written me that the interior capital was defended by anti-aircraft artillery, machine-gun nests, military troops, and private militias. Li Min paid attention to my words, asking about the Chinese and American pilots fighting. How many Japanese are they killing? She wanted numbers.

The farmers talked through the night, tossing rough words, hardening their anger into revolutionary acts. In the morning they were gone. They had decided to walk north to Ya'an and join the Communist guerrillas.

Holding my boy's hand, I hesitated. If we hurried, we might catch them.

My son looked at me. He could sense my indecision. He pulled me toward the retreating shapes in the snow.

My husband waited. My son's father waited. I left the girl and went back to the road. The girl followed.

Faces appeared on the stacked corn husks. My mother's crumbling eyes when she heard that her husband had been executed by the warlord. My amah's inquisitive look when I dressed in my school uniform, combed my hair, and left to walk to the government building where my father had been held. My father's serene expression on his head dangling from the light pole.

Squatting in the back of the truck, I shut my eyes, willing their faces away. The road to Chongqing was peopled by too many ghosts.

Mercifully, the faces receded into the peeling, yellow shells. My son slept soundly; his body no longer shaken by winter ice and gun shots. He needed sleep, the sleep of a child without war's hunting.

A smelly, stained canvas was stretched over the back of the truck to prevent people from seeing the cabbage, onions, and tins of cooking oil hidden beneath piles of corn and straw. The dampness of mold covered our hair, skin, and clothes. We inhaled the stink.

The ride had cost one gold coin.

We had not left the truck for hours. The driver was afraid to stop. There were too many people on the road. He needed to get out and check the sputtering engine and the half-empty petrol can. He was afraid and chanted to the Five Thunder gods as he touched the golden charm hanging from the rearview mirror. The lurching engine pitched us back and forth.

The ride was our savior.

Mountains rose on both sides of the narrow road. Snowy crags on jagged peaks thrust sharply into the sky. Scattered pines grew in cracks like forgotten soldiers waiting for the Yellow Emperor. These mountains were as old as China. Immortals were said to dwell within the granite caves pitched on the vertical rock faces. Legends described how the first emperors had built temples on inaccessible summits to honor these celestials, offering sacrificial animals to maintain balance in the middle kingdom. Even in the midst of war, solitary pilgrims still chanced the narrow paths to ask hermits and priests about their hidden future. Many fell thousands of feet to their death.

The truck drove slowly along the base of sacred Huashan. Li Min sat in front close to the driver, a stocky man whose chin stuck out like a pointed stick. He wanted the girl by his side. She was his good luck.

After weeks of walking, the truck appeared; without it we would have died in the mountains. In a small town where we joined refugees searching for food, the driver had stopped to get petrol. A desperate farmer tried to steal his near empty jerrycan for barter. As they wrestled, the petrol can fell. Seeing her chance, Li Min charged out of the gathering crowd and kicked the thief behind his knees. When the thief lost his balance, the driver punched him hard in the face.

The girl screamed, "Take us with you."

"Only you," he replied, staring at me, a filthy woman with a boy, standing next to her.

"She can pay," Li Min pleaded, wrapping her arms around me.

"You, only you," he said, pointing at the girl. "You are a spirit sent down from the sacred mountain, not a hungry ghost like that woman beside you.

A shrewd bargainer, Li Min exchanged my gold coin for a ride. The driver forgot his fear. He waved us into the truck, the girl upfront, at his side, and shoved me and my son in back between piles of straw and cornhusks.

We burrowed beneath the straw, our feet covered in sores, our lips cracked and broken. In a few minutes, my child fell asleep from the warmth of the engine. We had not been warm for months.

On the road, an old woman had told me that she could see the cold. She had watched it walk next to a child and seize him. The cold hovered over the boy, then bite hard, swallowing chunks of heat until the child's flesh hardened into a shell. She had seen farmers turn into cold logs and horses into blocks of ice. Cold tossed a beautiful girl on a frozen field and held her until her lips turned blue, her dead eyes questioning the sky.

In the back of the truck, I shoved straw around my son, tucking it under his legs and over his feet. I nestled close to him, his back curved near my heart.

"We will find your father," I whispered, my voice quivering.

Under the noise of the engine, I could hear the driver talking with Li Min. Many of his words were unknown to me, his dialect thick with jokes and curses. I had grown up in Suzhou, a Chinese paradise of canals and moon bridges, the Venice of the East. A world destroyed, a fading image on a movie screen. On the road I was forced to walk beside rickshaw pullers, cotton-mill workers, silk spinners, house servants, and farmers. I learned their words, the rhythms of speech.

Through a crack I could see the driver. He clung to Li Min, draping his arm on her frail shoulders. He might be one of those men who wanted young girls. His black hair plastered with clods of mud, he talked freely with the girl, not tripping over his words as he did with me. Curled inside his Luoyang speech were sounds I grasped too slowly. Struggling, I made signs with my hands that made him laugh.

He did not want me close to him. Only Li Min.

The truck finally stopped at a gutted Taoist temple, its fierce painted gods broken, the tiger guardian toppled at the gate. We unpacked quickly, the driver finding a good place to keep an eye on the truck. He started a fire. From inside a wooden case, he brought out a Mauser, its long, thin barrel set on a metal box. It was the dead scholar's gun.

"Find a place," he pointed at me with the gun, gesturing to move away. He pulled Li Min to his side. "The refugees bring sickness to this temple. The woman is sick."

Her mouth hidden by a torn scarf, Li Min whispered, her eyes avoiding me.

In the damp temple, I found a discarded carpet.

"Here," I said to my boy, pushing the carpet up against the wall and arranging a bed of straw. The temple filled with more refugees, but no one came close to us, their candles conjuring shadows in the dark. When I looked up, I understood. The carpet had been tossed below a painting of the Jade Emperor, defaced with excrement. The tribute vessels for flowers, fruit, candles, and incense were shattered.

An old man glanced at me, his wagging fingers warning me to move away.

I did not budge from the desecrated spot. The carpet would protect us from the damp floor. When did the Jade Emperor ever help my son and keep him warm? Was the Jade Emperor stronger than the stalking cold? What had I done to bring this horror on my family? Men, not gods, caused war. I wanted to shake the old man. There was no Jade Emperor.

My parents had forbidden me to read the Daozang books about Hua mountain or *The Emperor's Four Classics* with its beliefs in secret talismans that unlocked the spirit world. My father laughed at the old beliefs in immortality. Our home had no Taoist paintings of the mythical ancient emperor or those early gods who could stop demons or Wahuang who created the first men from the clay of the Yellow River.

At a distance, the driver sat near the fire with Li Min, a cigarette dangling from the side of his mouth. He jumped when a young man stood by the truck, sniffing like a dog. Cursing, he grabbed the gun, ran outside, and chased him away. Circling his truck, he patted his gun. Before he returned, he stared at the sculptures at the temple door, two fierce guardians, their task to chase away evil demons. When he sat back down, he yanked Li Min's arm. "Speak to the eight immortals," he commanded. "We are in their temple, my *tongji*, my young spirit talker. Speak to the immortal that turns stones into gold."

Afraid, Li Min froze. He yanked at her again. "Speak."

Something had happened to make the driver doubt her power. He had tired of his lucky charm to help bring his truck to the wealthy merchant in Xi'an. He wanted more. He wanted a shaman to guide him to riches like gold bells and jade amulets. Yelling, he mocked her as if she was already dead. He shook his gun in her face. "You are too clever. If there is a gun, there are bullets. You give me one gold coin like a witch. Where is more gold? Where are bullets?"

As if on command, Li Min rolled back her eyes; her body recoiled, her arm breaking his hold. She stood up, beseeching the desecrated image of the Jade Emperor, her voice transformed, a rhythmic rush of strange syllables. In a trance, she contorted her body, lifting one foot, then sweeping her arms as if reaching. She walked back and forth searching, then stood stiff, her body shaking. After minutes of what seemed excruciating pain, she collapsed.

The driver became quiet. He did not move. From his face you could tell he was puzzled. Was this magic or fakery? Li Min's eyes remained closed, her face rigid. For an hour he was afraid to go near her and kept away, tending a small fire and chewing on his cigarette butt. When she finally moved, he waited, watching her until she opened her eyes. He stared at her and then beckoned, offering food.

My boy twisted from my side and sat down next to Li Min, pestering her to twirl again.

"Quiet," the driver barked. "Or, you will have no food."

"You, come," he growled at me, as if he regretted a single morsel wasted on my life.

In silence, we squatted, sharing strips of bean curd.

From inside his pocket, the driver brought out a dented can of stew he had bought months ago from a British soldier.

The driver blew smoke in the fire. "He wanted money for this can of turnips and beef. He wanted money for a prostitute. Hours later when the British soldier died, he became a hungry ghost, wandering China." He opened the tin can balanced on his knee. "A whore, for this," he laughed, holding out the opened can.

He motioned, "Come closer boy."

"He is sick," I cautioned, my voice tense and grating.

Even beneath my rags, the driver could tell I was sick, not the boy. For days, I had coughed at night, covering my face to protect my son.

He handed my child two pieces of slimy turnip. Placing his hand on my boy's head, he told stories about how the ancient spirits could destroy evil in the world, how the Celestial Dog and the Transcendent Guardian who protected the Jade Emperor could devour demons that tormented human beings. How the Celestial Masters dwelling on the mountain could fly and change shape, helping humans to fight off enemies. My boy listened in amazement. His face glowed by the fire, delighting in the tales of the Yellow Emperor who could summon the eagle-faced Thunder God to punish bad men.

When my amah ironed my school uniform, she told wonderous tales of Hua Mountain, the magic herbs and sacred diagram carved on a hidden rock face, the fermented wines that nourished the spirits, and the tiger butterflies that guided pilgrims up the dangerous slopes to visit shamans and gain immortality. My amah died from a stray bullet of a British soldier fighting the Japanese in Shanghai. Her final gift: her clothes, a gift of disguise.

"We are close to Xi'an," the driver said. "If the mountain gods bless our journey, the truck's engine will last. But we must find more petrol."

He ordered the girl to prove her power and wander among the refugees to find the people from the east. A broken car sat at the temple entrance. Two trucks were parked in a grove of trees with a guard. If she was close to the gods, she would find more petrol.

Hours later she came back and sat down, tucking her legs under her. Her hair was cut short with straight bangs that made her look older. A bright red scarf was tied around her neck, scrubbed clean.

She leaned close to me and whispered, "Give me the other gold coin," pointing to my collar. One can of petrol for one gold coin.

The girl was clever, aware of my secrets while my mind was dulled by cold. She waited patiently as I ripped the seam and slipped out the coin.

She took it and said nothing. Her steps deliberate, she walked back into the temple darkness, reemerging with a woman carrying a large petrol can.

"It is enough," said the driver. "The gods have blessed us."

I took my son's hand and walked outside the temple. My amah would have told me to flee and find another way to Xi'an; the girl could be a *jiangshi,* planning to kill my son to steal his *yang,* the sun power in his body.

Night snow was falling on the dragon statue, its snaking spine, and ferocious, tongue licking the air. The milky sky hung low, hiding the mountain peaks. The wind began to howl, shaking the carts lined close to the gate. Snow fell on a crumbling rock wall, almost covering the face of a dead woman, her naked bound feet sticking out of her stiff black pants, her golden lotus shoes stolen. Other dead were stacked against the temple walls. Too many dead to count.

"We must stay together," I whispered to my son.

He tugged against me.

"You must listen," I repeated.

"Cold," he said, pulling harder, his broken fingernails digging into my palm. He yanked free and ran back inside.

In five days, we arrived at the ancient city of Xi'an, its thick Ming walls a protection against the thousands of refugees demanding entry. Impatient, the driver pushed his truck through the crowd, the gears crunching. He was in a hurry to get his money, but first he had to pass through the military area where nationalist soldiers checked trucks entering.

The driver had a plan. He barked at us to sit in front with Li Min. The closer the truck came to the gate, the more he was forced to slow down and edge through refugees squatting outside the city gates. He blasted his horn at a group of women with young children on their backs who stood in line waiting for a man to scoop gruel from a wooden bucket into their bowls. The driver nearly ran over two wounded soldiers sprawled on the ground who had been denied entry. They refused to move until the driver threatened to run them over.

"Act like family. Don't speak," he snapped, as we neared the outer wall. A bribed guard read his papers and waved the truck through the checkpoint at the east gate.

The tunnel through the thick city walls felt like a dark, suffocating cave. My trembling son panicked. He scrambled to get out of the truck, climbing over Li Min. She grabbed him, pushing down. "No!" she screamed. The driver turned around and hit him hard on the top of his head. He curled into a ball in my arms. I would never let him touch my son again. I would kill him first.

Inside the city, the driver drove the narrow streets bordered with stone walls and crammed with trucks and soldiers. Hawkers carried bags of sweet potatoes on shoulder poles, lighted shops displayed steaming lamb on sticks, hotel steps overflowed with officers in pressed uniforms, beautiful women hanging onto their arms.

Xi'an, the ancient capital of the Zhou dynasty had made a pact 3,000 years ago with the sky god to govern, and now it had made a new pact with the Generalissimo to create an island of plenty with machine guns to keep out the wounded and starving.

Turning a corner, the driver let out a stream of curses. They passed a three-story station where a police officer whipped a row of men in shackles. The driver sped past. "They betray for money. They catch everyone."

The police worked with the Generalissimo's agents hunting for communist spies that had infiltrated the city. Both the innocent and the guilty were picked up, beaten and jailed. The driver smoked and spit, hunching his shoulders, his knuckles white on the steering wheel.

He glared at me. "Unlucky," he spat.

"There," he said, pointing down a side street. Defended by a private militia, the merchant's warehouse stood like a brick wall.

Once there, the driver would barter me for trinkets and exchange my son for gold. The truck was carrying us to slavery.

I had to act. I would never let go of my son.

As if the war was not happening, a folk opera troupe appeared in the middle of the street, a moving theater with musicians striking cymbals, clicking cylindrical wood sticks, and trilling flutes. When an actor dressed in a brilliant red gown gave a piercing shout, the driver stopped the truck and gawked as if the performer was speaking to him.

I had only one chance. I flipped the door latch, grabbed my son, and jumped out, melting into the crowd of spectators. Two women laughed, trying to pull me into a store selling catties of roasted walnuts, fried donuts, and spun sugar. The smells intoxicated me. Joss sticks and deep red kites hung in clumps from stall ceilings, preparations for the Qingming Festival. Mesmerized, Andrew snatched a walnut as I dragged him back to the crowd.

Out of nowhere, Li Min appeared next to me, her eyes as big as moons.

"Bad man," she said, stealing a stick of spun sugar.

We ran through the throng past stacks of loquats piled high, rows of ducks hanging from wires, and steamed buns swinging in wicker baskets. Above a market stall, a beautiful acrobat playing Jade Maiden sang songs that drifted *high above fairy isles*. She floated on shoulders of fellow dancers next to the Dragon King, his tongue bright red, his crimson scales flashing.

The sound of a single erhu vibrated down an alleyway.

"Here," shouted Li Min. The twisted street brought us to a deserted plaza where a tall Christian church barred our way; a torn poster with large, smeared red characters swung above its wooden entrance.

避难所

Binan suo. Sanctuary.

We had nowhere else to run.

"There," she urged, pointing to the large doors. "Go. They can help find your husband. I head north to Yan'an caves."

In this strange land, I practice disappearing. The war only forced me to see it more clearly without the lie of longevity, the peasant's truth finally thrust on my silken shoulders. Was I worth a day's portion of rice? Li Min gone before I turned my head to see her leave. No parting. You alone know her name.

You alone gave me shelter.

My story you scribbled in notes placed in a folio of hundreds of stories, a way station of lives, their days scratched on paper after sanctuary was reached. And then where did we go? Did we find resurrection, death, rescue, or execution? When I leave here with my son what will happened to my story? What will happen to us?

I am not smoke. I am less than smoke. I am invisible.

21

An Offering

After Christmas, on the plane flying home, I had only one thought, I needed to contact Jin, a Chinese friend. I had to trust someone who would not bend the truth in the translation of Yaoming's letter. When Jin was in graduate school at Northwestern, she had visited us on Guemes Island, doing research for her dissertation on Andrew's poetry. Since then, she had stayed with us often, and when she returned to Beijing, we had spent evenings out with her, eating, and visiting the sacred geometry of the Temple of Heaven, her favorite place. I felt that she would understand the need not to censor any details, no matter how painful.

Three weeks later I received her translation. She had added a note telling me how upset she was, especially since she went to college at Fudan University, often walking past the iconic White House. She had visited the university's history museum and read the glowing accounts of Zi Ming and what he had done for the field of psychology at the university. Before reading the reprinted letter in the newspaper, she used to feel that his rehabilitation was a sign of how China was no longer provincial, stuck in a narrow ideology. Carefully constructed by the CCP, the rehabilitated Zi Ming was blown apart by the letter. The corroborating names of several well-known Chinese scholars and politicians had convinced Jin that Yaoming was telling the truth. The great man was the great monster. Anything we needed, anything at all, she would continue to help.

After comparing her translation with Chen's, I was reassured that the bulk of the letter was the same except for one key difference. In Jin's version, Yaoming claimed that his father, Zi Ming, had become "sexually involved with his student" when he was President of Zhejiang University in Hangzhou between 1933 and 1936. At that point, Yaoming was living on West Lake with his father, his mother, Cai, and their other children, Bill, Ida, and Ifong. In 1936, much to his and his family's shock, Zi Ming took his "illicit mistress" with him to the United States and abandoned his family, "leaving us behind with no one to take care of us." Fortunately, a family friend took pity, making certain they were "fed and sheltered."

Beverly, the historian of science, had uncovered similar 1935 accusations against Zi Ming when he was president of Zhejiang University. Students had denounced him as having taken a concubine and seduced female students. If Katherine was his mistress, then Zi Ming must have persuaded her to leave China somehow and given her reasons why he left his family behind. Is that why Katherine was so upset about returning to China?

There was another possibility. Katherine's childhood friend, Madame Wu, in a set of interviews late in her life, called Katherine the wife of Zi Ming. And nowhere in any of Katherine's correspondence did she or anyone else stray from calling her Zi Ming's wife. Had Zi Ming deceived Katherine by telling her he had a divorce decree from Cai, his first wife? By 1930, the divorce laws in China had changed. It was possible under the new Civil Code for a husband and wife to gain a divorce by mutual consent. All that was required was their written statement witnessed by two adults. Zi Ming could have convinced his first wife to sign such a decree. Was that why Ida thought her mother was "a stupid woman?"

Whether they were legally married or not, their relationship in the United States was under extreme strain. In a 1938 letter to LC, the American psychologist, Zi Ming reacted angrily to the news of Katherine's pregnancy, stating he "hated" what had happened. He had other plans for their union. He wanted a devoted research assistant by his side in the laboratory, not a mother of another child. He introduced Katherine to his American friends as his assistant, a fellow scientist, a young and beautiful wife, cultured, from a distinguished family who owned extensive ancestral lands. His projected life with Katherine had no room for mundane motherhood. His modern marriage was based on revolutionary love between two independent and equal partners who had freely chosen each other. Motherhood complicated everything.

Lu Xun had predicted in his writings that modern marriage in China was a thin veneer of liberation over an intractable past of traditional roles for men and women, husbands and wives. Katherine could be his modern "wife," but modern "mothers" were an oxymoron. Increasingly distant after the birth of Andrew, Zi Ming focused on his work in the United States, letting his relationship to Katherine ossify.

On the couple's way back to China in 1939, they had stopped in Shanghai and met Katherine's mother. In a letter to Mrs. Withington, Katherine reported on how this was the first chance her mother had to hold her grandson. The reunion seemed so ordinary I never questioned the relationships. Was Katherine's description of that moment ambiguous, the reality of her status hidden from Mrs. Withington? Could Katherine have been lying throughout her correspondence to her American friends?

Jin's translation of Yaoming's letter generated a thousand questions, none of which I seemed to be able to answer.

Would a woman from Katherine's social position become a concubine or a traditional second wife? It was possible since the concept of marriage to many Chinese men of Zi Ming's age was elastic, bending to new desires or demands.

Chen's earlier translation of Yaoming's letter had censored Katherine's status.

In his translation, Chen had referred to Andrew's mother as the second wife of Zi Ming, another ambiguous phrase. He had altered Yaoming's accusation that his father had seduced one of his students and taken his young mistress to the United States. Chen had tried to prevent Andrew from knowing his mother was a mistress not a wife, even though he did not mistranslate the speculation that the probable murderer of Andrew's mother was his father.

Did he think this additional accusation was worse than murder? Or did he think that the two combined, that his father had murdered his mother, and his mother was never married to his father, were so disturbing as to destroy Andrew?

Jin's translation was also clearer than Chen's about the sequence of events from 1944 to 1946. Julia's affair with her father-in-law, Zi Ming, went undetected for over three years and only ended when Yaoming discovered the truth about his father's unsuccessful plan to leave China with Julia, Peter, and Andrew. Yaoming had been duped into thinking that the foursome was merely traveling ahead, and he would follow after Zi Ming had arranged for Yaoming to continue his graduate education in the United States. Once Zi Ming was unable to receive the visas from the United States that he needed, the plan fell through. Only afterwards did Yaoming find out that his father never intended to include him in the journey to the States. His father had lied to him about graduate school help. Instead, the real plan was that he was to be abandoned in China. With this horrible truth, he struck back to avenge his betrayal.

In the spring of 1946, Yaoming decided to expose his wife and father's treachery. "I was initially worried about airing dirty laundry and had some vestige of love for my wife, so I forced myself to endure excessive pain." But when he remembered the "sudden and inexplicable death" of Katherine and how "distraught" Andrew was after "losing his mother," he became "increasingly terrified" of his father's "unfathomable and unrestrained diabolicality." To "protect my own safety and my son's future," Yaoming had no choice but to write a letter, exposing his father's deeds, intending to elicit "a just verdict" from his Shanghai family and the public.

I have since found out that in the tumultuous world of wartime Shanghai, it was not unusual for individuals to take their grievances to the press. If one could not achieve justice in the courts that were often in shambles during the Japanese occupation and after the war, at least one could strike back through public denunciation. Losing face or the threat of losing face was a powerful means to exact revenge if not justice. The timing for Zi Ming's exit from Shanghai would support that fact. Not more than four months later, Zi Ming had managed to liquidate enough funds to relocate his newly constituted family with enough household goods to a spacious apartment on Observatory Road in Hong Kong, crossing borders, customs, and legal barriers.

I have always believed that all families have secrets, some necessary, some malicious. Secrets can glue a marriage together or they can blow it apart. But the secrets uncovered in Yaoming's letter were not about human foibles, indiscretions, and infidelities. I was not reading about adultery or a lapse of judgment, I was reading about crimes that destroyed lives. Katherine was murdered and erased from her son's memory; Andrew's nephew, Peter, had been raised never to know his father and forced to live in a manufactured family; and Yaoming was robbed of his son, never seeing him again. For seventy years, exhausting lies, deceptions, and cover stories silenced the truth.

Could anything right these wrongs?

Conventional justice was not possible. Since everyone involved was dead, only gods of justice or retribution could punish the wicked. Only if you believed in powerful figures, like the Christian God or Yama the Buddhist king of Hell, could you feel any satisfaction that Zi Ming and Julia had received a just punishment.

But what do the living do? How do they find peace? And what to the living owe the dead that have been wronged?

I couldn't help feeling that Katherine had summoned me to help with the task of uncovering her past. At this crucial point, I couldn't let her down. I had to present a belated offering to her, not burnt paper money, oranges, nuts, or flowers, but a written record for her son and a circle of family and friends that would help calm her restless wanderings. Katherine and the crimes against her would not be forgotten because she was murdered twice, once in Chongqing by her husband/lover and again when she was erased from Andrew's life. Zi Ming and Julia's steady diet of lies, evasions, and midnight whispers would not bury her beneath their scheming. Only a complete uncovering of the past could shed light on what happened July 12, 1944. The last thirty years were a search to find details about his mother's life and the truth about her death, not the date, the year, or the multiple causes, but a more entangled truth that tugs at the heart.

Katherine's ghost had indeed come calling. She had disturbed my dreams, my daily life, even my moments of pleasure with Andrew. It wasn't enough to burn some joss sticks or build a family altar in our home. I needed to understand what Katherine would want.

I wasn't used to thinking in this way.

As a child every October 31, I would line up with my classmates in my grade school and march to St. Hedwig's cemetery to clear fallen leaves and stubborn weeds from the graves. Carefully, I would avoid stepping on them, walking around each one as if I was on an obstacle course, my friends often violating this taboo, playing leapfrog over gravestones, children's games among graves. A pious child, I succumbed to the spectacle of incense and candles, singing Gregorian chant in the children's choir, enchanted by the rituals of both weddings and funerals. Love and death were the great mysteries. But I never thought about what I owed the dead. What was my duty to them? Even the word "duty" was something I and, I would add, most Americans avoided. Rights and freedom were much more crucial, and certainly not as dreary and burdened as "duty."

Unlike traditional Chinese, I had not grown up thinking my ancestors had demands that must be fulfilled every year in ritual time through festivals like Qingming in the spring, Double Ninth in the fall, and that spectacular affair, the Ghost Festival, the highlight of an entire month. Held during the full moon on the 15th night of the seventh moon according to the lunar calendar, this festival enacted the web of regrets, resentments, and fears the living carry about dead relatives that influenced how they went about their daily lives.

My sisters and I still felt guilty that we did not do enough for my mother in the years before she died. Angry about going to a nursing home, she would always ask me when I visited if I was there to take her home. She hated the residents she was forced to live near, found the food tasteless, and resented the stupid activities the staff thought she would enjoy, silly crafts, dumb outings, and inane exercises. "They treat us like children," she would say. "I want to leave. Can I go home with you?" I can hear her voice after fifteen years, her discontent unforgettable.

The Ghost Festival allowed the living to help the dead, through offerings of food and paper goods shaped to look like luxury watches, yachts, designer handbags, and hard cash. These gifts helped to appease the dead whose demands can be overwhelming. Family members can have more psychological power after they die, haunting us with snippets of conversations, repeated expressions, and vivid images that undermine how we live and love. The Ghost Festival gave people a chance to pay tribute to their ancestors and reflect on the lives they shared with them.

Whether our relatives were vindictive criminals or inspired saints, we can still aid them while we live. Some Chinese believers called on Guanyin, the goddess of compassion, to have mercy on deceased ancestors. Or they performed acts of charity and sacrifice to help their deceased relatives to sort through the tangled web of unresolved emotions they died with. Their cruelty and kindness beckon us to reflect, understand and act, not disregard, or forget through elaborate acts of avoidance.

If she was murdered, Katherine would need to be appeased, the treachery against her exposed. If she committed suicide, she would need comfort. Zi Ming's crimes as a murderer or a betrayer would need our honest attempts to solicit compassion, not forgiveness alone, but a compassion that clearly sees the transgression and the personal costs of desperate deeds, his broken life, isolation, and lost status that plagued him in Hong Kong.

Attached to youth, most Americans avoid death, dead bodies, and grim ceremonies around the dying. We can barely stand to be in the presence of the dying and have only recently found a middle way through the hospice movement to administer to the dying.

Most Americans die in hospitals, but hospitals try to disguise this fact not wanting to upset patients and their visitors. Carts with fake bottoms haul the dead bodies out service elevators, invisible to the living.

Death is unpleasant. And we value our comfort above most human emotions.

We are a society afraid of the dark that relishes horror movies as a form of entertainment.

Was I no different than the typical American, unwilling to face the confusing emotions of death? I was at my mother and father's side when they died and was struck by the mystery of their passing. But I cannot say I return ritually to their memory to understand how to live and what I can do for them. They are inside me, that seems enough. Marrying Andrew, I entered a new equation between the living and the dead, an awareness of "debt," an immaterial bond that carried responsibility, closer to the celebrations I witnessed in New Mexico when an altar for the dead, an *ofrenda,* was built to honor the dead during Dia de Muertos each year in October. The act of remembering brought one near the dead, their struggles and pain, their hopes fulfilled and their dreams disappointed. The connection between the dead and living was never ending.

On the day my husband played bridge at the local club, I walked north on West Shore Drive on Guemes Island to a little park called Peach Preserve. On a Wednesday in mid-January, there was no one there, the winter light throwing into relief sand patterns and perched seagulls.

In three days, my husband would be eighty-one. We had already had several talks about our end times, what we wanted, what was possible. Each day was precious, our morning walks, our outings to buy local bread and berries, our support for each other's writing. He was almost finished with another long poem, wondering if it would ever find a home in an America that found poetry difficult if not impossible to read. It didn't matter to him. "What else would I do?" he would often say when we talked about how many bookstores had a shelf or two for poetry, at best, taken up by Shakespeare's *Sonnets*, Homer's *Odyssey*, or Emily Dickinson's *Selected Poems*.

I had to decide not only what to do with Yaoming's letter, but how to respond to what had happened to Katherine. No matter how many walks I took, it always came back to the same question. Did I simply hand over Yaoming's letter to my husband? What would I do after that?

The cold air made the metallic sheen of the water appear like ice. I knew it wasn't ice, but it looked like a solid surface. The unavoidable fact was that whether I gave him the letter or not, the letter was already between us. I could not look at Andrew without thinking about Yaoming's letter. I could not stop thinking about Katherine and Zi Ming on that fateful day, July 12, 1944. I could not walk past her portrait without sadness. The past would never go away.

Worse, if I didn't tell him what I knew, I would be continuing the dreadful reality of his childhood. At some point, I would have to lie and create cover stories. I would have to deceive.

In the end, there was no choice.

In my heart, I believed Zi Ming was a murderer. I did not come to this conclusion lightly. For days before handing over the letter, I thought through what happened to Katherine. I needed my own guidance before I thrust Andrew into the disturbing world of his brother's letter. I admit, there were problems with what I thought. I was wrapped up in my desire to protect Andrew and avenge the wrongs he suffered growing up. I was not impartial.

When Katherine returned with Andrew to Chongqing, she became Zi Ming's instant "enemy." If she had been with other men, as Zi Ming had at one point claimed, there would be no reason to feel such hostility to him. She would be the guilty party wanting to appease her lover. No, her rage was caused by rejection, not a confession of her betrayal. I couldn't accept Zi Ming's explanation for her suicide. It rang false. She was not the Hanging Woman who had killed herself because of an abusive husband or lover.

Overnight Katherine became Zi Ming's enemy, not a whimpering, shame-faced lover, or an injured cast-a-way, willing to abandon her child to the man she hated. A formidable foe, she could have threatened any manner of recrimination. Her rage fed her need to survive. If anything, I felt she could have seriously harmed Zi Ming's reputation. She was a threat. Maybe she wasn't Ng Mui, a woman warrior, fending off enemies with her White Crane martial arts style, but she was forceful, destroying the peace of the household, a fury intent on damage.

That's why Zi Ming had to find a second reason, a heart attack, to explain away her sudden death. Panic had seized Zi Ming. The explanation of a heart attack was meant to appease his family and friends, yet family and friends were immediately suspicious. They sensed that it was highly unlikely that Katherine had died of a heart attack. Moreover, the confusion caused by two reasons for her death made Yaoming and family friends sense foul play even though they could not prove it.

That evening after dinner I would hand Andrew his brother's letter. In the end, my reasoning didn't matter. My hours of fretting and analysis were finished.

Only Andrew mattered. Our love mattered. His mother had returned to our home.

The debt we owed the dead was partly paid through our halting and imperfect attempts to understand the past, an understanding that can deepen our own actions, giving us the freedom to love and the means to live deep to the bone.

About the Author

For 27 years, Joan Burbick traveled frequently to China and Hong Kong, teaching and lecturing. Puzzled about her husband's Chinese family that had erased the life and death of his mother, she decided to understand why. She began her research with personal letters from his Chinese family and then continued by searching archives in Philadelphia, New Haven, and Boston. She stayed  in places her mother-in-law would have lived or visited in the 1940s and immersed herself in the pathways of fleeing Chinese during the Japanese-occupation. She read histories of modern China and Shanghai wartime newspapers. *Erased* was based on these years of investigation.

Previously, Joan Burbick published books on Henry David Thoreau, rodeo queens, gun culture in America, and national narratives in the United States. She landed in the world of fiction later in life. *Stripland* was her first novel; *Erased*, the second.

Acknowledgments

This book would not have happened without the support and encouragement of my husband, Alex Kuo. Finding out about the past has its hazards. He is the bravest soul I know.

Writing a novel that drew from historical materials on China has been daunting. My first approach was mainly to read Chinese literature and history from the 1920s to the present.

If Lu Xun were alive today, I would write him a long, effusive thank-you letter. He was a brilliant writer that still is relevant today. My Chinese colleagues in Beijing and Shanghai have had to listen to my questions and often pointed me in the right direction for relevant materials. Their help in translation will be forever appreciated. Early reading of this manuscript has been crucial. For their care and attention, I want to thank Alex Kuo and Nancy Burbick. A thank you is simply not enough for my generous publisher, Kristin Summers, whose creative eye has enhanced what I have written. Not the least, special thanks to Greg Johnson for his careful and judicious editing.

I have plunged into various archival sources to find background material on Shanghai and Chongqing during World War II. Surprisingly helpful were: Harrison Forman Collection, University of Wisconsin-Milwaukee Archives, American Geographical Society Library; the Diaries of William Lyon Mackenzie

King, Library and Archives Canada, Government of Canada; Ross Granville Harrison Papers, Manuscripts and Archives, Yale University Library; Papers of Early American Psychologists, American Philosophical Society Library; Virtual Shanghai Project (Institut de Rechercher Asiatiques); Central Intelligence Agency Library, Center for the Study of Intelligence; and Office of the Historian, Foreign Relations of the United States: Diplomatic Papers, 1944, China.

....

ALSO BY JOAN BURBICK

Stripland

Thoreau's Alternative History:
Changing Perspectives on Nature, Culture and Language

Healing the Republic:
The Language of Health and the Culture of Nationalism
in Nineteenth-Century America

Rodeo Queens and the American Dream

Gun Show Nation:
Gun Culture and American Democracy

Beyond Imagined Uniqueness:
Nationalisms in Contemporary Perspectives (edited)

redbat
books

For other titles available from redbat books, please visit:
www.redbatbooks.com

Also available through Ingram, Bookshop.org,
Amazon.com, Powells.com and by special order through
your local bookstore.

www.ingramcontent.com/pod-product-compliance
Lightning Source LLC
Chambersburg PA
CBHW032347020726
47499CB00009B/3207